AN ACTIVE SHOOTER

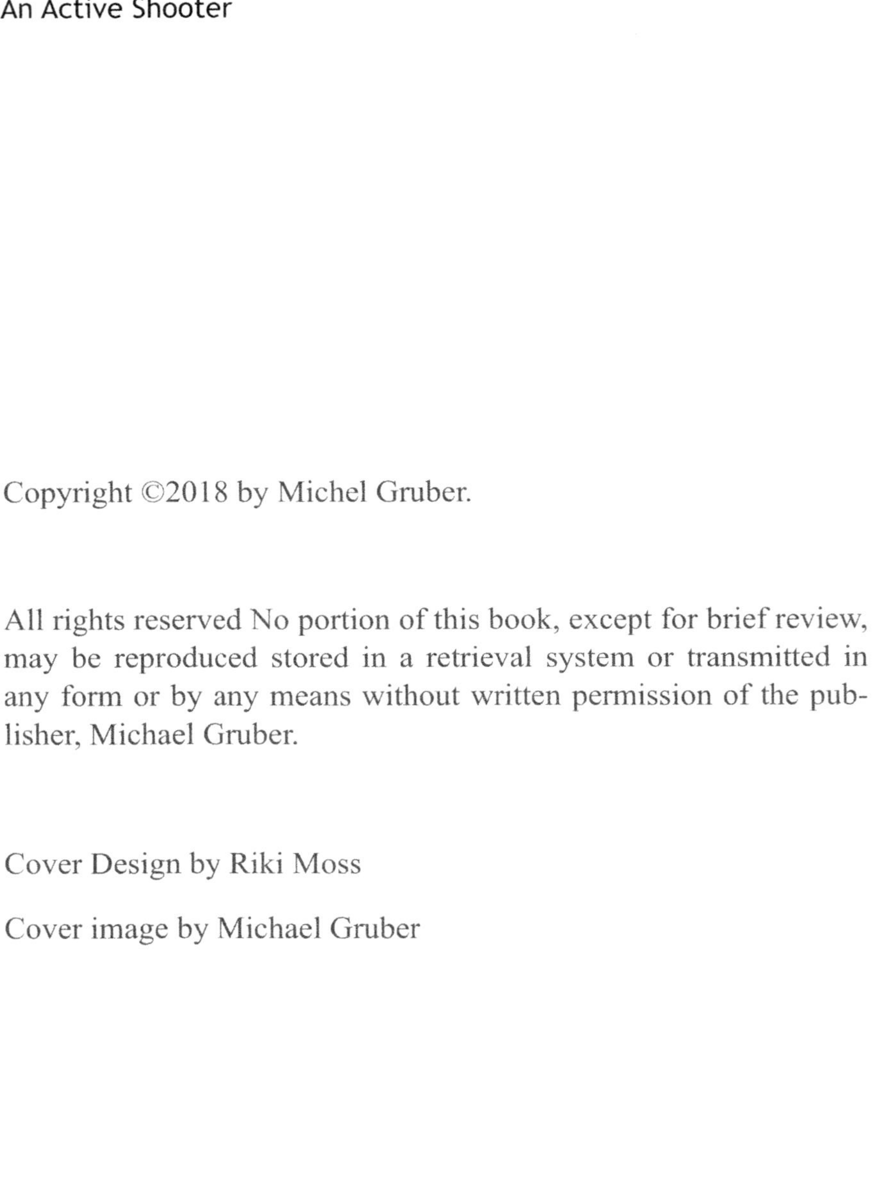

Cover Design by Riki Moss

Cover image by Michael Gruber

By Michael Gruber:

The Long Con
An Active Shooter
Amnesia Dreams
The Charles Bridge
Tropic of Night
Valley of Bones
Night of the Jaguar
The Book of Air and Shadows
The Forgery of Venus
The Good Son
The Return
YA The Witch's Boy

Ghostwritten/published under the name of Robert K. Tanenbaum

No Lesser Plea
Depraved Indifference
Immoral Certainty
Reversible Error
Corruption of Blood
Material Witness
Justice Denied
Falsely Accused
True Justice
Reckless Endangerment
Irresistible Impulse
Act of Revenge
Enemy Within
Absolute Rage
Resolved

AN ACTIVE SHOOTER

A Novel

MICHAEL GRUBER

1: At the Mall of Death

Nora Kehoe had done two tours as a Marine in Afghanistan and so when she heard the popping sounds coming from the lower level of the mall she did not think, like the other ladies in Sephora, that it was firecrackers. She threw down the tester that she'd been sniffing (*Bloom* by Gucci) and ran out of the shop.

The noises continued, a steady banging, like a hammer on an anvil, now joined by the howls of men, the screams of women, the maddening shrieks of children. She ran down the stairway to the lower level, heading for the Santa Claus lap-sitting area, where she'd left her husband and the three girls. Gretchen at twelve had judged herself too old for Santa and had wanted to come with Nora to fuss with make-up and perfumes, but Nora the wicked stepmother had made her stay with her dad and the babies, although they were not babies, were seven and creatively naughty and the older girl was required to control them sufficiently in public.

And also Nora desired a brief time alone in a place with no kids in the hell weeks between Thanksgiving and Christmas, especially desired in the mall because Nora had spent her working life in uniform and was not much of a shopper. She thought the world would be a better place if everyone was in uniform all the time, with symbols of their accomplishments attached thereto. She thought it would cut down mightily on bullshit in the world. Although she rarely wore perfume, she rather liked squirting herself with different scents; she considered it a form of aromatherapy, without the fees or mumbo jumbo. This tiny indulgence would expand into a choking lump of guilt later on.

People bearing the blank rictus of panic on their faces appeared before her, running away from the center of the mall, where the shooting was going on. Nora pushed through them, using her elbows and hips. The shooting grew louder, and the screams. Nora herself felt no panic. She had switched into what her fellow Marines had called iceman mode, or sometimes they said "ice queen," a state of mind where objects appeared with preternatural clarity, sounds seemed distant and muffled and time flowed slowly, as in a dream. It was a type of what the military called *coup de l'oie* , the ability to absorb a complex tactical situation in a glance—terrain, cover, dead ground, lines of approach, fields of fire, points of danger. It had been widely remarked during her service.

Now she was past the trampling crowd and encountered the first corpses. Nora had seen a good many civilian corpses in Afghan villages and these—a brown woman and two brown boys—had the unmistakable look of unoccupied flesh. A great pool of blood, already starting to gel up, surrounded them. She noted in passing that one of the boys had an exploded head, like an old pumpkin after Halloween. Few people comprehended what modern military rounds could do to flesh, the movies couldn't show it: this thought passed through her mind, a mental footnote, and also that the shooter was taking head shots, which suggested expertise with his weapon. She also noticed the spent brass on the ground: the familiar 5.56 mm. military rounds. The shooter had an assault rifle.

A few steps further, a chubby couple, lying together near an overturned stroller, both of them dead, she couldn't see the toddler in the stroller, had to suppress her EMT's instinct to offer help, and then three teens, all fashionably dressed in tattered jeans and bright parkas, the parkas blown open by the force of the bullets, the bits of released down spotting white on the red pools of their blood and turning red themselves. Two men, one lying supine with his face blown into red jam and the other alive and groaning.

She leaped lightly over these, skidded briefly in blood and stopped. She had reached the main intersection of the mall, in the center of which stood a circular information booth. A dead older woman was hanging head down across her counter like a coat flung on the back of a chair, her neat gray perm turned black with blood. Between this structure and where Nora stood was a field of bodies. Nora had seen a mosque bombing near Kabul that had the same look, a carpet of corpses, although there the bodies had been in hideous fragments. In a way this was more horrible than that, because you could see that they were dead people rather than shattered meat, and also that so many of them were children. For the first time she noticed that Christmas music was still playing over the mall speakers, *The Little Drummer Boy* just then.

The shooting had stopped for a moment, but now it resumed. Stepping delicately between the dead, Nora moved toward the short aisle in which the North Pole fantasia had been erected. Of course, Don was no fool, he would have rushed the girls out at the first shot, in fact, he was probably outside with them now, worried about her, and the smart move was to retreat with the others, away from the shooter. But Nora turned the corner, moving toward the bam . . . bam ... bam, and the wailing.

The mall's management had set up Santa's throne in a little cull-de-sac that was ordinarily used as a dining area for the nearby restaurants. A tall gaudy Christmas tree stood there, flanked by two lines of heavy planters containing squat fake Christmas trees decked with large silver balls. These had been arranged in a wide oval in which the waiting throng was meant to assemble, each party to wait for a turn on the Lap. At the far end of the oval stood the dais upon which rested Santa's throne, gilt and red velvet, with a pillow seat. Opposite was the entrance to this enclosure and there were the usual posts and cloth tapes arranged to manage the waiting lines.

Santa was not seated anymore, but Nora could see the soles of his shiny patent-leather boots emerging from a mass of white velvet that had been spread out as a field of snow to display a tiny, lighted village. Also in this wreck lay two girls dressed as elves, whose blood had turned the faux snow scarlet. From the loudspeakers Bing Crosby dreamed of a white Christmas.

The distribution of the twinkling brass cartridge cases suggested to Nora that the killer had opened fire at the entrance to the enclosure. The packed mass of adults and kids, restricted by posts and tapes, had been perfectly vulnerable to a man with a semi-automatic rifle, and the oval pen was three or four deep in torn bodies, the pile marked here and there by the handles of strollers. Many had tried to leap over the planters but the gunman had made short work of these, and the stiff plastic firs were festooned with the dead, like soldiers caught on barbed wire in the First World War.

Nora rejected the idea that her family was part of this bleeding heap, or rather the idea would not fit into her head. They were outside and safe. Instead she focused on the body of a mall security guard. She knelt and extracted the baton from his belt, then moved out of the Santa area toward the sounds of the continuing massacre.

These emerged from a restaurant called Thai O' Rama; its window was shattered and the dark interior was lit intermittently by bright red beams, which suggested that the gunman had a laser sight. The shots now came at longer intervals, meaning that nearly all the people who had taken shelter in that restaurant had been killed. A particularly loud cry came, somewhat muffled, but Nora thought it was "not my baby no no" followed by a shot then an impossibly loud scream, then another. Silence now ensued, except for Frank Sinatra singing *Have Yourself a Merry Little Christmas*. Nora crouched behind the big Christmas tree and observed the restaurant doorway through the lower boughs.

After a few moments, the gunman emerged, cradling his assault rifle in the crook of his right arm, like a gentleman out after grouse. He was a very large man, tall and broad as a door, and he was dressed as Santa. He was a good Santa type, with shoulder length hair and a full beard, although he was fungus-pale and his lips were not like cherries at all. Nora estimated he was in his early thirties; he must have powdered his light brown hair and beard for authenticity. Thick, clear-rimmed glasses magnified watery blue eyes. He looked tired; his face said, I am a man engaged in difficult, necessary, strenuous work.

The killer turned and started down the hall towards the next shop in the row, which sold T-shirts. Nora gripped the baton and tensed. His back was to her now. Five long steps and she would be on him. Even if he heard her and turned, it would take a second for him to bring up the gun and point it and by then she would have smashed his face in like an egg.

But now came a distraction: flashing blue and red lights shining through the glass doors at the end of the aisle, sirens sounding. The doors swung open and five people entered wearing the canonical black ballistic nylon gear, helmeted and carrying M4 carbines. "SWAT" was printed on their flak vests along with the seal of the Virginia State Police. They saw the Santa, they saw his weapon, they instructed him to drop it, he declined to do so, he raised his weapon. Five converging streams of fire reached out to the gunman, who instantly deflated and fell like a big red balloon.

Nora left her hide, intending to examine the corpse pile. She had to make sure that her family had escaped. Abigail and Adele were always having to go to the toilet and they delighted in peeing in strange stalls, whereas Gretchen would have begged Don to let her go down the aisle to Abercrombie's or Forever 21 and be twelve with clothing. So everything was going to be fine, she just needed to check it out . . .

But stern voices were screaming at her, telling her to drop your weapon telling her to get down get down now. She tossed the baton, but did not get down, instead turning toward the bodies that were not to include her family at all. She was walking very slowly now, her legs a-tremble, it was from all the excitement, she thought, and also, what if they were hiding down on the lowest layer of corpses, it would be hard to make sure they weren't there . . and her arm was grabbed hard and she felt a blow at the back of her knees, forcing her down into a kneeling position. Someone was pulling her wrists behind her back, at which moment she registered two bright red patches against the dark green of the plastic trees.

As a child, Nora had been taken to church in a red coat with a black velvet collar and had, in odd moments when she wasn't being a Marine or an EMT, mooned over one day having a daughter of her own and dressing her in just such a little coat. It happened eventually that she'd had two of them, identical, who looked almost parricidally like Nora, and were balls of fire, also like her, but had, thank

God, their father's sweet and mild temperament. The coats had been bought this day for church on Christmas, but at the store the girls had begged so piteously to wear them right away that the parents had relented, although they knew that Gretchen would sulk: you always give them everything they want.

So there they were, safe and sound, probably, although she had to go check, and if necessary provide first aid from her copious store of those skills, except these cops seemed to think she was associated with the bad Santa, being the only living person in the area and noncompliant. They were actually trying to take her away from her babies, which couldn't be right, and so she resisted vigorously, using Marine unarmed combat moves and hurting one of the policemen quite seriously before they were able to wrestle her into submission.

2: The Comforters

One hundred and forty-five was the total kill at what the media immediately began to call the Mall of Death, of whom 98 were under eighteen years of age. The youngest victim was seven months, the oldest eighty-two. TV vans had already set up around the perimeter of the mall and smooth-faced men and women were pointed microphones and cameras, cell phones and recorders at anyone who emerged.

The event was so news-juicy (Killer Santa! Dead children!) that the machinery whereby information leaks from the first responders to the press spun faster than usual. Thus, when Nora Kehoe left the mall, handcuffed and suspended between two big SWATs, everyone knew that Bad Santa had a Helper, and they knew her name.

She certainly looked the part. The cops had not been gentle with her after she had broken the nose of one of them and dislocated his jaw and his elbow. A bruise covered half her face and her mouth was swollen. She'd bled from the face and her white turtleneck displayed a ragged scarlet bib. Somehow her face and hair had been dragged through Santa's blood puddle, enhancing the Bitch from Hell effect. Her knee was messed up too, but the jackals couldn't see that because the cops barely let her feet touch the ground. A howling arose as they brought her out to the yellow tape and stuck her in a police van.

"Nora! Hey, Nora!" cried the journalists. "Was he your boyfriend? Hey, Nora, look over here, Nora! How many did you kill? Did you kill children? Was it for thrills? Hey, Nora, are you religious? Are you a liberal? Do you hate Christmas? Nora! How does it feel? How does it *feel*?"

Besides the press, some thousands of ordinary citizens thronged the parking lot, for the mall had been jammed for the holiday. Some of these were "escapees" from the massacre, and several of them had entered the hot-light zone and had attained the American apotheosis of a TV appearance, giving witness to their terrifying experience, with several unloading their opinion of what should be done to the surviving murderess. Others, not so fortunate, and perhaps pissed off that their shopping excursion had been ruined, screamed directly at the slowly retreating police van containing the alleged killer.

She didn't know how it feels. She had been hit enthusiastically on the head a number of times and she kept blanking out. At moments she thought she might be dreaming a nightmare, and that she might awaken at any moment next to Don's large warm body and tell him about it; and at others she was vividly present in the belly of the van, feeling the pains of her injuries, registering the details of the van's interior: a scrap of blue paper, a gob of spit on the floor, the texture of the slatted wooden bench, the wired glass of the rear windows, this alternate reality coming in quick flashes, as when you walk down the aisle of an airliner and catch glimpses of what the passengers are watching on their seatback screens. Her hands were cuffed behind her; chains shackled her ankles and ran up to a belt around her middle.

Nora knew a good deal about post-traumatic shock, having experienced trauma herself in Afghanistan and because she worked as an EMT, a profession where, as they say, nearly everyone you meet is having the worst day of their life. Of the two standard responses—batshit crazy nuts or suicidally numb—Nora understood that she was heading into the latter.

There were, however, aspects of nuts in the present situation. For example, she was no longer in the police van but riding in the shotgun seat of a Humvee out of the FOB at Khan Neshin. Chris "TP" Gomez was driving, more carefully than she usually did because Lt. Kehoe was riding next to her instead of Wart Gunther, who was in the back running the radio and the IED jamming electronics. Standing on the little platform to Nora's right rear was Peanut Cooper, manning the fifty cal up top.

In this phase of the war for hearts and minds, the Marines had established the Lioness Program, in which Marine women organized into Female Engagement Teams formed relationships with village women, doing various good works and gathering intelligence. The women knew everything, of course, and they were often willing to share information with the strange armed females who had dropped from the unknown.

The Humvee was going to Mir Puza, a place that Lt. Kehoe had been cultivating for six months. It was the second Humvee of five in the convoy, for the FETs had to be protected wherever they went by other Marines. Gomez said something to her and she had to lean over to hear what it was over the roar of the engine and then she was back in the police van, shuddering.

She had not had a full-color with stereo sound flashback for years, not since she had married Don, and it was almost always that scene just before the ambush in the strangely deserted maidan, but not this time.

This time she understood that what happened in Mir Puza had been demoted to a secondary horror. She found the cold little person who had taken control of Nora no longer cared about what had happened to the other Marines in that humvee or what had happened to her own body then or about what she had done later. That person said good-bye to those things. That person said good bye to Don and the girls too, and finally said good-bye to Nora. In the blackness behind her shut eyes she saw herself and her family as little figures waving up at her as she floated away from them. They were smoothed and smiling like Pixar characters. They shrank slowly into little blobs and then were lost in the general dazzle.

Well, that's over, she thought. I don't have to think about that again.

The Fairfax County detective who interviewed her later thought that she was just the kind of psycho bitch who might be involved with someone like the shooter, Duane Paul Hatch, and was disappointed when it proved otherwise. Some Marine colonel was making noise about the woman, it seemed, and since the police forces of America are thickly salted with ex-Marines, including the head of Major Crimes in the Fairfax PD, it was established more swiftly than it might otherwise have been that the supposed suspect was a victim. This determination still took most of the night, so reluctant were the cops to lose their live murderess. They fed her supper and breakfast, but she didn't eat. She drank coffee though. She wanted to stay up. She remembered that was also diagnostic: some PTSDs slept all the time, some never slept.

She was still awake therefore when Colonel Peter Kehoe, USMC (Ret.) came for her. Before that, when the cops arrived just after dawn, she noticed that they were treating her differently, deferentially almost, and also as if they were a little frightened of her. They took her out of her cell and let her use a real bathroom, with mirrors, sinks and toilet stalls. A female officer told her that her father had brought her a change of clothing and handed over a heavy plastic bag, containing, she found, a tracksuit, sneakers, socks and underwear. Nora changed into the fresh clothes and threw the bloodstained clothes into a trash barrel. The officer told her she was free to go, and after an embarrassed pause, said "I'm sorry for your loss, ma'am."

In the lobby of the police station were many agitated people clamoring, and there were desks with officers behind them and long bulletin boards had been set up, with lists pinned to them. This was where you went to see if your loved one had been among the victims. More then twenty-four hours after the shootings the process of identification and the distribution of grief had not yet been accomplished.

Peter Kehoe was a large man with a blocky, crew-cut head, broad shoulders and large capable hands. He muscled his way through the crowd and snatched up his daughter in a hug that lifted her from the ground. She didn't hug back, or say anything to him, or cry. *He* had cried, an astronomical rarity.

He helped her secure her belongings and then ushered her, still held close, out into the chill air. The press was waiting, somewhat more subdued now that they knew who Nora was. No one shouted apologies; they still wanted to know *how she felt.* Father and daughter climbed into the cab of his big Ford pick-up and left the shouting behind.

They were both Marines. They had both served in combat, the former in Vietnam, the latter in Afghanistan, and both knew that emotional language was insufficient to the present case. They drove through the brown Virginia roadsides, the father filling the noisy interior space with reportage. How he had learned; what he did when he learned; how he told Nora's mother; her reaction; how they reached Sally, Ben and Doug; their reactions; the scheduled arrival of the siblings, Sally from Quantico, Doug from his ship at sea, Ben from Santa Clara, and the logistics pertaining thereto.

Nora had regarded all this as if it were the news mumbling from a distant radio, but now she became aware that a question had been asked.

"Sorry, what?"

"I asked if you wanted to get out of town," he replied. "The goddamned media will be out, and maybe . . . well, staying at the house, you know, it could be rough . . . Ben has a timeshare in Maui you could use."

"No, I have too much to do. I have to dispose of all their stuff. And sell the house. I think I'll get a condo closer to work."

Colonel Kehoe stared at his daughter so hard and so long that he almost missed his turn. The calm of her face was far more frightening than hysteria would have been. It spoke of injury so deep that no balm could reach it. He had seen it before in combat. The ones who went nuts when their friends got hurt recovered faster than the ones w ho looked like they didn't care. The calm ones sometimes didn't last long, or did not adjust well to civilian life. Peter himself had early adopted a stoic approach to life, and he knew his daughter had followed him in this. Neither ever accepted the victim's role, and neither was easy about expressing feelings, but he thought Nora's current behavior was over the line. He hoped that her mother could do something.

The house was a big five-bedroom colonial in Herndon, with a large yard and three dogwoods out front. Don Chase, the late husband, had owned a prospering office-cleaning business and his house reflected his rise from humbler circumstances. It had white columns in front, a sure sign that a working stiff had made it big.

Nora's mother, Rose Kehoe, was waiting in the foyer when they came in. As a Marine wife, she was used to dealing with bad news, but *this* bad news had knocked the stuffing out of her. Her face was damp and red with weeping, and she began wailing again as she wrapped her daughter in her arms. Nora returned the embrace like you do when someone you don't know gives you an over-enthusiastic hug at a party. Yes, this was her mother, and she recalled that she had been close to her mother, but Nora felt she was now in a place beyond motherhood or daughterhood, where closeness was not a thing.

Rose offered food, a drink, both refused; Nora went to the stairs and when Rose went to follow, because you need your mother when something like this happens, Nora said that she'd like to be alone now because there was a lot she had to do. Again, the comment and tone in which it was delivered were more shocking than violent hysterics.

Rose fell against her husband and sobbed anew. She was a Marine wife, which meant that at any moment she could have learned of the death of her husband, or one of the three out of her four children who had spent time in harm's way, and she'd prepared for that, she knew how to behave had that day ever come. She had not expected to lose three of her grandchildren, though, and it undid her. She could not stop crying, this adding shame to her distress.

Nora went into her home office and closed the door. She kept the office military neat, because that's how she was raised and also as an example to her children. There were pictures of the three of them, from last summer at Rehoboth, splashing in the shallows aboard an inflated turtle, laughing, all three of them getting along for a golden hour. Next to it, in a silver frame was the wedding picture, Nora and Don coming from St. Rita's under an arch of Mameluke swords held by her grinning comrades, Don looking glad and a little nervous. Next to that was one of her with her Female Engagement Team, also grinning, squinting in the sun, draped around a Humvee. She slid all of these framed photographs into a desk drawer.

She thought about all the other photos, on the walls of their bedroom, in the upstairs hall and in Don's room, framed on tables in the living room, and how she would dispose of all of them, after the visitors left. The next week of so would be the hardest, dealing with the pain of her relatives and friends, and acting bereaved in an appropriate manner. And the funeral, a simple cremation. An orderly man, Don had written everything down, and he wasn't a Marine, so she would not have to endure the horror of an Arlington ceremony.

Nora lay down on the day-bed and pulled her grandmother's quilt up to her chin. It was a tree-of-life pattern. Her father's mother had embroidered the names of family members back to the early nineteenth century on the small leaves of the tree. The ones who had been Marines had their leaves decorated with the globe and fouled anchor, and tiny insignia of the rank they had attained. There were a lot of them. The Kehoe women had kept it up to date, and leaves on the tip of one of the brackets bore Nora's name and that of her brothers and sister, her nieces and nephews and her own dead children. Nora stroked the fabric and waited for what would come next.

A hesitant tapping on the door, her mother's voice asking if she could come in. Of course, Mom. The mother entered moving with unnatural care, like the woman descending to the basement in a horror movie. She was a tall, rawboned woman, like her daughter, with the same short pale brown hair and blue eyes. The daughter had the famous Kehoe beak rather than her mother's American-girl bobble, a disaster in high school, but now conveying character. She was a woman people called handsome or attractive, rather than pretty.

Rose sat on the edge of the day-bed. She clasped her girl's hand, frighteningly chill, like butcher's meat, and was silent for several minutes. She asked Nora if she wanted to eat anything. Nora wasn't hungry. Do you want to talk?

"About what?"

"Oh, baby," said the mother, and sobbed. She cried for a brief time and then stifled the crying.

"Are they still all outside?" Nora asked.

"Yes, the bastards. Four vans and a bunch of people with cameras and microphones out on the street. One of them tried looking in the dining room window, but your father chased him away. Can a bring you something? Your neighbors brought some kind of casserole. I could heat it up for you."

"That was fast. Do they keep dead neighbor casseroles in their freezers in case they're needed?"

Downstairs, the door bell chimed its double tone.

"More casseroles," said Nora.

Rose stood and looked out the window through the blinds.

"It's Sally. I'll send her right up. Talk to her, dear. You can't keep all of that inside you." A pause. "Let me know if you want something to eat."

She left, closing the door behind her. Nora heard a strangled cry from the other side of the door. Nora understood that she was not pulling her weight in grieving, and that her mother was picking up the slack, but she couldn't do anything about it.

Sally entered as she always did, bringing fresh air. Ordinarily, this would be accompanied by boisterous energy and a imperative to let's go out and do something., but not today. Sally was the senior child, was eighteen months older than Nora, the Irish twin, the captain of the kids throughout their childhood, the protector from harm.

First a blizzard of obscenity from the doorway, then Sally leaped upon the day-bed, grabbing her sister up in a near-asphyxiating hug. After that she held Nora by the shoulders at arm's length for an inspection.

"You're not crying."

Nora shook her head.

"You're numbed out. What's the matter? You howled plenty when Ryan got killed."

"Don't, Sally."

"Okay, okay, I'm sorry. Jesus! I suck at this. Here, let's have a drink."

From her big canvas messenger bag, Sally extracted a bottle of Wild Turkey over-proof and two squat glasses, into which she poured generous shots. She drank hers down and refilled her glass. Nora just looked at hers, as if she had never seen a glass of whiskey before.

"Drink it," Sally commanded. When Nora shook her head, her sister grabbed the back of her neck and pinched. "You have to. You have to do what I say. Mom left me in charge."

Nora sipped the liquor. She hadn't had any Wild Turkey for a long time. It was Ryan's drink. Ryan had been dead and buried at Arlington for over ten years. She had avoided Wild Turkey, or any bourbon, since then. She was a responsible young mom now and allowed herself only white wine. She took a larger swallow after this thought had occurred. Maybe that was a solution, to crawl into a bottle and stay there. She imagined that was what Sally would do in a similar circumstance, but Sally was always more of a drinker than she was.

The liquor made a warm path down her center. Ryan could do that, the warm path thing, although that usually terminated lower down, Ryan Graham could look at her across a room, or touch her anywhere, and her unit would light up like a toaster. They had laughed about it; he had the same reaction. When he deployed they had sent each other dirty videos. Then the thing at Mir Puza had happened and afterward a Marine officer had visited her in her hospital bed and told her that Lieutenant Ryan Graham, USMC, been killed in Iraq, at Fallujah. They were giving him the Navy Cross, posthumous, and the funny thing was they were talking about giving her the Navy Cross too, for Mir Puza, but then they found out about the civilians and they gave her a Marine Corps Commendation Medal with V instead.

Yes, she'd howled then, and thrown things, and broken stuff, and they'd had to come in and give her a shot. The numb had begun after that, she thought.

Sally was drinking and staring at her as at a stranger, though Sally was the person who knew her best in the world, the keeper of every secret, the only one who knew about Ryan and Don. A wonderful man, Don, as everyone agreed, and she had come to love him, as they say, come to, not instantaneous gut ripping passion, but a good life, with the kids, not the life she had planned on before Mir Puza. The best thing about Don, she had told her sister, was that he was not in the Corps, and thus unlikely to get his ass shot off. Well, the joke was on her, wasn't it?

Sally wanted Nora to be the person she'd been this morning, or at least the person she'd been this morning who had endured the great catastrophe. That person would have flown to her sister's arms, would have yelled and shrieked and keened and been comforted as much as such a thing could be turned to comfort, and the whole family would have rallied around.

But no. That person was gone. In truth that person had not really come back from Helmand Province. Nora had tried, she really had, to form a decent life with a decent man and had the kids and all and to be a good mom and step-mom and a loving wife and perform a socially useful function. She had been a good soldier in this, and her family had been proud of her. Now she saw how that had been an illusion, a trick the universe or God had played, like a cat with a mouse. Oh, you think you got away with what you did? You think you could just pretend all that hadn't happened? Take *this!*

Again, she had a kind of out of body vision, of that poor girl Nora Kehoe, so well-trained, so well-meaning, so doomed. She saw her walking toward the schoolhouse in Mir Puza, as if from above, the last moments of her innocence, dressed like a Marine in helmet and flak vest, holding her carbine. Nora felt her throat clench. Her eyes and nose prickled and tears appeared and flowed down her cheeks.

Her sister said, "Well, yeah, finally," and clutched her into a fierce embrace. Nora relaxed into it. Why not? There was still this body in the world and it must do what was expected of it: allowing condolences to flow over her, performing the ceremonies of grief with discipline and polish, like a Marine.

"We should go on a road trip," said Sally. "Just get in my car and drive. We could go to California and stay with Ben. We could go to Disneyland."

"I think we could skip Disneyland," said Nora and Sally gasped and placed her hand over her mouth. "Oh, Christ, I'm sorry! But you do you like the road trip. You need to get away from . . . you know, this life. The memories and all."

Nora said nothing in response, but allowed Sally to rattle on about a trip that would never happen, leaning against her sister as Sally stroked her hair. It was fine and shoulder-length. Don had wanted her to grow it even longer, but now she thought she would cut it short, the way she'd had it in the service. That was something to put on the list.

The list had been accumulating in her head for some hours now and it was getting too long to hold in memory. She had to write it down and she wished Sally would leave so she could do so.

"I could eat something, I guess," said Nora. "I haven't had anything but coffee since yesterday morning."

Sally thought this was a great idea and hurried out of the room to make it happen. Nora took a small black notebook from a stack of them she kept in a cupboard. This was from long habit: every project—the garden pool, the kitchen renovation, a wedding—had its own notebook. By the end of the project, these would be thick with business cards, receipts, samples of paint or whatever, to be carefully shelved for future reference.

The idea had popped into her head fully formed. It was when Sally had said she had to let it out. That's what she wrote on the first page of the fresh notebook: Letting It Out.

3: Funeral Rites

Nora's younger brother, Ben, landed at Dulles from San Francisco at just past one in the morning and was at her house within the hour. She was awake and writing in her notebook when he arrived. She heard the sounds of the arrival, the car approaching, the thunk of the car door, the ring of the door chime, and felt a moment of annoyance before she reminded herself that Ben was one of the people on the list she'd made of likely helpers.

She heard her father open the door. She knew her parents had both been up. They were staying in Nora and Don's bedroom, because why not? It was the most comfortable bedroom, and Nora doubted whether she would ever sleep in that bed again. It was next door to the home office, so Nora could hear the low burble of talk, and her mother's sobbing. Once her father had raised his voice: Rose! Burble *burble burble* burble. Even if she had been able to hear these conversations perfectly, she knew that they would have seemed to be in a foreign language.

They would probably put Ben in the girls' room. Sally was in Gretchen's room, probably still messy from the morning's prep for the mall visit, clothes on the floor, a wet towel. Gretchen was neat only with respect to schoolwork and her collection of American Girl dolls and accouterments. She had stopped playing with them, but was not ready to surrender them to her half-sisters. Nora wondered if Sally minded sleeping there with all those slightly creepy dead faces staring down at her, especially given the present circumstances. Ben would, of course, not mind being in the girls' room, except for the length of the beds. Ben was not sensitive to such things, or really, to much of the bright pageant of human emotion.

He entered, as always, sans knock.

"Bad time, Nora," he said.

Nora looked up at him from where she sat at her desk and smiled, the first such since she had smiled at a salesgirl before the shooting began. Ben was smiling too. She rose from the day bed and hugged him, which was like hugging an upright futon. Sally had once observed that loving Ben was a perfectly gracious act, because you got nothing emotional in return; except great presents.

She said, "Sit down, Ben. You're looming."

Ben was a loomer from an early age, when the Kehoes discovered that some kind of psychic cuckoo had visited their nest. Ben spoke late and when he started it was in full paragraphs. He had never developed a sense of privacy and was often to be found at dawn at the foot of someone's bed, staring.

What to do with Ben had been a subject of some concern to Peter and Rose and their other kids. He acted out in school. He hit. He had rages. It turned out that he was dyslexic, and when that was fixed, he became the smartest kid in the school, at least in math and science. With computers he was of course a natural, a genuine internet pioneer. At ten he ran a bulletin board chat room with a thousand adults on it, devoted to high-end discussions about computer communications and hacking. Large and soft, with a peculiar melon head and cottony pale hair, he made a perfect target for bullies, but he was only bullied once at each new school. After such event, two Furies would descend on the 'bully, beat him bloody and make him eat dirt. That they were mere girls made it worse, and no one ever bothered young Ben after such demonstrations..

When puberty struck, and he had to choose a clique, he went with the heavy metal black hat hackers. Peter Kehoe was out in the Sandbox while this transition occurred, and when he returned he found his youngest with a violet streaked Afro and a set of six earrings. He assessed this phenomenon with amusement. With a brood that included three perfect Marines in embryo, he felt one cuckoo was no big deal. The boy was in honor society at school and would clearly have no problem getting into a college, if not the United States Naval Academy, and earning a living. Besides that, Colonel Kehoe was genuinely interested in electronic computation and what it would mean for the profession of arms and the two had many conversations on the subject. Ben was thus not excluded from the general illusion that he was the favored child.

In the event, Ben destroyed the SATs, graduated with the predictable 4.0, and went to Stanford on a full boat scholarship. He founded a company that hired squads of hackers to break into corporate computers. Presented with the evidence of this hack, the embarrassed firm was glad to pay Ben's outfit lots of money to prevent others from doing the same in earnest.

Ben was probably on the spectrum, the Kehoe clan agreed, but if a weirdo, he was *their* weirdo and beloved, including the dozen or so piercings that ornamented his face, and the anime eyes tattooed above his eyebrows, and the Mohawk hairdo, now the color of cheap orange soda. Ben returned the love to the extent he could; he was particularly lavish with presents. He had learned to charm as he had learned Linux, and to act the part of the good citizen, although natively he was as amoral as a cat. Nora had no doubt he would help her.

Ben sat in the desk chair. Nora said, “Yeah, a bad time, the worst, and it’s supposed to make me sad, and I *am* sad because my Mom and Dad and Sally are sad and I love them, but I don’t know . . . I’m not exactly feeling sad myself. It’s like I’m on the other side of sad, looking through a frosted glass at something that should be inside me, but isn’t.”

“Welcome to the club,” said Ben.”Cool.” On his face appeared a smile disturbingly like the one on that plastic Guy Fawkes mask the anarchists wear, a strained chevron.

“Yeah, I see what you mean. You had to learn how to act like a human and I have to learn how to act like the victim of a tragedy. I mean, I had a loss so ginormous that no regular person can get their head around it. Everyone wants so bad to do something for me, but there’s nothing to be done. That’s why people have been trying to get me to eat something. Or sleep. And Mom and Dad and Sally have all tried to push dope on me since, since the Thing. You have to sleep, you have to eat, and if I did they would feel they hadn’t been totally useless. It’s hard for people to say this happened and life goes on. Except for you, Benji. You don’t give much of a shit, do you?’

“No, I feel the loss. They were great kids and I liked Don okay. But there’s blank place there. I don’t do mourning, like I don’t do sports. I know I’m supposed to be real sad, so I act that way. Most people can’t tell the difference. Like, for example, I don’t look people in the eye, but if I kind of stare at the bridge of their nose, they think I am.”

Nora looked at her brother and smiled again. His moon face was directed at hers, as he had learned to do, and it did seem as though their eyes met. He wore heavy hideous black horn-rims, very like the ones the Navy provides to enlisted Marines, who call them "birth-control glasses."

"Well, we don't want that, do we?" she said. "Did you eat on the plane?"

"I had Snickers. But they don't have Soylent on the plane."

"We don't have any here either, but there's a casserole. If it's Deborah next door's it'll be her famous mac and cheese. It's what regular people have instead of Soylent. We could sneak downstairs and mike some up."

Ben agreed he could tolerate mac and cheese, so they slipped downstairs as noiselessly as they could, and Ben worked the microwave; since childhood he could not bear to have a machine operated in his presence unless he was controlling it. (He had howled continually on car rides until age eight.)

Back in Nora's room, they ate mac and cheese from bowls. Nora had a beer with; Ben, water.

The casserole was delicious, beyond delicious, the best food she could remember eating. She wondered how she could be so alive to the taste of an ordinary dish and so dead to the feelings she ought to be having. My family is dead and I am loving Deborah Carling's mac and cheese. Poor Deborah! She must be crying sympathetic tears tonight. She saw Deborah Carling every day, her children were of an age with Nora's dead twins and were always in and out of each other's houses. If the same thing had happened to Deborah's husband and children, Deb would be prostrate with grief, screaming and wailing, and Nora would have brought over her famous four-cheese lasagna.

The thought made her laugh. Interesting: she could still do it. She said, "This is like being kids again."

"Yes, except it's a different house, and we're older, and your kids just got killed. Other than that we could be in Kailua."

"True," said Nora, interrupting. "How's your business doing?"

"It booms. Would you like to be bored by details?"

"That's an advance. A couple of years ago, someone asked you that, you'd recite spreadsheets."

"I matured. I started dealing with the V-caps. The V-caps can handle a little Asperger's but they get bored easily and they don't give you money for boring."

"But you still memorize train schedules."

"Of course. I mean, I'm not fucking *normal*."

He rose. "Sleep time."

"Wait! I need you to help me with something."

He sat.

She said, "Look, what do you know about identity theft?"

"Everything."

"That's good. Can you help me make up a new identity?"

"Sure. You want someone your age who doesn't have much web presence, maybe they just have a credit card they don't use a lot. If you have their social and DOB you can get a passport and a drivers license. Or you can just make up a fake person by hacking into state records and banks and employers and stuff. It's all on the dark web.

"Can I have three or four?"

"You can have a hundred if you want," said Ben. "What do you want fake ID for, by the way?"

"I'm going to do a lot of crimes."

Again the anarchist smile. "Cool," he said.

One good thing coming out of this, thought Nora, is that now I really *get* Ben. The not giving a shit, and the needle focus.

Nora managed to cry at the funeral, not during the Mass or the reception, nor at the graveside when the two little white coffins and one slightly longer went into the black earth, but later, in the limo driving home. It took her unawares; one moment she was sitting silently between her mother and Sally in the back seat, and the next her neck was snapped back in tetanic rigidity, her hands were by her cheeks in the classic Munchian position, while sounds at high volume shot from her throat.

She had cried before now, of course, but like a regular human. These were inhuman yawps, quonks, howls, sounds of ungainly waterfowl seeking mates, sounds of Pleistocene megafauna trapped in tar pits, quasi-industrial sounds. They came unbidden from her throat, scraping it raw, as her mother and sister, both of whom had been weeping conventionally for almost the whole of the event, hugged her from either side, and offered contradictory comfort noises—oh no oh no from Rose; good, let it out, yeah, let it out, from Sally.

The odd thing for Nora was that this paroxysm seemed to be happening to someone else, perhaps to the ghost of the woman who had died along with her family, but who still had some presence in the day-lit world. Or maybe it was something weirder—the goddess of grief had finally come on line, delayed by unusually heavy traffic or call volume perhaps, and had delivered her singing telegram.

The sons and the father, sitting in the forward rows of seats, pretended nothing was happening, as was proper. Nora wished she was sitting up there with them in the stoic forbearance of the Corps. This current display, it seemed to her, had nothing to offer, no connection to the past, no promise for the future. This is what it means to be beyond grief, she thought, and waited patiently for it to stop.

The men in the car also waited for it to stop, confident it would. Colonel Kehoe had observed a good deal of grief in his career, some of it caused by him, and was familiar with its varied manifestations. He had held in his arms Marines who had just seen their best friends reduced to red jelly. He understood the difference between what you felt and what you did, which is the heart of discipline. He loved his men, he would have died gladly for them, but also he would have sent every one of them to certain death if his duty had required it. He was a good father. He had the art of fostering in the hearts of each of his kids the sense that they were his favorite one. He felt for his daughter; he regretted intensely the loss of her girls. But he had five other grandchildren, Sally's two and Doug's three. In his heart he had already regrouped, had absorbed the losses, and he knew that Nora would as well. It was part of what he had taught his family to do.

Captain Doug Kehoe, USMC, was thinking about how soon he could get back to his ship. He loved his sister, but they were not close and he barely knew her dead children. He barely knew his own children. Every family has an addict, and Doug was it for the

Kehoes. He was addicted to flying F-18 Hornets off aircraft carriers, and while he cared very much for his wife and kids, if it ever came to a choice between flying fighter jets and them, he knew which one he would choose, and so did his wife. He thought he could with decency leave the next morning.

Ben was thinking that if they didn't increase their speed by at least four miles an hour they would not make the C & O level crossing on Route 123 before the coal train that was scheduled to pass there at 1:13, and they would have a long wait. He could do some work on his enormous phone while they waited, but he knew that his father would not approve of that. Nor would the Colonel approve of asking the driver to speed up. Ben was often in such situations when with his family; he sought relief by rocking, and by making his right knee vibrate up and down. In his head, he calculated primes and made to-do lists. One item was the fake IDs for his sister. He didn't think it would be much trouble. He would provide three, a nice friendly little prime.

Nora has stopped her noise. She is back in the humvee in the little maidan at the center of Mir Puza. Crammed around her is her Female Engagement Team. She looks out the dust-smeared window. There is the mosque, yellow-white like old bones, there is the police station and the school, a low green-painted building, and there is the street that leads to the market, all familiar, they have come here. many times, but today something is amiss. They all feel it.

Behind Nora, Wart Gunther asks, where is everybody? and Nora notices that the beggars are absent, who always gather on the porch of the mosque and hold out their begging bowls to the camo-clad male women from a distant planet. Nora looks up at Peanut Cooper, who is manning the turret and regarding the world from behind his M2, and asks him if he sees any movement. He says no movement; he says the school is closed, even though it's a school day. The door is shut and they have the shutters up.

She tells Gunther to contact Cowboy One. Cowboy One actual, Lt. Harrison, the convoy commander, comes on. Nora asks him what he thinks, should they unload, or what, the place looks wrong, no kids, no beggars, the school doors and shutters are closed. Cowboy One says he'll put some people on the rooftops, set up a perimeter. Continue with the mission, sir? That's affirmative. Nora glances at her translator, Zareena Deh Bala, and sees that her usual cheerful expression has been replaced with a pinched, rabbity look. They should book out, Nora thinks, but they have been ordered to deploy and Nora is a good Marine officer: aye aye, sir, is the only possible response.

The team begins to unload: cartons of baby formula, dried milk, books, paper and pencils, sanitary napkins, and other items useful to village women. Zulu Anderson, one of her FETs, asks where to move the load. The school? That's where they usually go, but usually the arrival of the FET is a big deal, women and kids swarming around, Bibi Lohani, their main contact should be there, being officious, taking charge of the goodies, offering tea.

Her mother said, "Would you like some tea?"

They had arrived at the house. How had that happened and where had she been? Another flashback, she had been completely gone this time, forty-five minutes at least, and no one had noticed. Sally and her mother both looked more relaxed; perhaps it was the wailing episode, perhaps they now felt that she was into the mourning process, that she had Let It Out. Nora spent the evening in her room; everyone seemed a little frightened of her, as if she were wearing a suicide vest, and were happy to leave her alone.

She lay on the day-bed in her office and thought about children, not her own children but children in Afghanistan, only some of whom had been shot dead. It had not occurred to her in her naiveté that there were people who would cause the death of a whole bunch of kids to make a political point, and so when children were present she and the other Female Engagement Team members would relax, would drop the psychic armor they wore all the time in Helmand Province.

Now she is among the women and their children on the banks of the Aryananda River just outside Mir Puza, they are at the woman's place, a broad beach and a hollow rock just right for pounding clothing. The water sparkles and gurgles, the children splash and shriek, and everyone is listening to Bibi Lohani tell stories. A merchant has a parrot that he sets to guard his wife's virtue while he is away. The wife pulls all the parrot's feathers and kicks it out of the house. Then, though a barely comprehensible set of events, the parrot pretends to be a saint in a shrine and gets the wife to pull out all her hair. *Thus he had his revenge!* Almost every Pashtun folk tale ends so, but the Pentagon did not think that was significant.

Bibi said that no one told stories in Afghanistan the way they once could because now they had DVDs from Pakistan and India, and who needed stories now? But she could tell all the old ones, the best ones, including the tales of the woman warriors of the Pashtuns, Malalai, a heroine of the Second Afghan War, who said to her beloved, "Beloved, if you don't fall in the Battle of Maiwand, someone is saving you for a token of shame," and Nahid, who helped start the jihad against the Russians, and died fighting, and Khatol Mohammedzai, the first Pashtun woman to become a general.

Bibi was the matriarch of the village and of the Lohani clan. The Lohani were one of the two major clans in the valley, the other being the Shiranis. Bibi had introduced Nora to the senior lady of the Shiranis, one Farishta, a dry and humorless woman, who surveyed the world with the absolute security of a Pashtun woman who has borne five sons. This was why Bibi, who had only one, deferred to her, or so Nora had thought. She had been wrong about that, as about so many things in that country. Still, she recalled the river, and the children and Bibi's moon face, and the stories and felt what she had felt then: joy and the sense of something opening up, a different life.

They got through Christmas finally, by pretending it wasn't, no gifts, no carols on the stereo, and by the twenty-seventh, only Sally was still there in the house with Nora. You can't spend New Years alone, Sally said to her, come down to Quantico with me and spend it with Barb and me and the kids. She asked, what are you gonna do in this big house with nobody here? You'll go nuts.

Nora said she wanted to be alone, that she was good with alone, she always had been. She saw her sister's face crumple up. They could always make each other cry, from the time they were babies, and when one cried, the other would always join in. It was their first lesson in empathy. Nora wished she was still that person.

She made herself shrug and smile. "I'll be okay," she said. "I mean nothing worse can happen, right? But I need to stay engaged, I need to do tasks, you know? I need to get with Andy Bannerman and see if he'll make an offer for Don's half of the business, and then I have to find one of those brokers that buys houses full of furniture, and sell everything, and then I have to sell the house and find someplace small and anonymous to live in, a condo someplace, I don't know where. But I'll visit you when all that's done, okay?"

"You're being a Kehoe, aren't you? Going it alone, don't need no help from nobody."

"I guess."

"That's so wrong." Sally began to cry now, not sobbing, but loosing fat helpless tears. "This is the worst, you know that? It's sounds crazy, but I always thought that whatever happened, *whatever* happened to us in our life, we would always be Sally and Nora, and now I look at you and nothing looks back. I feel like saying who are you and what have you done with my sister?"

"I'm sorry," Nora said. "It's the stages of grief. Denial. Numbness. Anger. Some others in there. It's the same as PTSD, I think it might be the same pamphlet, the stages and all. You could read it. The church sent a copy over."

"Oh, fuck your pamphlet!" Sally cried and left the room. Nora observed her sister's pain, but couldn't feel it. She lay on the day bed in her office and thought about those stages. They didn't say what happened if you were in one stage because of some post-traumatic stress and then something else happened, another trauma, maybe even a worse one, how did you know what stage to be in? Or maybe they converged, like superimposed synchronized sound waves, amplifying the peaks higher and sinking the valleys lower.

She thought she was in deep Numb now. She'd come back from Mir Puza numb and had stayed a little numb all through the aftermath, getting back with Don and having the babies, although she had learned to act like she was feeling stuff, fake it till you make it as they said in the counseling group sessions. And she had faked it and she had made it, although perhaps God was not fooled and had shifted her back where she belonged, to the zero, the nullity she deserved. But she felt some slow movement, she thought she was moving out of Numb. Numb had served its purpose, protecting the organism from dissolution in the acid of unbearable feeling.

After Numb came Anger, she recalled. Nora wrapped the Tree of Life quilt around her and let it come.

4: Making a List

Nora was glad to see her sister go, even though she loved her sister more than anyone in the world, really more than she had her dead kids, and being distant with her, as she had, as she *had* to do, was the final strangulation of love in her heart. The name of what had happened to her, the reality of it, had struck her on the ride back from the cemetery, which was why the mindless howling. But now that she was in it, it felt okay, clear and empty a polished wineglass of a person now, and also the sense that it was right and just that she should be that way.

It is right and just. That was what the people said in the Mass after the priest thanked God. Yes, and all that Catholic stuff still lived in her head now, from being always in a church school. God knew how they had afforded it for all the kids, but they had; Peter thought the discipline was worth it. Just-war theory, something she'd done a senior thesis on, *jus in bello, jus ad bello,* all that. Also St. Teresa of Avila, advice about what you do when you actually hear the little voice, the three possibilities, it's God, it's the Devil, you're crazy, how to tease those out.

The saint said, look at what the person does, how the person feels, that's how you tell. Well, clearly crazy, no one would do what she was planning except if they were crazy, God wouldn't ever license killing, except in a just war, and also: vengeance is mine says the Lord, *I* will repay. Not you. But the peculiar thing here was she felt neither hate nor the urge to revenge. She felt rather that she'd become an instrument, with another's will filling up the void where Nora had been.

She thought that St. Joan must have felt like that. As a female and a warrior, Nora had naturally a particular interest in the Maid of Orleans, and some questions: why did God care who ruled France? If God didn't care, then Joan's conversations with saints were mere hallucinations. But Joan had actually done what she set out to do. A teen-aged peasant girl had convinced the haughty chivalry of France to follow her, and she had taken Orleans and had the Dauphin crowned at Reims. Surely that was divine intervention; or maybe dumb luck and a medieval will to believe weird shit.

Or maybe Nora was just a nut. She entertained this idea too. It made sense—you lose your family in the most horrific way, on top of what went down at Mir Puza, and the mind snaps.

But Nora had seen people whose mind had actually snapped. There was a Pashtun woman in a village they'd stopped at after it had been bombed from the air by the Americans. She was sitting in front of a ruined house rocking a child, a girl of about five. The scene had caught Nora's eye then, because of the calm smile on the woman's face and the odd hat the girl was wearing, sort of a red beret with black lace trim, or so it seemed. Nora had never seen such headgear before and so she strolled over for a closer look.

It turned out that a piece of hypersonic metal, perhaps from the bombing, had shattered the child's skull and exposed her brain, which now sat like a red hat above her curiously untouched face. What looked like black lace was a horde of feeding flies. It turned out that the woman's other five children had been pulverized by the bomb and this huggable corpse was all she had left. She resisted fiercely any effort to take it away from her.

But Nora did not think she was crazy in quite that way. She didn't think her dead babies were alive, and she had no desire to sit and croon over their bodies. She knew what had happened, and why, and she was determined to act so as to reduce the possibility of it happening again. She thought she had a very small chance of causing any such reduction, but she felt compelled to try. She didn't care if she died trying.

For almost two weeks after the funeral Nora watched everything she could about the mass murder on television and the internet. There was a lot to watch. The nation and the world had been captured by the story of Duane Paul Hatch, the Santa Killer. It turned out that Duane had been for some years at the center of Active Shooter, a website devoted to the admiration, the connoisseurship even, of mass killings. The young men who attended this site desired to be thought outrageous and free of any social constraints, so they chatted about the killings they planned to do, and admired those with the courage to actually do mass murder.

Eric Harris, of Columbine infamy, was the patron saint here. Everyone wanted to be like Eric, except more efficient, so as to rack up a higher kill score than Eric's modest thirteen. A section of the site was devoted to weapons. Most of the boys and boy-men owned guns, some owned dozens, and they were all about giant magazines, laser sighting, suppressors, and full-auto mod kits. Crank, bump-stock or illegal tampering? Each had its advocates, and the debate was fierce.

In these debates, Duane shone. Nora thought his arguments in favor of the Robbins "Reaper," a 5.56mm copy of the military M4 carbine, and against the similar Patriot Ordnance Renegade Plus and the Mossberg MMR, were entirely convincing. He recommended the MVF-515 red modular vertical fore grip laser for the Reaper, and in fact that was what he'd installed on the weapon he had eventually used to kill Nora's family and 141 other people.

Duane wrote well, and was magisterial on both weapons and the history of mass killers. He could put down upstarts with a hail of facts and a clever insult. People asked him questions and he deigned to answer, at length and in detail. Active Shooter was a jolly place. It was so much *fun* to fantasize about mass killing: LOLZ as the boys put it.

Besides this trove, Duane had posted a manifesto, in the manner of his hero, Eric Harris, on his own website, Kill 'Em All! In it he proclaimed his view of the world and explained himself to an amazed nation. His position was that everything in the world was bullshit and everything that ordinary people valued was a scam and a delusion. Love was delusional, as was sex (how women controlled you) as was work (unworthy of the superior man) as were religion (especially that!), patriotism, the right wing, the left wing, cute animals, Facebook, Instagram, and Tumblr. He went into considerable detail on how every aspect of society had failed him, because society and humanity in general were unforgivably stupid.

Stupid was just about his favorite word. In his view, every person he had ever met was a disappointment and hopelessly lame. What then could the superior man do with his life? Grab the world by the neck and rub its face in the shit, was what, and the best way to do this was by killing as many people as possible in as public a manner as could be arranged.

He explained that to make the event even more memorable, he would do it just before the stupidest holiday of the year, dressed up as Santa Claus. He could hardly contain the hilarity: who was more stupid and in need of killing than the morons who brought their children to see Santa? And of course there would be plenty of child-sized targets there too.

He despised children anyway, the little vermin. The world would be well rid of them and he imagined with glee the sentimental fools whining over the little corpses. There was a long disquisition about whether he should kill his mother before going out on the prank (his word) and decided that it would be more nasty to let her be known for the rest of her miserable life as the mom of the greatest mass killer in American history.

Nora read this screed many times until it began to make a strange sort of sense to her, this urge to gain fame among online peers by outrageous violent action. She'd seen it before in young Marines downrange. They would tell one another to "get some" when they went out on patrol, and ask one another if they had "got any" upon returning. They mocked the dead civilians. They made jokes about murdering women and children.

This was her nation: what every other civilized land experienced once a decade, if ever, was a weekly occurrence in America, and weekly the politicians who made it possible sent thoughts and prayers to the ravaged communities in which these events occurred.

No one's mind was ever changed, it seemed. You would think that legislators from the towns and cities where these horrors occurred would lead the charge to ban mass killing weapons, even start a crusade to scoop up the millions of them now in the hands of Americans. But no. The relatively tiny industry that made and sold guns had a literal death-grip on American politics, such that throughout most of the nation no one could be elected who did not promise that, in effect, mass murder would continue forever because the Second Amendment somehow made the killing holy. Nora didn't think she could stop this, but she did think she could draw attention to the problem in a way that had not occurred to anyone before.

Besides this study, Nora found that she could mobilize the shell of the former Nora to interact with the world, a necessary part of her plan. Or the Plan, for she thought of it now almost as an institution that she served, like the Marines. She visited her neighbor, Deborah Carling, as she had done before the sad events, even though Deborah collapsed in tears at intervals, especially when her own living daughters were around. Nora was able to comfort her in her distress, although Nora was not sure just what her distress was. *You're so brave,* was something Deborah often said, although being a victim, in Nora's view, required no bravery.

Nora was extremely brave, in fact, had been brave her whole life, but she didn't think she was being brave now. A little manipulative, rather. Nora understood that it was her responsibility to make comfortable the people who cared about the person she had once been. Deborah appeared uneasy about contact between Nora and her own unmurdered children, but Nora put her at ease, and was outgoing and friendly to the three little girls, five, eight and ten. She answered their questions about Abigail, Adele and Gretchen in Heaven and corrected the youngest one's impression that Santa had killed them because they had been really really naughty.

After a decent interval, Nora put her house on the market and brought in a firm that bid on the contents. She sold everything. She also sold Don's Lexus and her Subaru Outback, trading both in for a three-year-old red Ford 150 with a camper back and a Masterbuilt motorcycle carrier. She bought a Suzuki GW250 motorcycle to go in it.

By February she had sold the house for a million-three, which netted her a little over six hundred thousand. This was in addition to the twenty odd thousand she got for the contents and the half million from Don's life insurance and the three million-six that Andy Bannerman, paid her to buy Don's share of Dominion Building Maintenance. That was on the high end of the valuation, but Andy was not of a mind to get over on the grieving widow. Don and he had been on the same high school teams, and he seemed to take his friend's death harder than Nora had. Tears brimmed in his eyes as they signed the papers, and he offered his services—anything you need, Nora, anything at all, just ask.

Nora had noticed this as a thing: people asking if there was anything they could do, and she wondered at this. What could they possibly mean? She had asked the same thing in similar situations and she hadn't known what she meant either. But now she said that there *was* something Andy could do. From time to time she met ex-Marines or their family members who were down on their luck, maybe there was a drug or alcohol issue in the past or a felony conviction that made it hard to find work. If something could be found for such people, cleaning offices, driving . . .?

Andy was nodding away. “Anytime, Nora, just call. Happy to help.”

And recommendations from Dominion to other firms in other towns? Not a problem. Andy could fake up a résumé and a work history on demand. Just call and it’ll be done.

By the end of February, Nora was living in a two-bedroom rental off Braddock Road in Centreville, a new unit with off-street parking for the camper, and convenient to the fire station where she worked. She had returned to work at around that time, to the surprise of her shift supervisor, who thought that the last thing Nora would want to do was to race out of a firehouse in an EM bus to treat drug ODs and gunshot victims. Nora told him that she thought that the best cure for suffering was to help others. She said she didn’t know how long she’d be staying in Northern Virginia, but she would like to pull a few shifts a week. The supervisor was inclined to be accommodating, and set her up with some plum shifts, no weekends, no graveyards. He called her a hero too.

Among the Kehoes it was said that boot camp began the day the babies came home from the hospital. Nora thus had all the discipline she needed to put a complex plan into effect. She had her black grid-printed notebook, which went everywhere with her, and in the notebook were sets of lists. It had been drummed into her during her childhood that any of life’s confusions could be allayed simply by breaking the problem down into an orderly progression of tasks. Even in the Corps, Nora had been known for her ability to bring order out of chaos, and this talent was now mobilized in furtherance of the Plan.

One list was headed “Resources,” and most of the items on it had been checked off. She had sufficient money, and the necessary vehicles. A list descended from the heading “Ordnance,” but none of the items had yet been checked off. The same with "Intel," and "Camo." The one labeled "Targets" contained a substantial number of items, but all of the little boxes still awaited checks.

Well, early days still—Nora had discovered in herself deep wells of patience, a virtue that had not previously distinguished her. When she had a family, when an outing was in train, she had always been the first one ready, jangling her keys by the open door and demanding haste be made (*Any day now, people!*) like any Parris Island DI. Now, she felt she had plenty of time. The problem she aimed to affect was not going away and she had nothing else she wished to do.

The first item under the heading "Personal" was "gym." Nora had been in shape almost since the cradle; having a Marine officer as a dad made it hard not to be, and of course as a Marine herself, she had done the usual crazy physical stuff that Marines do. But now there was a new seriousness, her notebook crammed with goals and measurements and speeds to be attained and weights to be lifted, the bench, the press, the curl. She had a good mental image of what she wanted to look like, and what she wanted to be able to do.

Beyond this, she sought instruction. She made a generous contribution to the Fairfax Theatrical Society, in return for which they let her participate in their performance of *Angels in America,* a small part, but she performed it well and learned how to apply theatrical makeup and use the various appliances actors employ to make themselves someone else.

She obtained coaches in motorcycle riding, marksmanship, parkour, and the Israeli unarmed combat technique, Krav Maga. A busy schedule; but on the other hand she wasn't dating, had no family responsibilities, didn't use social media beyond the bare minimum. She was no longer into television. She used her computer mainly to research subjects she thought would support the Plan. Her job gave her twenty-four hours off after each twelve hour shift.

She had lots and lots of time, and tried to fill each passing hour with achievements.

She might have quit her job--she didn't need the money--but she was trying to maintain the persona of a woman who had been badly hurt, but was tough and recovering. Normality was what she wanted people to remember, a normal person, not someone who would do what she was planning to do. For this reason too, she visited her family. She drove her camper to Nag's Head, North Carolina, and spent a week with her parents. Both were pleased that she had taken up so many new interests. They thought it was healthy, or at least her mother did. Rose Kehoe had spent so much of her child-rearing energy on her Benjamin that her other children had learned that the best way to please their mother was to be invisible and no trouble at all.

On several occasions Nora had found her father staring at her, like those people did in *Invasion of the Body Snatchers* after their loved ones had been taken over. Once she said, "What? Did I do something wrong?"

He started. "No, of course not," he said. "Just sometimes you seem not to be you, if that makes any sense."

"Um, well, I have PTSD, Dad. I'm *not* myself. And, like, losing my family to violence didn't *cure* the PTSD I brought back from A-stan."

Colonel Kehoe had been an enlisted Marine before he became an officer and so had a bullshit detector of unusual acuity. There was something *off* in his daughter, to be sure, but whether it was the kind of *off* you got from what happened in Mir Puza and the Mall of Death, or another and more dangerous off, the gun-in-mouth kind of off, he didn't know. This is why he stared at his daughter, nursing the absurd hope that the answer would somehow emerge from her skin and fly into his brain.

For her part, Nora had found that bringing up her tragedy usually served to distract the overly curious. As here.

Returning north, she stopped at Quantico, Virginia, to see her sister, Sally, who worked at the FBI's National Center for the Analysis of Violent Crime. Nora understood how important it was that Sally believed Nora to be just fine, because everyone in the family knew how close they were; if something were really wrong with Nora, they all thought, Sally would find it. Also, Sally had been for some years a special agent in the field, and she still had her field agent chops. Nora didn't want a light bulb to go off over her sister's head when the news of the Plan started to appear. Nora wanted to be the last person Sally thought of when that happened.

Nora was not much of a drinker, but it took a lot of beer and tequila to get through a weekend at Sally's now. Sally and Barbara Grant, her wife, had three children, twelve, nine and seven, Violet, Edmund and Lane, and it turned out that playing the aunt when your own children have been killed is harder than playing the maiden aunt or the aunt bringing cousins.

Barbara was a therapist, with that eagle eye the good ones have, and that might have been a problem, had *been* a problem in the past when Nora returned from the war. Nora had thought the false self she had constructed would pass, but Barbara had seen right through it and there had been scenes, thrown wine-glasses, some vileness.

Nora was better at it now, however; she had no conflicts inside her, there was not much of anything else inside her, or rather she was filled with the Plan, and since the Plan required that Barbara and Sally believe that she was a much damaged woman making a valiant recovery, she would actually become that woman.

So she leapt from the car grinning, and hugged everyone with enthusiasm, and distributed funny gifts (rubber noses, wigs, fart pillows), and, gathered in the living room with drinks, amazed them all with descriptions of her activities.

"What's parkour," Edmund asked.

"It's climbing around on urban architecture, walking up the walls, jumping across alleys, and like that."

"Like a ninja?"

"Sort of like."

"Cool, Aunt Nora!

It was cool indeed. Even Violet, who wore only black and had made a vow of ennui, regarded her aunt with somewhat more engagement. The kids wanted to have a cool and lively auntie, and not to have to think about their dead cousins, and Barbara and Sally wanted the old Nora back, old like before Afghanistan, and Nora let herself be empty and receive those projections and then reflected them back, to general satisfaction, she thought. Perhaps much of human interaction was like that, a stereotyped call and response, perhaps that was what really generated that much-desired emotional security. She didn't feel manipulative, if that even meant anything to what she had become, she felt like she was in a play and doing well and looking forward to wonderful applause.

On the last day of that visit, the Sunday, Barbara had taken the kids out to one of Virginia's perpetual celebrations of its colonial past, a fair, circa 1750: food, sharp tools, shootin' and hanging out among domestic animals--with candles, but without the slaves. This was a typical Barbara kindness, giving the two sisters an empty house to talk in. They watched the Nationals lose to the Orioles and drank margaritas.

Sally said, "I got turned down by the terrorism task force—did I tell you?"

"No. That's a surprise.," said Nora. "I thought you were Quantico's golden girl."

"Not quite golden enough, apparently. A rumor was going around that they looked askance at using victims of terror."

"But you're not a victim of terror," said Nora and then did a take. "Oh, you mean . . . *me* and all that?"

"That was the rumor."

"Then I'm sorry. Did you really lust for it?"

"Meh. It would've been neat to do it and it would've looked good in the CV. I guess I'll have to sit here for the next year and do profiling. After that, I'll put in for the field again and they'll be so guilty about screwing me on the terrorism thing that they'll give me my choice of assignments. So it's all good. And you, little sis, you've got plans of your own? You're going to be a ninja?"

"It'd make Edmund happy . . . but really, it's a little like that. I'm thinking of going back in."

"What, into the Corps? Christ, Nora, you think they'd take you?"

"I think yes. They opened combat specialties to women last year, but they're a little nervous about it, and not many women have a ribbon with a V on it. I've been in combat, they know I'm not going to break down and cry in a firefight. Combat hardened first looies w/vagina are not thick on the ground in the Corps. I think they'll let me in and when I tell the interview board about all my self-assigned training and let them feel my biceps--well, let's say I'm confident."

"What does Dad think about this? I won't even ask about Mom."

"The Colonel Dad approves. He totally gets it."

"What does he get?"

"The Corps is what I have instead of a family. I'll be the one to take the extra duty so that the other officers can spend holidays with their people. Not that he wasn't devoted, but it's different when there's no one needing you at home."

"What are you talking about, you jerko? *I* need you!"

"You know what I mean: besides, you've got Barb and the kids. Anyway, being free, and before I go back into the Corps, I'm going to travel. That's why I bought the truck and the camper-back. I want to visit some of the folks I served with and, you know, just drive around. I've never seen the Grand Canyon, can you believe? And I'm free to do stuff like that now. I have no ties."

Sally started to cry, and Nora hugged her tightly and offered comforting words. So this had worked out just right.

5: Rendezvous with Death

The phone rang at two-ten in the morning and when Nora answered it, her brother said, without preamble, "There are two kinds of false identity. One, you take over a real person's identity and you pretend to be them. Two is you construct an identity, someone who's not real, and pretend to be them. You want number two. I sent you a package with three, but you can have more if you want."

Nora didn't bother complaining about the time. Ben operated on a twenty-four hour schedule untethered to the rest of human society and called whenever. She said, "What's in the package?"

"Birth certificates. A guy I know from the dark web makes them up. Health departments are getting antsy about people using infant deaths to generate false ID, but their security is a joke, so he just goes into the systems and makes shit up. Bye."

That was an advance—Ben usually terminated a call without a word of farewell. As she had achieved full consciousness at the first ring of the phone, now she plunged immediately back into sleep. No dreams this time, a small blessing. She had not thought that any dreams could exceed in horror the Afghanistan dreams, but she had found that this was not so, that the ones with the children were worse.

The next morning there was a Fed Ex package in the condo's mail room. In it were three birth certificates, all with Nora's birthday, and originating in Virginia, the District, and Maryland. The names on them were: Jane Denise Bridges; Francine Susan Morgan; and Audrey Carol Franklin. Nora wondered briefly where Ben's pal had obtained those fictitious names and then concluded that they had been generated by a program optimized for bland. It was what she required, forgettable names for forgettable people.

With the birth certificates, some driving, and a lot of waiting around, Nora obtained social security numbers for her three phantoms, and Virginia driver's licenses. She opened bank accounts for each with varying amounts around ten grand, and on that basis three banks were happy to give her credit cards.

All this took a lot of time, but still well within schedule. At the beginning of April, Nora gave her notice to the county. She told her co-workers the same story she had told her sister: thinking about the Marines, wanting to travel. They gave her a nice party, with cake and sodas, and a little jokey gift: a first aid kit in a fake Vuitton bag.

It was no trouble to sublet her condo to a George Mason student at a favorable rent. The girl would have parties, she thought, and maybe trash the place, but Nora didn't expect to be returning. In the following days she sold her truck to the fictive Jane Denise Bridges, and reloaded her wallet to reflect the new identity. There was very little to pack. When her new truck registration came through, she drove away north.

Spring had exploded in the yards and roadsides, flowers abounded and so did blossoming trees, of which northern Virginia has more of than all of Europe. The air was wafting scent; she kept her window open and as she rolled north on Route 7 the poem returned to her mind, the springtime and the situation making it almost theme music. Ryan Graham had taught it to her. He had a bunch of war poetry memorized, and had a reputation in the Corps of declaiming it as his unit rolled into action on bird or humvee.

I have a rendezvous with Death

At some disputed barricade

When Spring comes back with rustling shade

And apple-blossoms fill the air

I have a rendezvous with Death

When Spring brings back blue days and fair.

And here she was, on a blue fair day, riding to a town famous for just the sort of quixotic, insane, but necessary action she now contemplated. Just about 170 years ago, a man driven to madness by the persistence of slavery staged a raid on the arsenal at Harpers Ferry. That he was quickly captured, that the slave rebellion he envisaged failed to happen, that he was hanged, didn't signify. John Brown won his battle, Nora thought, because he showed that the time for talking and compromise was over, and over also were the niceties of the law.

It was condemned as a crime, to be sure, but it was no ordinary crime, because if a white man was willing to kill and die to end slavery, then slavery could never be safe inside the United States. Everyone in the slave states knew this. It caused a panic; Lincoln's election was just the last mote that tipped the scales. A little over a year after John Brown was hanged, South Carolina seceded from the Union.

Nora knew a good deal about John Brown's story because her father was an American history buff who dragged his family across battlefields as the standard vacation treat. Of the four children, Nora was the only one not bored to the eyes by this, besides Ben, who was not entirely in a world where boredom signified. She loved the sense of being on the literal battle ground, seeing where *they* were and where *we* were, and imagining the unfolding of the battle on these actual cornfields and hollows and hills. She always thought that this was where she had obtained her eye for terrain, during these wonderful moments alone with her father, talking tactics.

John Brown himself was extra interesting because of the ambiguity with which her dad had discussed him. Nora had the sense that while what he did was wrong, he was also on the right side of history: slavery had to be destroyed and he had started the avalanche that buried it, added to which was the uncomfortable fact that Brown had been captured by U.S. Marines. Who, it went without saying, could do no wrong, so the oddness of the thing stuck in her head, and when the Plan had appeared to her, she thought immediately of John Brown's mad deed.

That her first target was in Harpers Ferry made it even more clear that this was meant to be. It was the kind of coincidental connection that crazy people make much of, she knew that, but she also knew she herself was in fact a crazy person. She was comfortable with the status. She thought that there were certain problems in life that required being crazy to fix and that this was one of them.

Her destination turned out to be a low concrete-block-stucco building in a strip mall on Route 340 just after it crosses the West Virginia state line. It had two slit windows barred with steel, each showing a neon sign, one saying GUNS and the other

AMMO. A large display sign squatted on top of the building, bearing a crude painting of a whitetail buck, with a crosshair sight overlaid on its chest. The top of the sign was cut to resemble mountain peaks; below these, rustic letters said "Mountain Guns" and announced an indoor shooting range. Nora drove by the place once, slowly, and then asked her phone to find her an RV park.

It was a nice one, sitting a woodsy bluff above the Shenandoah River, half deserted now except for some retirees living out of huge crate-like beige vehicles. After Nora had registered (as Jane Bridges) and parked, she walked down to the water and onto a dock. The river was in its spring fullness, brown, oily and dangerous. She skipped rocks for a while and then visited a Burger King in Harpers Ferry for lunch. It had WiFi, so she lingered and did some more research on her laptop. At a quarter to five she returned to the RV park, unloaded her motorcycle from its rack and rode it back to the gun shop.

Inside was a room with a glass counter displaying rental pistols, and behind that stood cabinets full of ammunition, and behind those a peg-board wall hung thick with weapons, including an antique Thompson submachine gun with the drum magazine and several copies of the Robbins Reaper 5.56 assault rifle that had killed her family. A door led to another room. Nora glanced in and saw more display cases full of pistols, and a wall full of long guns, and shelves full of accessories to make shooting more enjoyable.

Nora approached the fellow behind the rental counter, a husky youth in his mid-twenties. He had a military crew cut and a struggling ginger mustache and had dressed in a black jeans and a T-shirt. The shirt bore the text of the Second Amendment, with the words "shall not be infringed," in blazing red letters and underlined. He wore a nylon holster on his hip with a Glock 17 pistol in it.

She smiled and asked if she could rent a pistol for the range, and the youth told her they didn't rent pistols to singles. You had to come in with someone or bring your own weapon. Nora made a light remark about having to find another suicide venue, but the guy didn't smile. She said, "I guess I'll have to buy me a gun then," and moved into the other room.

Behind the counter stood the owner, Darren Oglesby, a large, soft, fiftyish gent, with a short black & white beard. His long, thin gray hair was tied behind in an attempt at a Minuteman pigtail, and his expression said he was nobody's fool. Under a black leather vest he wore a black T-shirt too, this one attesting to his determination to hold on to his guns until they were torn from his cold, dead hands. He packed a Kimber 1911 in a leather holster.

Nora was wearing desert digi-camo trousers and an olive drab USMC T-shirt under a worn green and gold George Mason hoodie. She slid a little country into her voice when she spoke.

"I'm looking for a Beretta nine?"

"The 92, I guess," said the man.

Nora said that would be okay if he had the SB version; he retrieved the pistol from a display case and set it on a black rubber mat on the glass.

Nora handled the gun, popped the magazine, racked the slide, looked at her thumbnail down the barrel and generally showed that she knew her way around the pistol.

Ogleby said as much.

"Yeah, I was with the 26th MEU in Afghanistan," she said.

This is making him uneasy, she thought, he's not sure what I am. I'm a gun person, but a girl. I shouldn't have been memorable. Close the deal.

"Really. I didn't know they let women carry weapons in the Marines."

"They insist on it. I'll take this. And, do you have the Robbins Reaper 5.56 AR?"

He did. He brought one down from a wall rack and handed it to Nora. Again she did the various things that people who know guns do when you hand them a gun. "I'll take this too," she said, passing it back.

Oglesby made out the sales slip and did not seem surprised when she paid in hundred dollar bills. He handed her a background check form and a Bic pen. She filled out the information in the name of Jane Bridges, a person she was absolutely sure had no criminal record. There was no box on the form that you checked if you were thinking about mass killing.

"There'll be a waiting period while I send the forms into the feds. Shouldn't be a problem—usually takes about a week. Lot of foolishness if you ask me."

"You don't believe in background checks?"

"Heck, it's just another government boondoggle. And it sure don't prevent crazy people from getting guns."

Nora agreed with him on that.

The week passed pleasantly at the RV park, fair days and blue. Nora hiked the Appalachian Trail and wandered through the Antietam battlefield. She bought fishing gear and fished in the river. She made friends, or Jane Bridges did, among the retirees and wanderers in the neighboring slots of the RV park. She made a special friend of a woman named Edna, a cheerful retired schoolteacher from Harrisburg, who was on a bucket list hegira to visit every one of the national parks in the continental U.S. One afternoon, Nora suggested they go together to the gun range at Mountain Guns and shoot targets.

"I'd consider it a favor," said Nora. "They won't rent me a gun while I'm on my own. And I'll buy you lunch after."

"Why won't they rent you a gun if . . . oh, right. I see. Well, Jane, I guess I'll do it. I haven't shot a gun since my brother gave me a try with his .22 when I was nine."

They went to Mountain Guns on Nora's motorcycle, which thrilled the hell out of Edna, her virgin ride, and at the glass counter Nora chose a Smith .22 revolver for the lesson and a Glock 19 for herself, with the appropriate boxes of rounds. They bought silhouette targets and Nora showed Edna how to set it hers up on the traveler and provided a quick gun safety and handing course. Edna proved as competent at making holes in the right places as she had been teaching English usage to fifth graders. Nora shot off a box of nines, blowing the center out of a short stack of targets.

Later, at lunch, which they took in a flowery upscale joint occupying a former brick mill, Edna asked her new friend whether she should buy a gun.

"I've never felt the need for one before, but I'm a woman traveling alone, camping in odd places. You seem to know all about this business--what do you think?"

Nora said, "You shouldn't keep a gun unless you're absolutely positively sure that you could take the life of a human being, and that you have the judgment to know when it's required. You should abandon any illusions that you can wing an assailant or scare him away by pointing a gun at him. If you haven't got it in you to kill a man, don't get a gun."

"Do *you* have it in you?"

"Yes," said Nora, in a tone that did not encourage further inquiry.

Saturday arrived. In the morning, Oglesby called and told her that the clearances had come through and she could pick up her purchases anytime. Nora asked her phone to find a gun show nearby and shortly thereafter was on her bike on the way to a big one in a field off Route 761 near Charles Town. A certain carnival atmosphere here in the Bazaar of Death, screaming kids running around with guns that nearly everyone hoped were toys, and a line of food trucks selling fried meals and sticky desserts.

From a flatbed, a country band with bad speakers held forth. Nora wandered the aisles, watching her fellow citizens buy weapons. You could purchase anything from a pistol to a gun that was not exactly a machine gun but the guy would sell you a kit with directions that if you followed them, would make it one. And since this was a gun show there was no damn nonsense about background checks.

There was a NRA table too, with a couple of friendly guys behind it making sure no citizen got infringed. Nora stopped and had a pleasant chat. It turned out that one of the men was a state NRA official and was able to provide Nora with much of the information she needed about the organization, its headquarters and its schedule of events.

A man was selling ammunition and accessories out of the back of a panel truck. Nora bought a 120 round can of Federal 5.56 full metal jacket and two thirty- round magazines for the Robbins Reaper AR. She was wearing her old field jacket and so was able to slip the magazines into the pockets that were, after all, designed to hold them. Then she drove back to her camper and waited, setting her phone to signal the time.

She was still enough of a Marine to consider wait time sack time. She lay on the camper's comfortable bed and fell into a familiar dream. She dreamed that what happened at Mir Puza had not happened, had been a dream, and that she had entered the school with her team to be greeted by Bibi and Farishta and the other village ladies and mobbed by the little girls in their embroidered dresses, and she had told Bibi about the dream of violence, and that Bibi had conveyed to her the inner meaning of the dream, but she awoke to the sound of her phone's tinkle without understanding or recalling what it was. This was one of her recurring dreams about Afghanistan, and while there was no blood involved, it was, oddly, particularly horrible to have.

She dressed in her camo outfit, washed her face, combed the knots from her hair, filled her magazines with bullets, stuck one of them in the breast pocket of her jacket, and went across the path to say good-bye to Edna. It was a normal thing to do and Nora wanted to seem extra-normal today. Edna told her she had decided not to buy a gun, and Nora said she thought that was a good decision.

Nora drove the camper to a disused gas station on 340 she'd spotted during her drives around the area, dropped the motorcycle from its bumper rack and took it to Mountain Guns. The kid at the front counter left at seven, she had observed, and Oglesby normally kept the place open for another hour. He caught up on paperwork then and served any late customers. The kid's car was gone when she arrived, so she went in, locking the front door behind her. She found the proprietor at his counter.

"I've come for my guns," she said.

"Got 'em right here, ma'am," said Oglesby, placing the cardboard Beretta box and the assault rifle on the rubber counter pads. He made her sign some papers with Jane's name and did not object when she said she'd like to check the guns out. She examined the Beretta and bought for it a box of 9mm rounds, a leather zip-up case and a nylon holster. She took the AR out of its plastic wrapper and checked it out, while Oglesby looked on benignly.

"You'll want some ammo for that, I guess," he said.

"No, I've already got ammunition," she said, crooking the rifle in one arm and extracting her wallet from her back pocket. She paid for the pistol stuff and stood there, looking at the man.

Who said, "Well, okey doke, ma'am, I guess we're done then. Unless there's something else, I'm about to close up shop."

"Actually, there is something else, Mr. Oglesby. I'm wondering whether you ever think about what happens to the guns you sell."

"What happens to them? I don't know, folks shoot them, don't they?" He smiled, a little uncertainly.

"Yes, they do. For example, on December tenth of last year you sold a rifle just like this to Duane Paul Hatch and he used it to murder 145 people, including my husband, Don Chase, and my three daughters, Abigail, Adele and Gretchen Chase. Do you have anything to say about that?"

On Oglesby's forehead appeared a sheen of sweat and he licked his lips. "Well, ma'am, I'm sorry for your loss, but I got no responsibility there besides doing the federal government check on a purchaser. They cleared Hatch, and if they clear him I got to sell him the gun. I got no choice in the matter—it's the law."

"I know. You also sold him four thirty-round magazines and five hundred rounds of ammunition. What did you think he was going to do with all that firepower?"

Oglesby shook his head. "Not my responsibility, no ma'am. The law is very clear on that. And . . .and . . . now I'd like you to leave my property. Hold on, you can't do that!"

In a long-practiced motion, Nora had pulled the magazine from her pocket, slammed it into the rifle and pulled the charging handle, jacking a round into the chamber.

"Yes, the first rule of firearm safety," she said, "never point a gun at anything you don't want to kill."

"I got a wife and four kids," he said, his voice going unnaturally shrill.

"They'll have my thoughts and prayers," said Nora, and pulled the trigger.

6: Return to Manufacture

Nora drove north and east, past Gettysburg, regretting not having time to tour the battlefield again, and got off the I-76 at Mechanicsburg. She filled the tank, parked on the apron, and studied the checklist in her notebook. She thought she had done everything, but it never hurt to make sure. It was something the Corps drummed into you: write down what you had to do and make sure you did it.

She had retrieved the single brass shell casing. She had cleaned the rifle and taken the dirty patches with her. She had placed the rifle in a soft case, $79.89, which she paid for in cash. She had taken the receipt copies with Jane Bridges's name on it, and found, on consulting the shop computer, that Oglesby had not recorded the sale of the rifle, the pistol, or the other things she had bought. She had expected this, one reason she had paid cash. Oglesby was skimming or hiding income from the IRS. It had been a reasonable bet, an anti-government guy like Oglesby.

The bullet had gone right through Oglesby's body and then through the peg-board and plaster behind him. It had lodged in the concrete wall and she had dug out and pocketed it. She had left the store copy of the federal background form where it was, in a stack of similar forms eight inches high in a plastic basket on the office desk. She had figured that they might check recent customers via background reports and she didn't want there to be a discrepancy that would point to Jane Bridges. She'd taken the car keys from Oglesby's body, and moved his pickup truck to the back of the building, out of sight of the road. She used Windex and a rag to wipe down every surface she had conceivably touched. She hoped the body would not be found until Monday, when the kid came in to open the store. Oglesby did have a wife and four kids, but he didn't live with any of them; Nora had checked.

Now it was time to terminate Jane Bridges's short life. She asked her phone for an RV dealer on her intended route, and it delivered one on Route 230, south of Harrisburg. Nora put on lipstick, blusher and eye shadow and changed her camo outfit for white jeans and a pale blue sweater that buttoned down the front. She completed with cowboy boots and an Orioles cap.

Thus rigged out, she smiled a lot and told the nice salesman that her current vehicle was too big for her now she was on her own, the kids moved away and finally got rid of Fred, ha ha. She was Francine S. Morgan (call me Franny) now, and of course she had registration for the camper, which she had purchased from Ms. Jane Bridges. She allowed the nice man to rip her off a little and put her in a four-year-old Toyota Tundra V-8 4x4, with an Adventurer 80GS camper mounted, for twelve hundred plus her current rig. He attached her motorcycle rack to the new vehicle for free.

Off she went to the east then, now as Franny Morgan, an altogether sweeter person than Jane Bridges, if a little dim. She took I-78 across Pennsylvania to the Garden State Parkway in New Jersey. Passing East Orange her cell phone buzzed. She ignored it and drove on, but it buzzed four more times before she got to Paramus, and when she pulled off into a service area to fuel the truck and herself, her phone showed that it was her sister calling.

She bought a couple of fish sandwiches, fries and a soda to go, reflecting that her enterprise was requiring her to dine at places she would not have allowed her kids to eat at, had she still had them. She considered eating fast food part of the sacrifice she was making, along with certain death, to make a difference in her nation. She had not called her sister or her parents in over ten days, a mistake. The former Nora would have called. She did so now.

"Hello, Sal."

"Where are you?"

"Jersey."

"What're you doing?"

"Crossing the state on a highway. Eating a fish sandwich. What are *you* doing? You called me six times—I thought someone had died."

"It didn't make you stop and call, though," said Sally. "Where are you going, anyway?"

"I told you. I'm doing a grand tour in my camper, seeing the country and visiting old pals, while I decide what to do with my life."

"That's not all you're doing, girl. You're up to something."

"Really? Like what, for instance?"

"I don't know . . . yet. But it's not just driving around."

"You're right. I'm visiting battlefields too. I was at Antietam the other day. Listen, have you ever thought that your job is getting to you? Like interns think they've got every disease they're studying? FBI agents think that every normal activity hides a crime."

"Very clever, but this is your *sister* talking to you. Your sister who knows everything, your sister you *tell* everything to. The fact I work for the Feeb is beside the point. You're up to something, Nora, you have a plan for something and you have to tell me what it is."

"You're right, but my plan is just to have a life, and driving around and seeing old Marines . . ."

"No. Just stop it!" Sally's voice rose into the screech zone. "I'm terrified, you jerk! We're all terrified. You're wandering the freeways all by yourself, and I see a couple of suicides of vets every fucking day, and this is the pattern—isolation, abandoning the family—I bet you're packing now."

"I'm not packing," said Nora.

"Liar!" Nora heard the hollow sound that a cell phone makes when it's removed from the ear and then heard the sound of a door slamming.

"Liar," Sally said again, "How can you do this? I don't understand you. We tell each other *everything*, that's like the core of who we are. You knew I was gay when I was twelve and you kept it secret until I came out to the family when I was twenty-two. I knew when you slept with Ryan the first time and I knew you didn't love Don when you married him. For God's sake, I know what really happened at Mir Puza. And now you're keeping *secrets*? You're the most PTSD woman in America, probably armed, riding around the country by yourself and keeping secrets? What the fuck, Nora!"

Nora heard her sister crying over the phone, and she recalled something that had happened when they were fourteen, fifteen. A group of tough girls from the public school had jumped Nora at a shopping plaza and taken some cash and stuff from her and she had come home crying. This was in San Bernardino, when they were stationed at Twenty-nine Palms. Nora had tried to hide it, but Sally had wormed out the story. She had taken a bicycle chain from the garage and made Nora get on her bike and come with her to find the girl gang and, having found it, wreaked bloody revenge with the bike chain.

After that, Sally had made Nora practice not crying, subjecting her to increasingly awful abuse over several days, or rather nights, when they were both supposed to be sleeping, until she was sure that her sister had been rendered cry-proof. It had worked pretty well until Ryan bought it in Fallujah. They had both cried then and both had noted it as an excursion from normal: but crying between the two sisters didn't really count. It only had to be suppressed in the world, because you can't let them think you're weak..

"Oh, quit that blubbering," snapped Nora."Yo mama ain't here, recruit." Which was what the family always said when crying broke out, and it still had the power to make Sally suppress her sobs. At which point Nora said, "I'm not going to kill myself, okay? If that's what you're worried about." She had to attest to this a number of times.

After that, the conversation relaxed into family gossip, work bitching—on Sally's part—and travel notes from Nora, as intimate and anodyne as an AAA magazine. When the conversation ended, Nora sat in the grease-scented cab of her truck and felt satisfied that it had gone as well as could be expected. Sally knew that Nora was off the rails, but did not know the nature of the derailment. Nora had been able to mobilize a simulacrum of her former self that seemed convincing enough to the person who knew her best, and it was good that, although worried, Sally was worried about the wrong thing.

The fix for the worry was more frequent calls, which would be heavily larded with trip anecdotes and tales of encounters with her old Marine buddies. She could pull off this part, she thought. Yes, it was the deepest kind of betrayal, and her fast food sat uneasy in her belly because of it, but the thing that had taken her over did not care much, and aside from some indigestion, neither did she. It was collateral damage; Nora knew a lot about that.

The new Franny Morgan drove her used camper up the length of New Jersey, traveled across New York state to the Hudson, and crossed the Tappan Zee as the broad waters were turned to rose by the setting sun behind her. She left the 95 at Westport and took older, smaller roads through the ruins of America's first industrial heartland. She found a forlorn motel on Route 58 whose clerk had no problem allowing her, in exchange for a hundred dollar bill, to park her camper on a corner of his parking lot and hook up to power. He was conveniently incurious about his guest's identification. As she had no WiFi with this arrangement, she drove the bike toward town until she found a strip mall with a Starbucks in it and traded a grande drip's worth of money for a couple of hours on the net.

For a surprisingly small payment, you can find the address of anyone in America who has a regular life. The address Nora found that afternoon—1018 Pequot Avenue--was the dwelling of William P. Schatz, who was the CEO of the Robbins Firearms Manufacturing Company, the firm that made the Reaper AR that Duane Paul Hatch had used to murder her family. Google gave her the street view of the house, a gray stone French-style chateau, and a shot of the property from above; Zillow gave her the various dimensions. The arms biz had clearly been good to Mr. Schatz with respect to real estate: a four million dollar, six-thousand square foot, 5 BR, 4B home, on 2.4 acres of extremely neat gardening.

Virtual was all very well, but Nora pined for a walk on the terrain. She mounted her motorcycle again and drove out to Southport. The house on Pequot was set well back from the street and protected by a ten-foot-high boxwood hedge. She parked her bike and went through the unlocked gate, keeping in the shadows cast by the tall line of rhododendrons that bordered the left side of the property. The security outfit Mr. Schatz had hired had posted signs on the lawn and on the front windows, warning of armed response to intruders. Nora was not worried about square-badge cops, but the firm had also installed CCTV cameras on the house and on several large trees. Nora counted four from her vantage point. It would have to be a night operation, she thought, and she would need to get into the garage.

Back in the camper, Nora called her brother Ben at a number reserved for the family. The call produced a default mechanical voice saying the number was not available and offering to take a message. Nora's message was "Iwo Jima," which the family had agreed was the word it would use when they absolutely required that Ben call back, and Ben had complied, almost always within a day or two. In this case, remarkably, he called back that evening. She was consuming her second Whopper when the warble sounded on her computer. In a moment she was looking at Ben's round face on her screen.

"What? I'm getting calls from everybody in the family about you. They think I have a special line to you because we both have a mental defect."

"I don't have a mental defect," she said.

"Sally thinks you're going to kill yourself. Are you going to kill yourself, Nora?"

"No."

"Then why are we talking? Why the Iwo Jima? It distresses me. I have stuff to do and when I get into the people channel, the code channel just goes to shit."

"I'm sorry. I just need to break into a garage and I thought of you."

"That's nothing. That's just a cheap toy."

"It is?"

"Yeah, a Mattel IM-ME toy, it's like a really primitive personal assistant for kids. It sucked as a toy, but it has a twelve-dip-switch array that mimics the array in almost all garage openers. Twelve switches gives 4096 combinations, and you can brute-force a solution, except if you don't want to be sitting in your car for a couple of hours trying them all, there's a neat kluge using a bit-shift register and De Brujin sequencing. So it works by, um, let's say your code is 010 . . ."

"I don't need the explanation, Dr. Asperger. Do you have one?"

"They're around. I'll send you a copy. You can get into any garage in about ten seconds."

"I need it yesterday."

"Even if you had a time machine, that would create a paradox. If you had it yesterday you wouldn't have called me today, and then you wouldn't have it at all, But if you called me yesterday . . . ."

"Ben? Just do it as soon as you can," she said and gave him the address of the motel. She saw him nod. His face blanked for a second or two, then, as if prompted by an inner checklist, he asked,"How are you doing, Nora?"

"I'm doing fine, Benjy. I'm wandering this great land of ours, seeing people and sights, and eating fast food."

"What sights?"

"I went to a coal mining museum. They had every kind of shovel."

"Cool. I'm fine too. Well, I have to go now, Nora. It was nice talking to you."

"Same here. I love you, Benjy."

He stared and bobbed his head. His face went away and the Skype home screen returned.

The next afternoon Nora drove into Bridgeport, to a mega-store, and bought a yellow coverall, a hardhat, two pairs of rubber boots in two different sizes, a clipboard, a backpack, a forty-pound bag of sand, various office supply items, and a portable color printer. Back to Starbucks, where she did some research, had lunch, and put together a card that might look like the ID card of the Southern Connecticut Gas Company to someone who had never seen one up close. It showed an unsmiling selfie of Nora and the SCG flame logo and a bunch of phony information. She went back to the camper, printed it out, cut it to size, laminated it with the kit she'd purchased and attached the clip. She donned the coveralls, boots and helmet and rode the Suzuki back to Southport.

Mrs. Schatz was a pale, slender woman in yoga pants and the kind of designer sweatshirt that costs five hundred dollars. A blond girl of around four clung to her thigh as she stood in her doorway and dealt with this interruption of her day.

"Gas? Really? I haven't smelled any gas."

"Well, ma'am we have reports in the neighborhood and we have to check every house," answered Nora, radiating harmlessness and routine.

"Do you have to come inside?"

"No, ma'am, just got to check the meter and the outside lines and test for fumes. I'll be out of your hair in ten minutes. Um, and I notice you have a security system—I'm not going to be setting off any alarms am I?"

"Oh, no, we keep it off during the day," said Mrs. Schatz. She seemed to want to continue the conversation, asking about gas leaks and the dangers therefrom, but the child grew restive, and Nora, smiling, made her escape.

Out on the grounds, Nora made a thorough inspection of the security arrangements. She counted eight CCTV cameras guarding all four borders of the property, but only one of them was pointing toward the rear neighbor's property. The danger was apparently supposed to come from the mean streets, not from a nearby estate. She calculated and walked a route that would take her from the thick plantings in the rear of the property to the garage without tripping a motion-sensor light or appearing on a CCTV camera. She walked the route several times until she was certain she could run it in the dark.

She spent the next few hours driving around Southport and its environs, scoping out the roads, and familiarizing herself with the terrain on which she would be operating. Around five, she drove back to the Schatz home and pulled into the opposite driveway, concealed behind a large rhododendron bush. At six-ten, a

Mercedes 500 series car appeared and turned into the Schatz driveway. The target was home.

She drove into Bridgeport the next morning and found a public library, where she read *USA Today* for the last few days and the *Washington Post.* The former failed to cover the Oglesby killing, but the *Post* gave it three inches in the Metro section. The locals were shocked. Apparently, Oglesby was a pillar of the Baptist church, coached a local junior football team, and didn't have an enemy in the world. The police were treating it as a robbery gone bad and were checking inventory against missing weapons. Gangs from DC had been knocking off area gun shops and they assumed this was another instance.

The library had provided armchairs that proved too comfortable; Nora fell asleep. She awakened with a start, reaching for a pistol that wasn't there, and found herself ravenous. She went out to look for a place to eat, spotted golden arches and headed that way. There was a playground attached to the restaurant and a child was wailing in it, the hopeless cry of a toddler deprived. Or several children wailing together, she thought, those peculiar harmonies evolution had shaped to be maximally disturbing to the adult human. She entered, sniffed the familiar pong of boiling grease, realized that it no longer quite sickened her, ordered, sat, and addressed her Big Mac.

Men were digging up the street outside, and a pneumatic drill was intermittently banging away, the explosions and the ring of steel on steel, so similar to what a fifty caliber M2 machine gun sounded like when you had your thumbs pressed on the triggers, that and the wailing, there must be a dozen kids crying in that playground, what in hell are they yelling about? In the next instant she was gone from there.

7: Stress Disorder

They were firing from the rooftops, the flat-roofed houses of Afghanistan being ideal for this, having mud-brick walls surrounding them with often an upper room added, so convenient for storing ammunition or stealing away after an ambush. The Taliban knew what a command Humvee looked like, so that was the first one they took out; an RPG scored a direct hit and that was it for Lt. Harrison and his radioman and his radio. Properly, Gunnery Sergeant Hosto should have taken over, but he had been speaking with the lieutenant at the time the rocket hit and so was unlikely to be of use. Nora yelled as loud as she could to mount up, mount up, move the cars and return fire. She repeated the message via radio, identifying herself as Cowboy One actual, thus announcing the new commander.

Some seconds after she did, a machine gun sited on a roof across the square opened fire and killed Peanut Cooper in the turret of Nora's humvee. His body collapsed on top of Nora, soaking her with blood. She pushed and kicked the corpse out of the doorless vehicle as T.P. Gomez tromped on the gas.

"Go left, go left—across the square," yelled Nora, and then used the radio to direct the other humvees to positions where they would be most protected and most able to use the firepower of their turret fifties and grenade launchers. She felt neither fear nor panic as bullets clanged against the thin metal skin of her vehicle.

The insurgents undoubtedly wanted the convoy to attempt escape and Nora supposed that they had certainly placed IEDs on the exit routes, but she had no thought of escape now. She was going to kill them all right here in Mir Puza.

As the humvee dashed across the square, Nora climbed into the turret and pointed the M2's muzzle at the rooftop where the fire had originated. She saw the man, saw his black turban and the sparkling end of his machine gun, bullets snapped by her head, making that horrible broken stick noise, and when the shooter ducked down behind the wall, she opened up.

Later, she concluded that the unit that attacked them had probably not yet learned that you couldn't hide behind a brick wall if the person you were hiding from was shooting a .50 caliber machine gun at you. Nora fired at the wall, turning it into dust and fragments and turning the shooter into a large red stain against the wall of the rooftop room behind him.

The firefight continued. Nora was firing the fifty when she felt her leg jerked. It was Zulu Anderson, yelling above the noise that she had to come down, get on the net, take command.

"I'll shoot it, ma'am," said Zulu and Nora knew that she was right. Her place was commanding her team and directing the Marines in the convoy, a difficult enough job, but now she was doing it, all the while under fire from the enemy. The noise was terrific, the huge bang of the fifties, the rattle of the M4s, the regular slow boom of the M19 grenade launchers and the echoing slam of their explosions.

She remained on top of the tactical situation, moving her vehicles and troops around like chess pieces in response to the changing threats and calls for aid coming over her headset, surfing on the edge of chaos, unafraid. That her life might be over in the next second meant nothing, was rather the drug that was making her feel more alive than she ever had. She understood her father now, and why guys persisted in war, signed up for tour after tour until they died or were too badly smashed for military use. There was nothing like it, nothing she had ever experienced before, better than drink or sex or dope.

She sensed a slackening of the insurgents' fire as the superior weaponry of the Marines reduced their number. A dozen or so red stains showed where men crouching behind walls had been jellied by the heavy machine guns. The maidan was now ringed by partial ruins, the work of the Mark 19 grenade launchers. The few Taliban still firing were doing so by sticking their Kalashnikovs at arm's length over walls and out windows, shooting at random. They were going to break, she thought, and moments later they did break, a group of fighters appeared on the street, running away, some firing behind them.

"Get 'em, get 'em!" she yelled to her driver, "don't let the bastards get away!"

But she felt no motion, something was wrong. Was Gomez hit? Was the humvee disabled? "Gomez, talk to me! What the fuck is wrong?"

"Ma'am? Ma'am, ah, can I help you?"

Nora opened her eyes. She was at a table in a McDonald's, holding a Big Mac in her hand and looking at a worried young man in a white shirt and clip-on bow tie who had a little black tag with "Kyle" and "MANAGER" engraved on it.

"Can I help you?" he said again. She noticed that the other twenty-some people in the restaurant were staring at her too.

"Excuse me?" Nora said, placing her burger on its paper. It was still warm; she couldn't have been out more than a few minutes.

"You were shouting, ma'am," said Kyle the manager. "You were shouting, um, bad language and stuff. I haven't called the police, but I'd appreciate it if you left right away."

Nora noticed he was holding a cell phone. She mumbled an apology, shoved her meal back in its bag and walked rapidly from the restaurant, onto her motorcycle and back to her camper, cursing herself into the wind of her passage all the way. Thank you for your service.

This was a major blunder; the idea was to slip into town, stay anonymous, do what she had planned, and vanish, but now a couple of dozen people had seen her go bat-shit in public and they would remember it, and it would not take Sherlock Holmes to make the connection between a wacky stranger and an unusual crime. She should have used the take-out window. Abort the mission?

She considered this briefly. If the point was to continue a criminal career without getting caught, then the smart move was to leave and return some time in the future, when memories of the crazy lady in the fast food joint would have faded. If the point was to make a statement, then it didn't matter if she was shedding clues. And maybe it wasn't that bad. She was operating in different states. It would take some time to make a connection between Harpers Ferry and Bridgeport and she didn't need a lot of time. She was moving like a Marine assault team—go in fast, blow shit up, get away fast. Except for the last part, as she had not realistic expectations of getting away. So she would go ahead with the plan. Meanwhile she had to wait for the delivery of a toy.

Which arrived the next day via Fed Ex. The device was a purple plastic box the size of an old GameBoy, with a pigtail antenna emerging from one corner and some wires sticking out that were clearly not part of the original equipment. A Post-It had been taped face-down to the front of the thing, with a big red arrow drawn on it, pointing to a button. "Push this!" it said.

Nora did, a few minutes later, having taken her motorcycle to a nearby street with a rank of garages. The doors opened and closed on her command. Then she drove to the Schatz house in Southport to see if it worked there and it did. She loitered, hidden, and observed the master of the house arrive at six-twelve.

Nora was there at six the next morning and waited under a low-hanging mulberry until William Schatz left his home at 7:15. She accompanied him to the office building in downtown Bridgeport where his company had its headquarters.

When he turned into the employees lot, she drove to the downtown public library, where she spent the next few hours reading everything they had on William P. Schatz in magazines. (No computer searches related to the Plan was her rule. Sally would be monitoring her searches, probably against laws thereto applying, and Nora didn't want to make it too easy.) He was 49 and had married into the business, although he'd had a career in arms-making before he won the heart of the fair Phyllis Gail Robbins, the founder's daughter. After old Robbins passed on, William had taken over, shaken up the company, introduced the AR line, increased Robbins's political influence and contributions, and expanded sales by over five hundred per cent in a decade. The handsome couple had two children, Georgie, six, and Patsy, four.

He was certainly a good looking man, Nora thought: tall, broad-shouldered, a high-school standout in football, she learned, a

Bridgeport kid, too. He looked decent, she thought, a solid citizen, and an example to us all. She was looking at a color spread in one of those magazines about how rich people live, an article about his lovely home in Southport, equipped with a soundproofed and ventilated indoor shooting range as well as a pool and squash court. In one picture, Schatz is posing with his son, who is pointing a miniature toy Robbins Reaper AR 5.56 at his Dad, who is holding his hands up and grinning proudly. Charming!

After this research, she waited at the company until his Mercedes emerged and followed it some cars back as he headed home, arriving at six-eleven. Perhaps a creature of habit, Mr. Schatz? She would count on it; she saw no reason why the following evening shouldn't be the day. She had studied him enough to almost get to like him, and more of that would be counter-productive.

This was like war, she concluded, long stretches of boredom and preparation speckled with short bursts of action and terror. When she considered what had happened at Mir Puza, she estimated that from the first RPG barrage to the final revelation, not more than ten minutes had elapsed. It was upsetting that she was having these fugues or flashback or whatever they were. The surprising thing was that she had not had one during the ten years of her marriage. Dreams, yes, screaming nightmares, but these had been infrequent and less so as time went on.

She had no idea why this new thing had arisen and there was no one she could ask. Or maybe there was. She recalled that Zulu Anderson was from Vermont, and made a note to check if she was still there in Brattleboro. It might be good to talk to Zulu after this was done, and it would add verisimilitude to her journey—after all, she was supposed to be visiting old comrades.

Around four the next day, Nora gassed her truck and drove to a construction site in Fairfield she had scouted some days ago. Lots of construction workers owned pickups with camper backs. She parked behind one that was a lot like hers, but dirtier. Inside her own camper she put on a black nylon coverall and black sneakers. She had filled a canvas duffle with the tools she would need, and took it with her, along with her helmet, when she left the camper. On her back was the pack loaded with the forty pounds of sand. She rolled the Suzuki from its rack, strapped the duffle to the back rack, and drove off.

Marine Avenue, the street to the south of Pequot, where the Schatz family lived, was the last street before Long Island Sound, so the people fortunate enough to live there had their houses facing the water, and showed walls, fences and hedges to the street. On the north side of the street, where the Schatz property stood, was a low iron fence; a thicket of dwarf pine, Japanese maple, and boxwood lay behind it, filling the rear of the Schatz property. Between the end of the fence and the next yard was a wide space on the road, deeply shadowed by an overhanging oak, just leafing out. Nora parked her motorcycle there.

She tossed her duffle bag over the Schatz's fence, following it herself a moment later. It was a little clumsy with the heavy pack on, but it was twenty pounds lighter than a combat load, and she had climbed plenty with that much weight on. She was wearing rubber boots two sizes larger than what she normally wore. She found a soft place under the rhodies and made sure she made some good prints in it. The cops would be looking for a 170 pound man.

Ben's IM-ME toy worked again--the garage door rose; she went in and closed it. It was a three-car garage, with a storage area to the rear and a door leading into the house on the right. One of the three parking stalls was taken by the wife's white Volvo station wagon, the second awaited the master's Mercedes, and the third was pristine, and might stay so until the little girl Nora had seen was old enough to drive. Whom she was depriving of a father tonight, who would grow up without a father because of her. Nora thought about this while she waited, while she expertly and unthinkingly assembled her Robbins AR and loaded a 30-round magazine into it.

Too bad for the kid and her brother, but Nora decided it was acceptable collateral damage, just like in Afghanistan, where they were taught not to think of kids deprived of dads; or of life, for that matter. She had considered escorting William P. Schatz into his home and shooting his family in front of him before she shot him, or even leaving him alive to experience something like what she had experienced because of the killing machine he had caused to be manufactured and sold.

But she had decided that whatever she had become, it was not the kind of creature who could do that. She had herself happily killed men who could do that and worse, and did not want to be in that surprisingly populous sector of the human race, and also she had killed many children too and did not want to add any now.

Besides, this was not about revenge, but justice. She had no desire or reason to torture Schatz. He had to die, and he had to know why. That was important to her as well, although when she thought about it, why? Why did it matter that a man's brain absorbed a certain set of words, information about the cause of his death, the murder that would take place right *then*…

And afterwards, what? Nora's parents were military Catholics. They did the rituals, respected the uniforms, followed the rules, felt guilty, expected bad stuff to happen as often as good stuff, and when bad stuff did they would accept it as the will of

God. The afterlife was not much discussed among the Kehoes, although Nora always had the sense that there was a further world beyond death. It stood to reason: you followed the rules, didn't screw up too badly, and you got promoted, just like in the Corps.

So she thought that Schatz would have a further career after she killed him, and when, probably in a matter of weeks, she followed him into violent death, she would also experience divine judgment on what she had done with her life. She couldn't make herself care about the outcome.

Meanwhile, shafts of headlight coming from under the garage door announced the man's last homecoming. Nora retreated to a dark corner where the storage racks ended, among the Schatz family's skis and other winter sporting impedimenta. She donned her helmet and chambered a round. The door opened. The gray Mercedes rolled in. Engine off. Garage door down.

William Schatz stepped out of his car, reached in for his briefcase, and started toward the door that led into his house.

A voice said, "Mr. Schatz."

Schatz said,"What do you want? I'm happy to give you all the money you want, anything in the ATM, I mean. I think it's a thousand dollars. We could get back in my . . ."

"I don't want your money. I came here to kill you."

"Kill *me*? Why would you want to kill me? Who *are* you?"

"I'm one of the many victims of this rifle you manufacture. My husband and my three daughters were murdered by a rifle of this make." She could see in his face that he knew exactly which rifle that was, the one used by the bad Santa. Nora imagined that the massacre had caused some concern in the Robbins Firearms boardroom, but in fact the notoriety produced a bump in the sales of that rifle, so it was all good for the firm. She imagined Schatz smilingly pointing that out to his board.

He said, "Wait, uh uh, you can't, I mean because a Robbins rifle was used in a massacre, you're holding me responsible? How can I be held responsible? The weapon was sold legally and bought legally . . . "

"No, you're responsible, Mr. Schatz. You thought it was a good idea to put a military weapon in the hands of any civilian at a gun show with a grand in cash in his pocket. It made you rich."

"He could have used a different rifle. He could've used a Ruger or a Colt or a Daniel's..."

"In which case I'd be having this talk with a different greedy bastard," said Nora, taking aim.

Schatz flung his briefcase at Nora's head and took a step toward the door to his home, but Nora shot him twice while the thing was still in the air. Schatz lay dead on his back with his eyes and mouth open and his leg bent under him. He had two small red holes in his white shirt, inconspicuous, but Nora was sure that the exit wounds had opened him up at the back like an anatomy lesson.

The door to the house opened. A woman's worried voice: "Bill? I heard a noise."

8: Bad Terrorist

An actual terrorist would have killed the wife, Nora thought as she raced away on the Suzuki, and would have gone into the house and shot the kids too. It was simple operational security and also more terrifying when you killed the whole family, but Nora had not done that. She had actually loosed a round, but something had moved the point of aim from the instinctively-sought center of mass to the door frame above the woman's head; the bullet would have gone right through the wood and ended up who knew where. The wife had fled.

The cops would find that bullet, though. At this moment, the widow Schatz would be on the phone with 911, telling them that her husband had been murdered by a terrorist, without adding that it had been an incompetent, inefficient, overly sentimental one, who had stupidly allowed her to live. She might even have heard the motorcycle that Nora was now driving back to where she had left her camper. If the cops started looking for a motorcyclist, it would severely cramp her plans. As she rolled the Suzuki up the ramp and secured it to its rack, she realized that the arrangement was no longer safe. She's have to trade in the rig for one that kept the bike concealed.

She got out of town on 63, then took I-84 to Hartford. Along the way she stopped at a freeway rest stop, scrubbed the AR, bagged it, tossed it in a dumpster. She put her coverall and boots in another, thus severing her forensic connection with the murder scene. Now it was time to lie low for a while and observe the response to the latest phase of her plan. Guided by her phone, she found a truck dealer near the airport. She parked in a long-term lot there and slept until awakened by the rising sun.

Breakfast at a Denny's and a look through the local paper. Nothing yet about last night, but the local morning news on her phone was full of it.William Schatz had been a local magnate and a prominent spokesperson for the gun industry and for the most gun-adoring interpretation of the Second Amendment. The Bridgeport police were thinking carjacking or home invasion gone wrong. At the press conference the cops held early that morning, a reporter asked the chief of police whether Schatz's business or his politics might have been a factor. The chief did a lemon suck impression and said that there was no indication of anything like that at this time.

But the murder of a gun maker in his own garage by a masked figure using an AR was just the sort of local story that got picked up by the nationals. Any morning anchor-beings with a taste for irony got to comment on the news that one of the chief pushers of powerful semiautomatic rifles had just been slain by (apparently) a powerful semiautomatic rifle.

They had a comfortable waiting area at Gannon Trucks and Canopies, equipped with a big television tuned to the local news, so Nora got to view this comment while she waited for Greg, her new best friend, to finish the paperwork that traded her truck and camper for an almost new Ford commercial van. The remark led to a brief discussion about whether the irony would be lost on the NRA, and the anchorperson and the sidekick agreed that nothing done with a gun would change the minds of those people. Nora thought, we'll see about that.

Greg had thrown in a steel ramp that hooked to the rear bumper, enabling a motorcyclist to ride a bike directly up into the van. Nora did this with the Suzuki and went to sign papers as Audrey C. Franklin, who had recently purchased the Toyota camper from Franny Morgan.

"Well, you're getting a good deal on this vehicle, Miss Franklin," Greg said. "I was going to have to paint it because of the signage, and you saved me that trouble and I passed the savings on. Motorcycle get in all right?"

"Yes, thanks, Greg—it worked great."

"And you really don't mind the sign?"

Nora looked out the window. The van bore a large drawing of a surveyor's theodolite on a tripod, and the legend, "Wade P. Hogben, Chartered Surveyor." The late Wade, according to Greg, who had told her the whole sad story. Had a bellyache on Sunday, went to the docs on Tuesday, dead in a week. Cancer. Didn't have the van hardly a year.

"No, I don't mind," said Nora. "In fact, I might take up surveying. I could change my name to Wade P. Hogben and just leave the sign."

Greg thought that was pretty funny. He laughed and made some flirty remarks, but she did not respond in a friendly manner. Nora saw from his expression he thought she was probably a lesbian of some kind, what with the bike and the van.

At a mall in Manchester, Nora bought new boots, a blue coverall, a nylon duffle bag, and a narrow mattress. She already had a pillow and a sleeping bag. She would sleep with her motorcycle, which she thought appropriate: she felt like something made of steel and rubber herself.

Interesting how luck made a difference in plans, why Napoleon always asked if an officer was lucky before he made one a general. The wife coming in was bad luck. Finding a van with a surveyor's logo on it was good luck, and Nora wondered why she hadn't thought it before. A surveyor's van was a perfect cover for any gathering of intel about a target. A person dressed in work clothes and hard hat, humping surveying gear, could hang around a street corner for a week, scribbling in a notebook and peering through a scope, and no one would pay any attention.

So perhaps she was in for a run of good luck now, or perhaps there was no luck. Firefights tend to foster superstition among their participants, because death comes so randomly in battle, with so little regard for level of training or who everyone in the unit thinks is the best Marine. Nora's combat history was only minutes long, perhaps not long enough to require magic against terror, and she had remained a pragmatic rationalist. You make your plan using the best intel on hand, making the fewest possible assumptions favoring success, and then you gave it everything you had and if that wasn't enough then fuck it. Next time try something different, if you happened to survive.

Whatever, she seemed to have made a clean getaway from the Bridgeport area. She reached Brattleboro and spent the night in a former gas station parking lot south of the town. Her tiny screen failed to tell her her that law enforcement was looking for a woman or an ex-Marine, or anyone who'd been involved in a mass shooting, or the late Mr. Hogben's van.

In the paranoid end of the Twitterverse, however, at least some of the followers of #whokilledbill? were urging the cops to look into relatives of victims of mass shootings where the weapon was a Robbins Reaper AR rifle. The number of people who believed this theory was about the same as the number who believed that it was terrorists trying to weaken America by assassinating the makers of the guns that keep us free.

The following days brought some local coverage of the grieving widow and the kids. The Hartford PBS station did a sad story about those left behind by gun murders and they included the Schatz killing to show that it was not just low-lifes and those of dusky hue who were murdered: look, a respectable, wealthy, white family and *they're sad too!* Nor did they neglect the by-now obligatory irony of Schatz's occupation.

Nora, at a public library computer, made herself look at the Schatz family, stopping the video and letting it roll, over and over. The widow, in black, emerging from a big car, the stunned-looking girl on left hip and little boy grasping her other hand. A handsome woman, Phyllis Schatz, and very rich. How long would she be alone? How long before another man drove his car into her garage every night and played father to her children?

Not long, thought Nora. She recalled the time she had gone to Eubank, Georgia to visit the widow of Lt. Henderson, who'd been blown up in the first seconds at Mir Puza. Nora had thought that a widow would want to know about her husband's last moments from someone who was at the scene, but no—the widow Henderson thought it was morbid to dwell on death. She wanted to move on. While Nora had sat on Mrs. Henderson's vinyl sofa, twitching with awkwardness and resentment, Mr. Moving On himself walked in to the house, laughing and joking with one of Henderson's kids.

So it would be, she thought, with Phyllis, after a decent interval, but so it would not be with her. She had sort of remarried already, but not to anything of flesh. Her new husband was more demanding than the dead one had been, and his grip on her was far stronger, stronger even than her desire to please her father or to be a good Marine. She hadn't thought there could be anything more powerful than that, but here it was. She thought often of John Brown, and how he felt at Potawatomi hacking the pro-slavery men to death with his cutlass. Did he think it was right? Did he feel the pinch of Christian charity as he shattered skulls and made the bloody gobbets fly? Probably not. Probably he thought it was a necessary evil, necessary to the defeat of an evil a million times greater.

She thought about how she had lost it after Mir Puza and Ryan, weeping for days afterward, unable to keep food down, so that they had to push the undesired nourishment into her with tubes. She didn't feel anything like that now; her new husband told her it was fine and she believed him. She could feel him moving inside her, his thick serpent coil filling her spaces, the pressure of his fangs and claws urging her toward horror and doom.

But her new husband didn't discuss much with her, and she found that she was terribly lonely now. She had never been this lonely before; when Ryan got killed, her family and the larger family of the Marines had rallied around her, and after Mir Puza, in the hospital, Don had been there with his comfort and his sincere lies: you're a hero, you're the best girl in the world, they were terrorists, they wanted all those people to die, it was war, things happen, no one can control a battlefield, it's not, not, not your fault. He'd worn her down; it wasn't hard, there was just a little nub of her left.

In the morning she drove into Brattleboro and had breakfast at a diner. Over coffee, she called Zulu Anderson, but got only the whistling squeal and the robot message that the number was no longer in service. She drove to the last address she had for Anderson, which turned out to be a large, worn, clapboard house on a big lot on the wrong side of the tracks. A leaning barn of a garage stood nearby, with a backboard and hoop hanging above its door. Nora mounted the sagging, unpainted porch and rang the bell.

The woman who answered it was around sixty, the kind of hard sixty that happens when you've spent your whole life doing physical labor in rural America, and she had the yellow skin, abyssal wrinkles, and nicotine stink of a heavy smoker. She was not smoking at the moment, but clutched a pack of Newports in her hand just in case.

Nora asked if Maureen Anderson was at home and the woman, suddenly suspicious, asked her who wanted to know. Nora explained who she was.

"The Ice Queen," said the woman, and Nora, smiling, agreed that that was her handle in the Marine Corps. She was invited in then, and seated at the oilcloth-covered kitchen table and offered coffee and spice cake from the store. The woman was Anderson's grandmother, Lorena McIntosh, called Mac by her granddaughter and everyone else. She used Zulu's real name, Maureen, possibly the only individual still to do so. Zulu Anderson was six feet tall and an all-state basketball player, who had taken on the affect, fashion and slang of the ethnicity that dominated her beloved game. Her nickname was explained by that and by her hair, which appeared in blond corkscrews, and which she grew out into the biggest honky afro in New England high school sports.

Mac brought out the scrapbooks, and Nora was allowed to view the archive: Zulu on the court, racking triple doubles, leading Vermont girls' B-ball in scoring two years in a row. There were pictures of her in the air, dunking, others of her driving down the paint, with a familiar fierce grin on her face.

"She was going to get a scholarship and go to UConn. That was her dream," Mac said. "To be on a championship team."

"Did she apply?"

"Uh-huh. But she had problems in school. She couldn't sit still, they said. Anyway, she couldn't pass her grades well enough to get in there. And she didn't want to go anywhere else. She went into the Marines for the college money. She thought she could do a tour, then go to CCV down the road here for a year to show she could do the work and then get into UConn and just show up for the team as a walk-on."

"She could still go back to school," Nora said. "It was a good plan."

"I told her that, the very same thing," said Mac. "You know what she said? They don't want no one-arm ball players there, Gran. Always been just as stubborn as a mule. When she came back from the service she wasn't the same person . . . she drank---why before, she wouldn't hardly touch a beer, and now she was out at roadhouses all night, coming home stinking. She stopped using her prosthetic, stopped going to counseling at the VA clinic. I told her I wouldn't have it. I wouldn't go through what I went through with her mother again, and she said, okay then, I'll move out. And she did."

Nora said, "I'm sorry for your trouble, Mac, but stuff happens in a war zone that's hard for people at home to understand. She's seen some bad stuff."

"And I haven't? My baby died a crack whore in Boston, froze to death leaning against a dumpster behind a A & W with a crack pipe in her hand. I had to go there and identify her body. I saw my beautiful little girl lying on a slab, she couldn't have weighed more than ninety pounds and covered with bruises and awful tattoos. You seen any worse sight than that over in Afghanistan? Or anywhere?"

"I guess not," said Nora kindly, although, of course she had.

"Everybody's got some trouble, Lieutenant. But you're not supposed to give in to it. I would've thought that would be the one thing they'd teach you in the god-damned Marines. Don't give up!" She pounded a fist on the table, making a harsh domestic clatter of crockery and tableware, and then let out an embarrassed laugh. "I'm sorry. It upsets me so. You know, one and then the other. It's a lot to bear." A long silence after this; then:

"You were with her when it happened."

"I was, yes."

"She says she can't remember nothing. She was shooting a gun at the terrorists and then she was in a hospital room with her arm gone. It's hard to imagine. I mean not remembering."

"It's very common. It's called traumatic amnesia. I have it myself."

This was a lie.

After a pause, Nora said, "But *you* want to know what happened, yes?"

Mac nodded.

Nora told the simple tale: an ambush—and L/C M. Anderson, trained as an infantry person like all Marines, and expected to excel as one at need, had jumped into the .50 cal turret when its gunner was killed and directed fire at the enemy position until she was herself gravely wounded by enemy fire. She contributed greatly to the victory the Marines had won that day, over a hundred terrorists killed and a town liberated from their influence. Five Marines had died and ten, including Nora, had been wounded.

All the time Nora was telling this she was hearing Zulu's scream in her ears, the scream that wouldn't stop, and seeing in her mind's eye Zulu's red-soaked arm hanging straight down against the blood-spattered tan camouflage paint of the turret, impossibly far down because only some uniform fabric and strips of flesh held it to the ruin of her shoulder. The remarkable thing was that by some fluke, the palm of the dismembered hand was quite clear of blood and stood out white against the reddened metal like something on a coat of arms. Nora saw this in her mind (and sometimes, terrifyingly, in hallucination) almost every day. It was not the worst image of that day, however.

After she finished, Mac said, "And do you think it was worth it? All the death and pain. And girls too! Girls! So, is that town still liberated from their influence?"

"I don't know, but I kind of doubt it. We pulled out of the district ten years ago. It's a heavy Taliban region now, I understand."

"Then why?"

"That's not a question we get to ask in the Corps," said Nora. "You're supposed to ask your Congressman if you're interested in why."

"I'm asking you."

"And I haven't got an answer for you. She did her duty. I did my duty. Aside from that, it was just something that happens in that line of work. You know, I would really like to see Maureen again. That's what I'm doing now, going around and visiting all the people I served with in Afghanistan, maybe . . . maybe even try to make sense of it all. Do you happen to know where she's staying?"

"Mm hm, she's with a guy, lives up on the mountain, out by Wilmington. I have to say, a pretty decent guy. She didn't inherit a taste for bums, thank the Lord. I'll give you the address. They're in Zarb."

9: In Zarb

Nora drove west across the state of Vermont, in rain, often heavy. She stopped in Wilmington, a pleasant village, for a burger meal. From there, she drove north on Route 100 and then roughly northwest, the road gently rising to the hill country that bordered the Green Mountain National Forest. Spring lagged in the hills. The buds on the trees, though fat with promise, were waiting for go, or at any rate for a cessation of the freezing rain. The little hill streams were rushing brown, tossing foam at their banks, carrying tree limbs and dead cats, and everything terrestrial was brown, slick and sticky. The season was called "Mud" in Vermont for good reason.

Zarb made Mir Puza look like Chicago, a stop light and a gray shack of a gas station, with the kind of electromechanical pumps outside that Nora had not seen since Afghanistan. She stopped and went in to buy some gas, candy, and aspirin. The place smelled like all the other country stores: kerosene, cheese, and a stagnant smell of no apparent origin, perhaps the odor of the rotted corpse of 1923. A two-year-old calendar hung above a rusted tin thermometer, perhaps because the picture it bore of a rising trout was too precious to toss.

A wall-eyed middle-aged woman in a flowered housedress and white apron rose heavily from a worn sag of an armchair and stood to serve. Nora handed over her real credit card and asked for a fill-up—she never let it get below half a tank—but the woman shook her head and unapologetically demanded folding money. This was unfortunate because Nora wished to leave for her sister Sally a trace of a legitimate location near a former comrade. It was a joke in the family, always denied, that Sally routinely used what they used to call "national technical means" to keep track of her near and dear.

Nora's hundred-dollar bill was spurned, and Nora was directed to a greasy sign that stated the store policy of never breaking anything larger than a fifty. Another sign nearby said that we had a deal with the bank—they don't sell bologna and we don't cash checks. Also, in God we trust, all others pay cash.

Nora did so, and thought that this store would survive even the total collapse of civilization and they wouldn't ever have to raise their prices. Ordinarily, Nora would have slipped on the nice American lady persona and had a conversation with this woman, chat about the area and maybe get some information about the place she was going, but it was clear from her prune of a face that the shopkeeper lived in a constant state of rage against Away, and disdained any engagement with beings that were not of Zarb. Nora thought it was just like Afghanistan.

She followed the directions of the Google maps guy on her phone, turning onto increasingly rutted and mud-choked roads. A misty but soaking rain continued to fall. Her new van complained, it shook and skidded alarmingly. A commercial van had no business on these roads, it seemed to be saying, and in one particularly deep wallow, it gave up.

Could have been worse, Nora thought as she left the van. She must be close to where Zulu lived, for she could smell and see a small column of white smoke rising above wet black trees beyond a bend in the road. She re-entered the truck, came out wearing wellingtons, and began the squelching trudge.

She had not been on the road for five minutes when she heard the familiar yet unexpected clinking of brass bells and the nasal moaning of goats. Around the bend came a goatherd with a dozen floppy-eared goats capering around him. Or her, Nora observed as the herd drew closer, and closer still she saw that the goatherd had no right arm and that it was Zulu Anderson.

Nora said, "You know, I was just thinking this was a lot like Afghanistan, if Afghanistan had trees, and here I run into a girl herding goats."

Zulu stopped short and stared a hostile Zarb stare. When recognition dawned, she grinned and said, "Lieutenant Kehoe. What the fuck!"

“I’m not surprised you’re a goat person, Anderson. In Helmand I noticed you looking at the goatherds with admiration and envy.”

“Don’t tell me—the Crotch wants me back and they sent you to convince me.”

“That’s correct, Lance-Corporal. You’d be surprised how many goats the United States Marine Corps uses in an average year.”

The two women had been wading closer to one another through the tan mass of the goats until they were close enough to embrace. This they did with a passion that surprised both of them. Zulu was wearing a hooded parka, but now the hood fell back and Nora saw for the first time in real life the true Zulu hair-treatment, a bushel of dusty blond dreads somewhat larger than the face they surrounded. Nora felt her heart stir with actual human feeling for the first time since the Mall of Death happened. It felt strange, like drinking an unfamiliar but powerful liqueur, and she was able to enjoy it as an exotic pleasure. She was relieved that Zulu seemed happy, healthy and glad to see her old C.O.

As was Nora happy, absurdly happy, to see Zulu. Because no one who had not been at Mir Puza understood, and here was one of the survivors; Nora felt relax in her something she had not known had been tense.

“Yo, but for real, Loo. And . . . wait, how did you know where I was?”

“I shamelessly manipulated your gran, is how. And I came to see *you*, Zulu. I’m on a road trip, I’m trying to go see anyone I can find in the old F.E.T.”

"No shit? Who've you seen?"

"You're the first."

"And the best. I got to take these beasts down the lower mowing. They're making it bigger for us, they're clearing all the brush away--ain't you, ain't you?" She scratched the bell-whether under her chin. The goat baahed affectionately. "After that, we can go up the house and you can meet Thomas."

They met Thomas in the dairy instead, a low-ceilinged concrete building with a lively stream of icy water flowing through it. He was a very tall, latté-colored man, wearing a white coveralls and a shower cap. He greeted Nora with an oddly formal courtesy (he was the type of Thomas who is never called Tommy or Tom.) spoken in the true strange-voweled, glottal-stopped Vermont accent.

As she learned in the next few minutes, Thomas Bigelow's family had been in Vermont since 1847. The tale emerged from the man in familiar periods: the founding ancestors escape slavery in Maryland, travel via Underground Railroad to Canada, passing through Vermont. They come back to the state after Emancipation and stay put. The generations pass with increasing education and prosperity, eventually yielding Thomas, Dartmouth, B.A., English Lit.

Thomas seems amazed at his luck. His parents are both professors at the University of Vermont. He himself was a poet and goatherd. His parents waited patiently for him to get over it.

When Nora asked where they'd met, Zulu said, "At the Y in Burlington. I was at the VA there getting rehabilitated, and the shrink said we should try to return to our regular activities, it would help to orient us to normal or some shit, so I went down there, sort of like a joke? But also I wanted to see, I lost my arm, did I lose my eye? And it *was*, like, my only regular activity besides the Marines.

"So I got to the court, and the feeling . . . it was really weird--embarrassed, but also, fuck you, who gives a shit any more? Loose, you know? And I can still palm a b-ball. So I started shooting—like people are always going, oh you lost your right arm, extra bad, and I'm like, I'm a lefty, asshole. So, I started shooting and I go brick, brick, brick and then . . . did you play ball, Loo?"

"A little soccer in high school. My main thing in college was fencing. But you have to call me Nora."

"So Nora, when you're fencing, do you ever get to a place where you can do no wrong? A groove? Everything's fucking perfect?"

Nora indicated that she had, without mentioning that the last such a moment for her had come when she directed the battle of Mir Puza.

"Right, so I start sinking shots. It was fucking surreal. I have one arm, I should be off balance, fucked up, whatever, but no, I start sinking them. Five in a row, ten in a row. And he was in the gym playing horse with another guy and they stopped playing to watch me."

Nora said to Thomas, "You admired her ball-playing skills."

"Uh huh. She sinks like fifty foul shots and then she starts shooting three-pointers. She goes four in a row. My mouth was hanging open. By the way, this was like six-thirty in the morning.

Me and my cousin Calvin had a regular game before class and we usually had the place to ourselves, and, um, you don't really expect to see a six foot, one-armed black white girl channeling Steph Curry in the Burlington Vermont Y. I mean, I would've been interested if she couldn't shoot worth shit. So she finally missed one and the ball got away from her and I picked it up. And, also, you have to know, all the time she was shooting. Calvin was all over me, the way kids do, like, you should go play horse with her, she'd whip your sorry ass, and shit like that, and so of course . . ."

"I did whip his sorry ass," said Zulu.

"I was weak with love," said Thomas, with a fond smile at his maimed girl.

Later, having left Thomas to the curds, Zulu showed Nora the house. It was old, well-made, and too small for a pair of six-footers, but it had been in Thomas's family for over a century and was dear to him. It sat on a ridge with a view toward the national forest, a near chunk of which used to be the family farm. She discussed his family too, their warm embrace of white trailer-trash her, their worries about him, their unwillingness to accept that their brilliant boy might be content to write poetry and keep goats on the scraggly hill farm his ancestors had fled more than a century ago.

Zulu cracked a couple of beers and they sat on an old glider on the front porch and talked about Thomas. Zulu was more than willing to sing the praises of her guy, and Nora was happy to talk about anything but herself. When pressed, she made up a version of the story she'd told to her sister, at loose ends (the cause for the ends being loose not mentioned) and visiting old Marine pals.

"Can you stay? There's a bluegrass thing in Wilmington this weekend. You can hear Thomas play the banjo."

"Yet another talent! You lucked out, girl. Tell me he beats you and cats around."

"Not yet; I mean so far, so good. He's a Quaker, actually, the whole non-violent thing, kind of strange of him falling for a trained killer like me. His family's been Friends since forever, since they all started quaking around here. We go to meeting."

"Really. What's that like?"

"It's good in a strange way. We go in and sit and nobody talks, except when the spirit moves them. It ain't like any church I ever been to, like, you know, nothing's *happening*? On the up side, nobody's yelling you're gonna go to hell for doing shit there ain't nothing wrong with. I like going with *him*."

"Did the spirit ever move you?"

"Once. I was just sitting there, thinking about shit, you know? About nothing, really, and then . . . I can't explain it, I just started to bawl, tears and snot, the whole waterworks. And talking, like it wasn't me, just something inside that had to talk *itself,* all about what happened over there, when I got hurt. But not about me —it was about all the killing we did, all those hajjis we wasted, the hajjis I *personally* wasted. I can't remember a lot of what I said, but Thomas said it was pretty rare and with, you know, the kind of language the Friends don't get to hear much. Salty. I got nauseous and had to run outside and puke in the parking lot. I guess it gave *them* something to talk about after."

Nora had no response to this. Zulu finished her beer, got up and tossed the can in a wastebasket, then studied her former commander.

"So, tell me, since it came up, you still have the nightmares and hallucinations?"

"Mmn. I zone out from time to time. Mainly when I'm in a car. It brings back the ride in the village and all that. And loud noises can set me off. You?"

"No, not any more," said Zulu, "not after that thing in the meeting."

"So you recommend religion."

"Or goats. Or someone who loves you. So will you stay for the weekend? Thomas is an unbelievable cook."

"Of course he is," said Nora with an eye roll and they both laughed and made up some more fantastic talents for Thomas, including naughty ones and they were nearly crying with it when Thomas came in and asked what was so funny.

"Nora's gonna stay till the weekend," said Zulu, and Nora saw Thomas smile and also the small wrinkle in his brow as he began to consider what to feed her.

Nora said, "Provisionally staying. Let me get my laptop and check my schedule."

What Nora meant was picking her next target. She had a short list already prepped and a few minutes of study in the small but neat bedroom she'd been placed in gave her the man. His name was Arthur M. Pauling, and he was a businessman in nearby Keene, New Hampshire; he was also the state chairman of the National Rifle Association. There were few people in the region more vigorously devoted to stopping any infringement on the right to carry guns of any make anywhere at all. He was particularly devoted to the NRA's current campaign to make firearm suppressors sound completely legal.

Nora studied the photograph of the man in an NRA magazine she had lifted from a public library in Hartford. Pauling was a big-bellied gentleman of sixty-one with a prominent nose and a mass of thick white hair. He had served two terms in the state senate and was a familiar fellow in regional conservative circles, a major funder with his name often mentioned as a gubernatorial possibility. She made some notes, then came down and told the couple that yes, she'd be happy to hang with them through the weekend. She thought hanging wouldn't be hard; they were a pleasant pair, their love obvious and simple, like running water.

That night Nora discovered that Zulu was a woman loud in the sack, calling upon the Deity often during the passages of the night. She was glad her old comrade was happy, and relieved that she herself could still generate a normal persona, so that decent people like Zulu and her man did not run screaming from her and bar their doors. She wondered how long she'd be able to manage it as she descended deeper into her project. In the moments before sleep she surprised herself with thoughts about Ryan Graham, and about what it had been like to be in love. She did not think about her dead family at such times.

She rose before dawn, thinking to slip away across the state —it was less than thirty miles to Keene—but there is no slipping away early on a dairy farm. She descended into a kitchen smelling of coffee and frying things and had to sit for conversation and enthusiastic face-stuffing. Nora endured the pleasant atmosphere as if it were a television show playing too loudly in another room, until she thought it was reasonable to excuse herself and leave. She said she was going to Boston to handle some old service paperwork at the federal building. Thomas hugged Nora, kissed Zulu and went to milk. Nora was at the door when Zulu said, "Loo . . . uh, Nora?"

"Um?"

"What the fuck happened?"

"Happened . . . ?"

"Downrange. When we got hit in Mir Puza. What happened?"

"Hell, Zulu, you were there . . . "

"No! I mean *why*. I thought we were doing okay. The locals were friendly. We all thought that, everybody in the FET. We were ready for IEDs, maybe getting hit on the road, but not in the village. I mean, no one warned us. And I thought I *knew* those people. Bibi and Gul Mina and Farishta and that little kid with the yellow dress, you know the one . . . she brought us flowers every time we showed. Nara something."

"Nazanina," said Nora. "Yeah, well, I don't know what to tell you. It looked good, it turned out shit. Life happens like that, especially in a combat zone, especially with the Pashtuns."

"And you never figured it out? Why they fucked us up?"

"What I figured out was it's better to forget all that shit and get on with your life. Look, I got to go—I want to get in there when they open."

Zulu was still talking when she went out the door. Nora could hear the staccato bleating of the goats as she trotted past the dairy to her van, she was nearly running now as she had been, figuratively, since Mir Puza, although she knew that Mir Puza could run faster, would always catch up.

10: Helmand in the Spring

The goats, that was one sound always in your ears there, and the slap of *rotis* being made, coming from every house with a woman in it, and the odor of them cooking on hot iron. She had come to Afghanistan in the spring, the best time, the dust laid by the rains, the roses blooming in the gardens of the compounds, the valley farms white with apricot blossoms or pink with opium poppies. If you could get past the wind and the dust, and that you were far from home amid a generally hostile people, the rippled harsh landscape had an undoubted, near visceral appeal to some arrivals. Nora was one: she fell instantly in love with the land. It happened, according to old Afghan hands, and was not necessarily a good thing. The affection was rarely returned.

Nora had arrived in Bagram as a logistics specialist, but having seen a little of the country, she was reluctant to serve her tour locked in a room with computers and paperwork. Since at the time the Marines didn't allow females to have combat-type military occupation specialties, she'd volunteered for the Lioness program when it started.

Nora had always been good as a trainee, always coming out at the top of any rankings, and she now excelled in the orientation course the Marines provided about Pashtun life and how to be accepted in Pashtun communities, how to perform useful, ingratiating services for women, how to search them for weapons or contraband, and how to generate actionable intel from women's local knowledge.

Nora had approached this training with her usual unrelenting focus. She actually tried to learn to speak Pashto, which her superiors thought was waste of time because her team would be supplied with a translator. Nora ignored this advice, instead insisting that Zareena Deh Bala, the team translator, teach her to speak Pashto.

She remembered . . . no, she did not want to remember the pleasant, the interesting, the wonderful times she'd spent in Afghanistan, she only wanted to think about the present.

This was now Tuesday, she thought, and it would be good to do it on the Saturday. She'd attend the bluegrass concert, establish a presence, slip away, do the thing and return to the concert. She'd be away at least an hour, maybe more. If they asked, she'd make up a story. She'd grown up in a family where a lie was despicable; lying was about the only crime for which punishment by Dad would be severe and implacable. You could screw up and get a Parris Island style chew-out from one of the parents, provided there was a full and frank confession and an apology. If you lied, on the other hand, and were found out . . . oh, brother! None of the Kehoe kids had tried it more than once.

Now she lied all the time, easily and without compunction. Her life was a lie, but she felt no guilt at all. The Thing that was driving her bore all the responsibility, just like when you followed an order and shit happened it got written off, because what counted was the mission. Away in the back of her mind's closet was something that knew this was wrong, but it was small and all crunched up with sorrow and couldn't even tug the sleeve of Nora's fierce resolve.

She was in Keene by eight and found Mr. Pauling's house soon after. It was some miles north of the city off 12A, a much larger version of the late Schatz's grey stone mansion. This one was set on a substantial wooded estate, with several outbuildings, a swimming pool and a tennis court. It connected to Matilda Lane by a long driveway, guarded by a high, motorized wrought-iron gate, which was in turn guarded by an intercom and a CCTV camera. A quick inspection of the gate and its surround was all she needed to devise a plan.

Back in her van, Nora checked the weather report, which was more than satisfactory. The coming Saturday would be fair and mild, with temperatures in the upper sixties. A perfect day for golf; she knew that Pauling was an avid golfer, and she assumed he would be a member at the sole private club in the area, the Keene Country Club.

She called her brother. It would be six or so in the morning in California, but Nora was sure that Ben would be up. It had never been entirely clear that Ben slept like regular people.

"I need something that will spoof caller ID," she said.

"There's an app," he said.

"Can you send me the . . ."

"Doing it now. Done. How are you, Nora?"

"I'm feeling good, Ben. How are you?"

"I'm good, too. I have to go now, Nora. I'm doing something with some guys in Shenzhang."

"Wait. I need three more identities."

"A couple of days," he said, and closed the connection. At almost the same time her email tone sounded. She loaded the app that appeared.

Representing the Keene Country Club, Nora called Pauling's office, using Ben's app to generate the correct number on the recipient's screen. She asked the secretary who answered whether Mr. Pauling wanted his regular slot on Saturday. Of course, said the secretary, the reservation had been made. Nora: Oh, and sorry, our computer is down, was that ten o'clock? No, Nine-thirty. Sorry, again—these machines! He's confirmed for nine-thirty—bye bye!

Her phone then led her to a gun shop, one of the very many in the Keene area. She (as Audrey Carol Franklin, of spotless record) bought a Robbins Reaper 5.56 AR, a padded rifle case, and a Griffin Recce 5 suppressor. For cash.The clerk, a burly middle-aged fellow with odd bushy sideburns and a waxed mustache, told her there'd be a three day wait to clear her details through the feds. He commiserated with her about the unbearable tyranny of this; she allowed it was a burden.

He added as he put away the rifle, "These have been flying out the door since he got killed. I can't keep 'em in stock."

"Killed?"

"Robbins. The guy who made your weapon. You heard about it?"

"No. I don't follow the news much when I'm traveling."

The clerk was happy to fill her in, getting many of the details right.

"Did they catch the guy?"

"Not yet, but it's only a matter of time. The company posted a fifty K reward. They say it was the gun grabbers done it. Because of the shootings?"

"Well, it's a crazy world now," said Nora as she took her receipt and the bag full of her other purchases.

"You said it, sister. Stay careful, now."

"Stay careful now," she reflected later was what Lieutenant Commander Wylie always said when he dismissed his students from his class on *pashtunwali*. Wylie, a tall, professorial, but extremely hot, bearded man who was at the time the Navy's premier authority on Pashtun culture, having been in-country almost continuously since 2001. He was a SEAL too, and had participated directly in the original rout of the Taliban. All the FETs were in love and giggled about Commander Wylie in public, so that salty old gunnery sergeants rolled their eyes and wept into their beers at what the Corps had come to.

Nora thought she might still have the notes from Commander Wylie's short course for officers somewhere in the storage locker where all her personal stuff sat now. What had she learned? The Pashtun were the largest tribal group in the world. That was one fact. Every Pashtun belonged to a *tabar*, and every *tabar* was divided into clans, or *khels* and *khels* consisted of *kahols*, which were extended families descending from a common male ancestor. There were over four hundred *khels*, all having intricate histories with one another, which every village child knew, which no foreigner ever figured out.

Three pillars of Pashtunwali: *melmastia; nanawati; badol* . Hospitality: A man was obliged to defend a guest to the death, even if the guest is a sworn enemy. Forgiveness: if an enemy asks forgiveness in humility, a Pashtun is bound to grant it, and to offer asylum to anyone who asks it, even if that man if a fugitive from the law. Revenge: a man had to protect his honor with his sword. Tribal feuds, clan feuds, went on for generations. Causes of feuds: *zar, zan, zamin*—gold, women, land.

Nora was his prize student. She ate that shit up, as they say, because it had struck her powerfully that the Pashtuns were off on their own thing the way that the Marines were: insane bravery, an antique sense of honor, pride in peculiarity, fidelity to the group above all. Wylie pointed out, when she mentioned this, that there were as many assholes among the Pashtuns as there were in the Marines, and plenty of hypocrisy and lip-service to ideals. He warned against falling in love with them.

In the event, this proved impossible for Nora. Perhaps it was her own honey being in Iraq that made her vulnerable, and lonely, and longing for some zone of deeper feeling, or perhaps it was the perfect fit between the FET program and her own sense of mission. In counterterrorism, intel was what made the difference between success and failure, including the ghastly kind of failure that occurred when the vast power of the Americans was falsely or mistakenly directed and civilians died. FET was all about better intel.

She reflected that the twelfth of April was fact approaching and that it would be the tenth anniversary of the first time she saw Mir Puza. Everything she had hoped for on that day, riding in with a green FET, had proved ashes, although it hadn't been a total loss from the personal development angle. Her visit to Pashtunstan had schooled her in the connoisseurship of revenge. "Vengeance took me a hundred years; I regret my haste." That was one saying of hundreds on the subject. She hadn't understood all of that in Mir Puza, but she did now.

During the rest of the week Nora made herself useful among the goats and around the house. She herded and cooked and shoveled shit. She drove Zulu to the dentist in Brattleboro. She pretended to be a real person and tried not to think poorly of the couple for being taken in by her. On Thursday she returned to the gun shop and picked up her rifle, then used the shooting range they had there to blow off a box, to zero the sights and check out the suppressor. It was more than satisfactory; it made the shots sound very much like a hard strike of a wooden ruler on a wooden desk.

She drove back to Zarb, parked at the base of the hill, and took the motorcycle into Wilmington again. She parked it behind the general store and chained it to a maple tree. Then she jogged the eight and a half miles back to the goat farm. The day was brisk, the air was wine, the birds chirped their enticements to each other and the trees wore the heart-rending green of another spring.

She thought it would be her last spring. She felt the sting of tears, and laughed bitterly there on the gravel road; I don't cry for my dead, but for the world in bloom, how fucked up is that? Thinking so, Nora was hard put to maintain a human countenance and often failed. Luckily, Thomas was constructing a larger and hopefully fox-proof chicken coop and Nora helped on this task with vigor. It involved hammering and a degree of isolation, both apparently necessary for her just now. Neither of the others asked her what was wrong because they thought they knew.

Saturday came and the three of them went to town for what was billed as the Third Annual Mud Festival, sitting abreast in Thomas's weary red Dodge pick-up truck. They sang "I Shall Be Released," going down the mountain. Nora, shoulder to shoulder with Zulu, was acutely conscious of the woman's missing arm. Still, they sang.

The concert took place in an old, white clapboard Congregational church that the town had taken over when the Congregationalists died out. There was a scant midway set up in the old church's parking lot, the usual fried food and baked goods and a sprinkle of local crafts on sale. It was early, but a small enthusiastic crowd had gathered, a demographic of gray pony-tail hippies, young people who had missed hippie by a generation, but still thought it was cool, a few actual country folk, and musicians.

Thomas played in a jug band with four locals. The Mob from Zarb as they called themselves, specialized in high-speed bluegrass versions of modern hits by Drake, Cardi B and Chance. They were more than good enough for rural Vermont and (by report) hilarious besides. Nora was actually sorry to have to miss the show. Making an excuse—upset stomach—she slipped away to retrieve her motorcycle. She was in Keene by ten-thirty; twelve minutes later she lay in wait, concealed in shrubbery near Arthur Pauling's automatic gate.

It was a simple plan. Pauling would drive up after his golf game. He would tap his remote; the gate would jam, because Nora had placed a rock on the rail it traveled on; he would leave his car to see what was the matter and Nora would step out, have a brief conversation, as with her prior victims, and shoot him dead.

But, as she knew, no plan survives the first contact with the enemy, especially when the intel is no good. Nora did not know that Mr. P was in the habit of bringing his foursome home for a little brunch after golf (strong Bloody Marys and omelets made to order by his staff) and so he was not alone in his car. Worse, a second car rolled up the drive, a black Crown Vic trailing Pauling's white Escalade. The second car bore a two-man state police security detail. Even so, given complete surprise and with the handy suppressor suppressing the sound of rapid fire from her AR, Nora was able to kill them all with no trouble.

11: Another Flashback

There was screaming in her ears, a woman's voice telling of the last extremity, and on top of that the yelling for the corpsman and the continuous roar of weaponry as the Marines poured their fire into the green painted schoolhouse. Fifty cal and M4 fire and the bang and explosion of the grenade launchers. It should have deafened everyone, but everyone who was there remembers how Zulu Anderson screamed.

The shots that hit her had come from the school, a two-floor, mud brick building painted green. More fire struck Nora's humvee, the windshield shattered, and Wart Gunther cried out. From the turret, the screams continued.

Now Nora made an error. Maddened by the screaming and the battle-lust, she failed to follow doctrine, which was to assault an enemy-occupied building from the roof. In fact, she should have pulled away from the enemy fire and sent squads to the nearby buildings to clear the rooftops and descend through the school. Instead, she ordered every weapon under her command to fire on the building. This the Marines did with enthusiasm; again the noise reached extravagant levels.

Then came one of those odd intervals that are mentioned in many accounts of battle. The firing ceases, all of a sudden, and the stunned participants hear the singing of birds, for example, or the groans of the wounded. Here, from the silence of the guns emerged the thin wailing of children. Nora shouted orders into her headset. Her people raced forward with breaching charges. They blew the doors and barged in. . . .

Nora pulled the bike onto the shoulder and sat there shaking, dripping sweat down her flanks. This was a new one, a waking flashback while driving, combined with a little amnesia. She recalled shooting Pauling and the others, but nothing between then and the present instant. She had no idea of what she'd done at the shooting site. Maybe she'd dropped her wallet. Maybe she'd autographed each corpse.

No, stupid thoughts—she dumped them. Then the discipline kicked in, and she put the van in gear. In thirty minutes she was back in Zarb and ten minutes after that in Wilmington, concealing the motorcycle under the tree where she'd left it before. She'd been away for eighty-six minutes.

Another bluegrass group was playing "Foggy Mountain Breakdown" when she entered the old church. People were dancing on the worn planks in front of the stage, including Zulu and Thomas. Nora watched them and tried to think of the last time she had danced. Don had not been a dancer. One of her parents' anniversary parties? Something like that, and the partner had probably been a brother or a cousin. She'd been drunk, which is what it usually took to get her wriggling and stomping.

But she wasn't drinking now, and when a guy with a backwards ball cap and brown teeth asked her to dance, she smiled a shy smile and shook her head.

"Not interested, huh?" This was Zulu, who had appeared at her side, smelling of musk and ganja. "It's a shame. I happen to know Craig has a Daytona with a 426 hemi, painted purple candyflake with flames. You'd be the envy of every girl in Zarb."

"He dips snuff."

"And he's got a girl and a baby in a trailer out by Readsboro, but that just means he's an eligible bachelor around here. Where did you go?"

"Out in the Porta-Potties. You remember what my gut was like in Helmand. It hasn't improved."

"All that time? You were gone for hours."

"Not hours. Because time flies when you're having fun. You're loaded, girlfriend, and weed messes with your time sense. I was talking to some people out at the craft fair and then I took a walk. I was gone maybe forty-five minutes. Also, no offense, but bluegrass really isn't my thing."

"Yeah, me neither, but I like hearing Thomas play."

Zulu chatted on, Nora was elsewhere, keeping only enough attention present to make the right noises at conversational pauses. She thought Zulu was not convinced enough to stand as an alibi, but probably enough not to have suspicious thoughts when the news about the shootings broke. Speaking of which, Nora was dying to get to a place by herself with good Internet so she could see what the authorities made of her small massacre. She also had to get her van and her bike together again, all the while hoping that neither Zulu nor Thomas noticed that the bike wasn't in the van. She waved good-bye to Zulu and left the building.

She would need a fresh identity, and expected that one or more waited for her at the tiny Wilmington post office in the back of the general store. This proved so: a three-pack again, neatly wrapped and sent by Ben. Of these, after some study, she chose Cathleen Mitchell as the new her.

Sunday the happy couple went to meeting, and Nora collected the Suzuki in Wilmington and took her laptop down to the lowlands to seek media. She drove to Brattleboro and found a coffee shop with WiFi. They also had the Keene *Sentinel* there, which had led with the massacre, presenting a screaming banner headline set in a font probably last used for the assassinations of the Sixties.

The interviews with the head of the local police and the man from state police homicide added little real information, which was good, although Nora knew from her sister's tales that the cops often did not tell the press all they knew. In any event, there was no police sketch of a woman, no mention of a woman, and no search announced for any particular vehicle, a surveyor's van, for example. The state cop noted that there had been reports of gunfire by neighbors at the time of the murders, the return fire from the victims, obviously, which was good. No one seemed to suspect that the killer had used a silenced rifle.

They would know, soon enough, that she'd used a 5.56 mm rifle, and they would hypothesize, from the number of rounds fired at the vics, that the shooter would have needed a semi auto with a big magazine. The weapon she had used at Keene was currently in many pieces, wrapped up in black plastic bags, distributed among several dumpsters, but that didn't mean some parts wouldn't be found. So far, no one had put together the shootings in Harpers Ferry and Bridgeport, also done with a 5.56 rifle, but someone would, and that someone would be, as likely as not, a member of the FBI.

Now, as she thought this, her cell phone dinged its tune and Nora found, in one of those weird coincidences that makes some people think the world is ruled by forces beyond human ken, that it was her very own FBI agent on the line.

"Plate o' shrimp," said Nora. "I was just thinking of you."

"Oh? Why is that?" asked her sister Sally.

"Probably guilt rays from your powerful transmitter. Now I'm talking to my sister and I feel *much* better. How're things in lovely Quantico?"

Sally told her how things were, the annals of yet another happy family, this one with really terrific and interesting children. Nora asked the questions about them that a loving aunt would ask and Sally responded like a doting mom should.

And at the same time, both women were conscious of how perfectly wrong it was for the sister whose children survived to speak about them with joy to the sister whose children had been slain. Yes, life went on and one had to move with it despite everything, and yes, both women were bred to stoicism, but it was also the case that every time Sally Kehoe looked at her living children she imagined her dead nieces, and that after she got off the phone with Nora she would walk with gritted teeth to the ladies room serving the FBI's Behavioral Analysis Unit Four, where she worked, and there lock herself in a stall and weep almost silently into a towel, rocking back and forth and banging her head against the steel wall.

For her part, Nora was also gritting teeth, fighting an insane but powerful urge to confess all to her sister, as she had done throughout her life. It was like standing hip-deep in the Shenandoah when they were kids, braced against the power of the current. That was the game—to stand it as long as you could and then let go and let the brown water take you downstream. Now, however, she had to fight it without hope of relief, and yet seem not to be fighting anything at all.

The conversation rushed to its conclusion. How's work? How's Mom and Dad? How's Barbara? Heard anything from Ben or Doug? Nora received information, commented like a normal person, then answered Sally's interrogation blithely.

"I'm heading south and west now. I'm going to see Jolae in Kentucky."

"I thought you were trying to get back into the Corps."

"There's no rush. We don't seem to able to end wars anymore. I might try to pick up some shifts down there. Everyone always needs EMTs."

"You can't be short of money."

"No, but I like to be useful," said Nora.

Before the conversation ended, Sally urged her to call her parents, and she did. She spent fifteen minutes speaking with both of them, and did her regular-person imposture to good effect. Both seemed to accept the damaged but plucky daughter she presented, and she felt no tension at deceiving them. She was careful to leave commitments vague. She avoided direct lies.

Nora did some more web cruising and when she looked up from her laptop she thought she'd gone over yet another edge of madness because Bibi Lohani from Mir Puza had just walked into the coffee shop. The woman was moon-faced, black-haired, and massive. She wore a gold shalwar kameese and walked from the door to the counter with the same ponderous authority that Bibi always showed.

As the woman came closer the illusion dissipated. It was a tan African-American in a gold ski parka and tight ochre corduroy jeans. The woman must have felt Nora's stare, for she looked over at her somewhat sharply. Nora felt a blush start and quickly directed her eyes back to the screen.

Now, not precisely a flashback, but a deep musing., aided by the photographs stored in the machine. There was an album devoted to the second tour. Nora had not looked at it for many years, but now she brought it up, searching for a specific shot, because . . . there was no because. She just felt driven to find it.

Memory lane: should be sweetly nostalgic, but in her case the lane was littered with IEDs. Here was a nice one, her FET at the beginning of the tour, grinning and dressed for action--helmets, flak vests, camo fatigues, web gear, scarves, sun-glasses, weapons —leaning against the side of their humvee. There was Zulu, of course, towering, and little Chris Gomez out of Pilman, Texas, half her size, just as tough, and Jolae Ambling, the corps person, always called Doc, a self-described hillbilly from someplace in Kentucky or Tennessee, who looked doctorish enough with the specs and the red buzz-cut, and Wart Gunther, from Colorado where she had a husband and a toddler, and Zareena Deh Bala, their translator, who always had a worried look and smiled only a smile's ghost here. Did she know something even then? Stupid. Stupid to speculate at this remove. Her comrades. At that moment, Nora understood that she had actualized her cover story and would visit her surviving team for real.

Okay, here was the one. Two women in shalwar kameezzes and dupattas on the street in front of a bright green wall. It was the front of the freshly painted, just opened school, not the madrasa but a government school, in which girls would be educated. One of the women was Bibi Lohani and the other was Farishta Shirani.

Nora studied the photograph. Both women were smiling, Farishta showing her gold tooth. Nothing there, as there was nothing there in Mir Puza. The women, the two senior females of the two most prestigious khels in the region, appeared to be friends, appeared to be enthusiastic about what the FET was doing in their town. Nora checked the date of the photo: it was four months into the mission, the progress reports she sent up the line glowed, they seemed to be doing so well.

Against Commander Wylie's advice, Nora did fall in love with the country and the photos showed it. Here was one with her and the children. That was one thing, the wonderfulness of the Pashtun kids, that and the hospitality. Nora had read about *melmastia*, but the thing itself transcended any description. They had little, but what they had was yours, unreservedly. The guest was dearer than the family; any man or woman in the village would sacrifice a son to protect a guest. Nora had to tell her team not to admire anything because it would immediately be presented as a gift, no matter that it was a family heirloom two centuries old.

And the intel was terrific. Farishta especially was a rich source. She knew who was Taliban and who was leaning that way, and the times when the Taliban made their rounds to collect tribute and dispense punishment. Several successful ambushes and airstrikes were down to intel from Mir Puza; the brass were pleased. Nora was given more resources and told to keep at it.

Then Nora could not bear to see the photographs any more. She closed the laptop with a snap that attracted the attention of the false Bibi, who had taken a nearby seat. Nora gave her a smile that hurt her face and hurried from the place and soon hurried too from Zarb.

She left without saying good-bye to Zulu and Thomas, instead placing a note on the enamel kitchen table expressing her gratitude and apologizing for running off like this, adding an anodyne excuse. The actual reason for her exit was the sense that her presence might be a danger to the couple. Nora had much experience of the dangers of hospitality, and felt grim amusement at the thought that although she was murdering people she still retained these delicate sensibilities about harming her friends.

Nora crossed the Washington Beltway just after six-thirty in the evening, and checked into the Fairfax, Virginia, Comfort Inn, as Cathleen Mitchell. She showered and dressed in a new t-shirt, flannel shirt, jeans, and boots, adding a holstered Beretta to her belt. She was tired, but she couldn't go to sleep without seeing the place. And besides, it was close by, just down the road.

She took the motorcycle. In eight minutes, she was in the parking lot of a modern blue-glass building consisting of two long wings converging on a rectangular central column. Nora thought it looked like a winged rifle end-sight, which she supposed was not an accident. At the top of the rectangular column the letters N R A appeared. She considered going in, but recalled she was packing and the NRA building was famously (of course!) a no-gun zone, and she had no place to stash a loaded weapon on the bike. Instead, she sat on her motorcycle, looking at the building for a long time, and then drove back to her motel.

11: Gunsub

The people who worked with Sally Kehoe at Behavioral Analysis Unit Four all understood that at certain times and especially after certain phone conversations, their brilliant colleague had to go to the ladies' room and bang head. They knew what had happened to her sister, knew that Agent Kehoe felt, however irrationally, responsible. Agent Kehoe had from infancy been in charge of making sure her younger sister was okay, always had been, always would be, and then the Thing happened. They understood this because they were all professional adepts at reading people, and they cut Sally some slack on it; nor were her fits a subject of Bureau gossip. The unit valued Sally highly, for she shared with her sister the ability to see a whole, where others saw only bits.

Some years ago, the Bureau had decided that various smart people within its ambit should be given the time to think seriously about crime: what it was, where it came from, how to stop it from happening, how to catch particularly clever villains. Some leaders of the FBI thought this was a good use of resources, others begged to differ: anything not involving actual accumulation of evidence for the prosecution of a particular crime was hogwash. The debate continues today.

During Sally's time as a regular grunt Special Agent in Baltimore, she had sometimes shared the latter opinion when the guys she worked with held it, because she wanted to be one of the guys. Then they had rotated her through the brain factory at Quantico, because she was considered one of the smart ones, and after some time there she had grudgingly changed her mind. Yes, gosh, data could expose patterns that might actually lead to grabbing some bad actor. Her first love was field work, but this was fascinating.

At the moment, she was exploring whether seven murders of prostitutes in a swath of states from Kentucky to Oklahoma were connected, perhaps even the work of a single man. The tool she was using to do this was called VICAP, the Violent Criminal Apprehension Program, an enormous data collection and dissemination project founded on the idea that criminals repeat patterns in their crimes and that knowing these patterns enables law enforcement to focus resources on the most likely places and people.

Sally had discovered the delights of getting lost in data and allowing the patterns to emerge, like a figure emerging from fog in a horror movie, the unknown culprit in this case, the *unsub* in the parlance of the Bureau, gradually taking on definition. The commonalities here included: vics all prostitutes; all vics manually strangled; all vics but two tortured with burning cigar or cigarette pre-mortem, on breasts; all but one body arranged naked in a clear spot in a public park; all but one body had face covered with vic's underpants. All bodies discovered over a nine-month period, with the westernmost corpses being discovered later than those in the east.

She had a board in her office with the crime scene pictures of the women pinned up, including close-ups of the torture zones, with the other information, like date and approximate time of murder, written in her precise, angular script next to each photo. An industrial degreasing agent had been found on two corpses, in their hair, and one theory had it that the unsub was a salesman or driver dealing in such chemicals. Or a janitor. Or a factory worker. Or just someone who had to deal with lots of grease.

Anyway, not much help. Sally thought it was one guy, but she couldn't really say why. All the working girls were the kind of hooker who specializes in truck stops, and the consensus in the Bureau was that the unsub must be a truck driver, but Sally didn't think that was so, for several reasons. The dump sites were far from major trucking routes and no one was going to bring a semi up the road to Big Flat in the Ozark National Forest unnoticed. Witnesses had mentioned a black van, others a red panel truck with some logo. Was *that* a pattern? How did the sightings relate to time and place?

She was riffling through her notes with growing excitement. Maybe two guys working together? That would explain certain anomalies, for example, two of the murders were far apart and quite close in time—where was that table?

"Sally? Sally!"

Sally emerged from her analytic trance to find her boss, Stewart Nelson, standing in her office door.

"Oh, sorry," she said. "I was engaged."

"I see. You weren't answering your phone either. I thought you might have had a stroke."

"I did," replied Sally, contorting her face strokeishly. "What's up, boss?"

Nelson's characteristic frown deepened a little at the bad taste. He was a stocky, neat, pale, bespectacled man of the old-school dark suit/white shirt FBI, who had a doctorate in psychology, but always gave the impression that he'd rather be up on the running board firing a tommy gun at Pretty Boy Floyd.

He said, "I got a call from Op Support—they're organizing a task force on this Keene shooting and they want one of us on it."

"What's the Keene shooting?"

"You didn't read the morning alerts."

"Guilty, sir. I'm pretty engaged with the Ozark Strangler. I've been working sort of non-stop. Besides, I thought Ken Daley was next up for task force duty."

"He is, but he's tied up in Phoenix testifying on those post office bombings. I think it has to be you, Sally."

"Really? Damn it, sir, I am getting close on this one."

"Also, with all due respect, this one is bigger than a string of hooker killings. There's a plane leaving for Boston at 1640 today."

"Today?" This word came out with more volume and shriller than Sally had intended, and Nelson gave her a look. "Read the alert," he said, "Now," and departed.

Instead, Sally immediately called Barbara, who knew before she had heard half a sentence that, once again, her life and the lives of her children were going to be disrupted by the absence of her partner, all the intricate schedules and rosters carefully engineered to produce a perfect balance of child care, couples time, and professional development, were scrap paper now. Barbara's voice was tight on the phone and Sally's heart vibrated in tune with her anger and frustration.

No matter how often they had discussed it, no matter how often Barbara attested that she could handle it, every time it happened it drove home the itchy truth that Sally's job was about life and death under quasi-military discipline and Barbara's job was making the comfortable life of well-off teens somewhat more comfortable by resolving their neuroses; a cancelled appointment was no biggie. The aspirational equality of their lives together would remain chimeric as long as Sally worked for the Bureau.

"I need a wife," said Barb.

"Don't we all?"

"Actually, you have one, as now. Christ, this is the weekend of that seminar at Georgetown. Oh, shit and damn!"

"I'm sorry, babe . . . "

"Could you like, solve it in a couple of days and be back Friday?"

"Not a problem."

"You're a worthless slut, did you know that?"

"I do. I'll call you from Boston."

Sally kept a go bag in her office, so she could leave directly from her desk, and it had a down jacket and boots in it, so she would be fine for Boston. Or Keene, apparently. She turned to her computer and brought up the alert.

She read it, then read it again, with a sinking heart. This

was a bad one. Like every law enforcement person in America, Sally understood that while murder was always important, some murders were more important than others. Heinousness always counted, as did the murder of children, and the social status of the victim weighed heavily as well. No kids here, but aside from that it would be hard to imagine a more pressing quinella of homicides.

Three of the victims were prominent politicos. Arthur M. Pauling, who owned the driveway where the killings took place, was one of the largest political donors in the northeast. (Sally looked at the crime scene portrait. He looked like every murdered guy, his last expression one of surprise.) Milton P. Evans (he's flat on his face, with the back of his head a gory hole) was the chairman of the state Republican Party in New Hampshire, and just above his corpse, hanging from a seat belt, shot through the face, was Louis X. De Paul, the Lieutenant Governor of that state.

The other two victims were state police officers, a security detail for Mr. De Paul. Sally studied their fate with particular interest. Cpl. Frank Otono had been driving the unmarked state police car. He lay beneath the open drivers-side door, killed also by a shot through the head. The other officer, Sgt. Gerry B. Martin, was lying almost twenty feet to the left of his vehicle. Beneath him was the Browning BPS shotgun he had obviously yanked from its rack near the car's passenger seat. Sgt. Martin had been killed by two bullets through the center of his chest, his weapon unfired.

This had happened on Sunday, just before noon. The bodies hadn't been discovered until after five that afternoon, following a comedy of errors. When Pauling and his party had failed to show for brunch, his housekeeper had called her employer's cell, and when she received no answer had called the golf club. When she learned from the club that Pauling and party had played and departed on schedule, she called Mrs. Pauling, who was unfortunately engaged in her usual game of mixed doubles; her cell sang a futile tune in her locker. The housekeeper, having discharged her duty, put away the brunch things and attended to other tasks.

Mrs. P. finished her set and went to a brunch of her own with her three tennis partners. She did not check her voice mail, for she was of the generation who remained uneasy with the smartphone and its ways; nor could she imagine an important call on a Sunday. Her husband would be eating with his golfing pals, which was fine, it was his house, but she did not care to be there while the meal went on. She didn't care for the cigar smoke and the loud male braying, and she *especially* didn't care for Louie De Paul, a toad who had once pinched her buttocks at a political do some years ago. She liked to stretch out her absence from home on such Sundays and so she ordered Champagne at brunch and the brunch became one of those things that lasts and lasts, hilariously, into the late afternoon.

She called her husband twice during this time and was not particularly worried that he didn't pick up. The boys usually watched a game or played poker after brunch. Arthur would have checked the name on the incoming call and sent it off to oblivion or voicemail. She understood that her calls would not be returned while Arthur was watching or playing games.

She happened to mention this electronic silence to her companions and the woman had laughed and suggested that maybe they got a bunch of hookers in and they're having an orgy, to which Mrs. Pauling had laughed and replied, "Really, but nothing could surprise me anymore."

She reached her driveway at 5:22 p.m.. when she discovered how wrong she was on this score.

Sally finished reading this witness statement and the others and the initial forensic reports. Two cops dead, three prominent taxpayers ditto, all with political connections, and not merely political—New Hampshire political. The current governor had decided to run for the U.S. Senate and so Mr. De Paul was now governor of the state for practical purposes and likely to be governor after the upcoming election. The election after that was a presidential election and the three men who had been killed had *ex officio* more of a say than just about any other Americans about who the Republican nominee for President was going to be. Was there a connection? Was this a political assassination? Also, what about the fourth guy in the foursome? Didn't he brunch?

No, put that out of mind—there wasn't enough information yet. She spread out the crime scene photos and took up the initial forensic reports from the state police. All the victims had been killed with rounds from a 5.56 mm military rifle; it remained to be seen if it was the same rifle. A scatter of brass casings had been collected from a spot to the left of the gate near one of the thick decorative pillars that supported its hinges. The gate was set into an eight-foot-tall gateway that described an elegant curve flowing back to the wall proper. This switchback had provided the shooter or shooters with a secure place to lie in wait and a field of fire that commanded the whole of the foregate apron on which the two vehicles sat.

The killer had wedged a stone into the track the gate ran on. The supposition was that Mr. Pauling had stepped from the driver's seat of his car to see what was wrong and been shot through the left chest. Mr. Evans had left the front passenger seat to see what had happened to his friend. Seeing the bullet wound, perhaps, he had drawn his .380, popped off a few rounds at random and been shot through the head.

Mr. De Paul had thrown the rear door open and tried to exit the car, but had forgotten to unbuckle his seat belt. He had his own gun, a Colt Commander, out and cocked, but was not able to return fire before the shooter, had fired through the front windshield and killed him with another head shot.

Meanwhile, she surmised, the two cops must have been taking defensive action. Cpl. Otono had obviously thrown open the driver's side door, crouched behind it, and began to fire in the general direction of the wall. There was no evidence that any of the ten shots he had fired from his pistol had come anywhere near the shooter's position.

Sgt. Martin had pulled out the shotgun, run around the back of the car and charged at where he imagined the shooter to be. Sally figured that the two cops had formulated an instant plan. Otono would lay down a base of fire from behind the car door and Martin would circle around to the left and attack from the flank. She flipped through some pages now to check an obvious idea: yes, both men had been Marines.

It was a good plan, but hard to bring off against an opponent with an assault rifle who was also, on current evidence, an expert shot. A professional hit: the thought came unbidden, tinged with embarrassment. That was a movie idea; in real life you didn't see professional assassins executing politicians and cops, or not in the United States, or not yet. Sally hoped that it was instead something stupid, like one of the vics was porking some guy's wife and he'd defended his honor and had unfortunately been obliged to take out all the witnesses.

Could a single marksman have done all this damage against five armed men? If so, they were looking for someone who knew his way around military rifles, which suggested a vet, or a hunter, or both. Sally was already thinking of the profile she would help develop and the things she wanted to take a closer look at when she got to the scene.

Six hours later she was at the FBI's Boston headquarters, on Maple Street in Chelsea, where she met the Special Agent in Charge and the rest of his team. The Bureau now had many more female agents than it did when she first joined, but they were thin on the ground, especially in high-profile investigations. Sally was the sole female here among a couple of dozen men.

The SAIC was named Brendan Meagher, a man of around Sally's height and ten years older, with a red cannonball of a head on a short neck, a mouth full of yellowish tombstones and large, meaty hands. He was clearly not happy to have a female on his team, but that's what they had sent from the weirdo shop in Quantico and he was clearly determined to make the best of it. He had studied her record beforehand, found it unobjectionable, indeed sterling, and had resolved never by thought, deed, or inaction to reveal his mild misogyny or his somewhat more fervent dislike of lesbians.

He had a brief private meeting with Sally in his small office, whose door he pointedly left four inches ajar. He said he ran his investigations by the book, and Sally agreed that it was good to follow the book. He asked what her impressions were so far, and she said they were looking for a guy who really knew how to handle a rifle. He said they had come to the same conclusion and had started to call the perpetrator GUNSUB. Sally smiled as expected at the cuteness of this, opened the fresh notebook she'd brought, and wrote that on the top of the first page.

12: Acts of Corporal Mercy

To her surprise, Nora found that the excuse she'd given her family, that she wanted to drive around the country visiting her former comrades, had turned into an actual desire. It had done her good to see Zulu getting on so well, and she wanted to see if the other Marines who had endured Mir Puza had put their lives together. She wanted to be in their presence once more before she died, and if she could help any who were down, it might make what she was doing not entirely awful.

It was like checking the kids before you went to bed. She actually had this thought, and it summoned up a short, loud cry, like a bird call, that hardly seemed to come from her throat, it was that involuntary. She shook herself and turned again to her task, which was spray-painting her motorcycle matte black. She had bought two cases of paint cans, having thought to do the van as well, but decided to stop with the bike. The bike might have been seen in New Hampshire; she was sure the van hadn't because if it had she'd be dead by now, and she still thought a van with a commercial logo aroused less suspicion than a blank-sided one. When the paint was dry, she affixed a large Marine Corps globe and anchor decal to one side of the tank and a skull and crossbones one onto the other. Tacky, yes, but with the virtue of honesty.

She left at first light, when military operations always begin. She liked driving through the dawn, the symbol of hope, even though she had none just now. It recalled for her the voyages of her childhood, also always begun at dawn, Colonel Dad being in charge. Mom was always in the back of the van with Ben, who required constant attention, lest he try to grab the wheel or the gear shift, and the three older children wanted only more sleep, so Nora got to ride in the front with Dad, and have him all to herself.

These dawn rides, when Peter Kehoe would converse with his daughter as if she were an adult, or at least more than seven, were the golden memories of her childhood. She got to push the cigarette lighter in and retrieve it when it popped for his waiting Lucky. She had her questions answered, the mysteries of life and death, whether animals went to heaven, where mountains came from, the reality of vampires, the possibility of getting a kitty at the next posting, the cruelty of the Marines for not allowing same in officers' family housing, why the light seemed to creep into the world even when you couldn't see the sun.

As now, except there was not an admirable man next to her who could make her feel safe and provide a satisfactory answer to every question. Nevertheless, she enjoyed sunrise on the highway and the damp freshness of the morning air pouring through her van. The road was open, little traffic this early on a Friday morning. She took I-68 through the Cumberland Gap, then switched to I-79 as far as Charleston, and then I-64 into the state of Kentucky. At Grayson she left the freeways and took state route 7 to the south. It was past noon, she'd been on the road for over six hours and she was hungry.

A roadhouse served her a dish of Kentucky fried chicken that was colossally superior to Kentucky Fried Chicken and she joked about the name with the waitress, a woman of middle age whose heft attested to her enthusiasm for her own food, and the waitress replied that everyone in a Santa Claus suit wasn't Santa. Nora disguised the feeling that this common observation engendered in her and asked whether the woman knew of the Licking Valley Health Co-op. The waitress said, "Oh, my goodness, yes. We'd all be goners without the Co-op," and closed with a concise version of her own medical history. She knew Jolae too (Oh, my, yes! God *bless* her!) and gave Nora the address of the Co-op in West Freedom.

As she drove through the green farmland and the hillsides dotted with black cattle, she thought about the woman she was going to see. Jolae Ambling had been the Naval medical corpsperson assigned to Nora's FET. Basic health care got you through the door, as they said in the Female Engagement business. The village women found ways of taking their kids to the doctor, even if she was only a corpsperson, and after they became familiar with her, shyly confessed their own problems.

It worked fine until it didn't. Jolae was the only person who was there that day who was off the hook for what had happened in Mir Puza. She had saved a number of lives, of Marines as well as of locals, had risked her own with the casual, unprompted valor common among Navy corpsmen, and had not killed anyone, although she did get shot. She won the only Navy Cross of the day.

West Freedom, KY, was a T-shaped town formed where one highway butted another. It had a single shopping street with a

Dairy Queen-Hardy's at one end and a Texaco station at the other. In between were a bank, a feed and tractor agent, two nail places, three church charity resale shops and half a dozen boarded storefronts, these attesting to the arrival some years ago of a Walmart not far distant. Next to the bank stood the town's sole commercial structure, a two-floor job from the 1920s faced with distressed brown stone and the title "J.P.M.Taylor Building" deeply incised over the entrance. Here Nora found the storefront housing the Lick Valley Health Co-op.

The window held a dusty plant of some species highly resistant to neglect and a large cardboard-mounted photograph topped with the logo of the LVHC. The photo showed a line of presumably healthy children of the various races people came in, dancing along the banks of the presumably eponymous river.The photo had faded and warped in the sun, making the children appear a disturbing space-alien green.

Nora entered and found a waiting room of the kind she expected, facilities catering to the poor being of a type, although in rural Afghanistan a place as fine as this would have served only the elite: scuffed green tiles on the floor, an unmatched set of chairs in a few ragged lines, these holding a dozen or so patients,. These were either absurdly juvenile women with children in tow or in carriers, or rural elderly poor, on average the sickest demographic in America. Their liquid coughing served as the bass to the high whine and cry of the kids. The room was divided by a counter, behind which sat a large woman with an aggressive gray perm and harlequin glasses on a chain. *Beryl* was the name engraved on the plastic strip affixed to her desk.

Nora asked Beryl if she could see Jolae Ambling and Beryl replied that patients didn't get to pick what provider they wanted to see, they had to take the next one open, and Nora explained that she wasn't a patient but a friend. From the Marines.

"Oh, well, Jolae don't work in here no more. She's out in the county on the circuit? But she usually checks in around five or so to drop off records and such and pick up supplies? I could tell her you stopped by."

"No, don't bother. I'll catch up with her later. And, um, would you know of a place to stay in town?"

"In West Freedom? Well, there's the Bonny Brae around the corner on Taylor, or if you wanted something more fancy there's a Motel 6 out on 460. There was a real hotel here once, they had a doorman and everything. The Depot? But it closed."

Nora thanked the woman and drove to the Bonnie Brae. The cadaverous fellow behind the desk could not get his credit card machine to work, so Nora paid in cash, which he did not seem to mind one bit. The motel was a traditional one, with separate cabins, painted white, with chintz curtains on the windows. The wall-to-wall was, inevitably, avocado, but the bathroom, a relic of the 1940s, worked reasonably well. It was good place to lay up if you were Bonnie and Clyde on the lam, and while Nora was not yet on the lam, she thought she might be one day, and have to spend time in places like this.

She washed, took a brief nap, awakened with a yell, sweating, and washed again. She changed her t-shirt and walked to the Dairy Queen down quiet streets lined with trees bearing fresh green and yards full of forsythia, honeysuckle and dogwood. She bought a flame-broiled burger and a strawberry shake, sat at a concrete table outside, and observed the scene.

High school was out for the day, or these kids were ditching. Parked in the lot were two well-worn pick-ups and a 2003 Malibu with yellow flames painted on the hood. In and around them a dozen or so boys and girls congregated and acted silly at some volume, aided by a car radio. The music was country.

Nora cast her eye over the youths, idly trying to pick the ones who'd go directly into the service after high school. Without towns like this the United States could not have fielded a substantial military. It would not be fun to come back from Afghanistan to the Dairy Queen in West Freedom, but they didn't know that and she was not of a mind to tell them.

A gray Toyota SUV covered in dust and bearing the LVHC logo was parked in front of the health co-op when Nora returned. She supposed it was Jolae's rig and it was. Jolae was fuller in the face and body than she'd been downrange, as who was not? She'd let her hair grow out into dark red swathes, which she kept tied up in a top bun, like the girl in the Toulouse-Lautrec poster. She still had an expression that combined compassion with preternatural intelligence.

Just then she was talking to Beryl, who must have been informing her that she'd had a visitor, because when the clerk caught sight of Nora she said, "Why, there she is now."

Jolae turned and saw Nora and Nora observed a short film strip of expressions pass across the woman's face: surprise, horror, the quick assemblage of an appropriately neutral persona, accessorized with a wan smile.

"Lieutenant Kehoe? Wow."

"You're surprised to see me."

"Not really. They say that if you hang out at the corner of Main and Taylor in West Freedom, Kentucky, long enough, everyone you ever knew in your life will show up. What brings you to this neck of the woods, Lieutenant?"

"It's Nora. I haven't been a lieutenant for a while. What brings me is you. I'm sort of on a tour, checking in on all the old team. I was in Vermont last week, visiting with Zulu."

"Well, lucky me," said Jolae in a tone not exactly hostile, but lacking all warmth. Nora was taken aback; she had always enjoyed Jolae Ambling and had probably spent more time alone with her than with any of the others. Jolae was the most intelligent member of the team, not excluding Nora herself. Every corpsman is called Doc, but in Jolae's case this was barely hyperbolic. She always had her nose in a book, usually one with disgusting photographs of wounds, or of nasty diseases in their final stages. In Afghanistan she had done surgical procedures she had no business doing, all with good results.

Nora's face must have reflected dismay, because Jolae reached out and touched her arm.

"And yeah I'm being a bitch after you came all this way. Sorry. Look, let me finish up a few things here with Beryl and we'll go somewheres and talk."

Jolae turned to the clerk and Nora passed the time reading posters. There was one about PTSD and Nora learned she had four of the five major signs of it. She also discovered from another poster that she was not eating properly and was in danger of contracting diabetes and heart disease. Nora assessed that in her case the danger was remote.

She was reading one about sexually transmitted disease and wondering vaguely if she would ever again have the chance to catch one, when Jolae tapped her shoulder and led her out to the street.

"We'll take my rig," said the medic, and when they were in the vehicle, added, "We'll go to the bad side of town and drink. If I don't get a tequila and a beer real soon, I'm gonna spit brick."

The bad side of town was five minutes down Route 460 and a sharp left turn away, a three block commercial strip that housed a *carneceria*, two *taquerias*, a discount store selling *mochilas, maletas and targetas,* a check-casher, a package store, a pawn shop, three storefront churches, a massage parlor, two nail and hair places, and four bars. The action on this street, as evidenced by the number of cars and people moving around, was substantially greater than in the rest of the town.

Jolae parked in front of one of the bars, labeled *Tio Sal's* in red neon in the window. Inside it was dim, cool, beer-stinky and supplied with a dozen or so drinkers and two big, flat screens, one showing international football and the other baseball. The men there wore hoodies and work pants and there were hard hats on tables and under chairs and bar stools. The conversation was in Spanish.

Several men and the barkeep greeted Jolae in that language, and jokes were traded. She ordered shots of *reposado* and bottles of PBR for herself and Nora, and they both sat down in a booth. The black vinyl seat was sticky and patched in places with duct tape.

"I forgot you spoke Spanish," said Nora. "Now I remember you were always yakking away with Gomez. Where did you pick it up?"

Jolae threw back her shot in a gulp and took a long pull from the Pabst. "In bed, the only place to really learn a language. Julio Martinez, my high school honey. Left me with a case of crabs and a working knowledge of the loving tongue. Turns out useful—I guess you picked up on the demographics hereabouts."

"Mexicans moving in?"

"Uh-huh. And they're still having lots of kids, unlike the white folks. The schools are seventy per cent Latino now and that's not going down anytime soon. The big employer is the dog food plant. We're close to horse country here, and in horse country you have to find a place for the runners who don't finish in the money, and Americans don't care to work in slaughterhouses, especially in those that process horse meat, so there's a draw on account of the jobs.

"And they open businesses. Besides the dog food, I bet half the employment in Mitchell County comes from Latino businesses. They saved the town, basically. You notice there's just West Freedom, and not East Freedom or just plain Freedom? Gone with the wind. They shrank, the stores closed, the young people bailed, the old people died, the school went, then the P.O. and that was it. It didn't happen here, and the white folks are so grateful that their asses got saved that they all voted for politicians who want to kick the Mexicans out of the country."

"It sounds like Afghanistan."

"It's the same crazy anyway." She drank again, then caught the barman's attention and gestured for a refill. She stared balefully at Nora, who, after standing this for a couple of long minutes, said, "And if you got a beef with me I'd like to know what it is."

Jolae dropped her eyes and a red bar appeared on her cheeks.

"Yeah, Lieu . . . Nora. My beef is I'd like to know what the fuck happened. We were doing great—I thought. I mean I had patients. I had connections to families. I was treating kids who'd never seen a doctor in their lives and the moms were so grateful. Little baskets of *kulka*, little pots of *qabili pilav.* We get there that day and right away I knew something was wrong because when I set up my clinic, there was no one waiting and usually, you know, the line was out the door. And Zareena wasn't there either to translate."

"That's true. She faded into the background right away."

"Right, so I went out to see what was going down and that's when they opened fire. Anyway, if *I* knew something was going sour, how come you didn't? How did you let that happen to us? And why the fuck didn't any of the moms who I saved their kids' lives come out and warn us? Why didn't *you* warn us? It was *your* command. You were supposed to know all that shit. I mean, let's face it, aside from all that happy horseshit about hearts and minds, you were a goddamn spook. You were there to collect intel on the hajjis—how come you didn't see what was going on? That was your *job*! We lost five Marines and then the thing . . . the thing in the schoolhouse."

Jolae's voice had risen during this speech, it was clear that she'd been storing this for ten years and here it all was, very like the same accusation Nora had made against herself innumerable times, only much milder, barely a reproach in comparison. Nora forbore to mention that she hadn't been in command at all; the late Lt. Henderson had and he had given clear orders to proceed with the FET's normal operations.

As to why she had not known about the ambush, well, the short answer was that she'd been played. American lieutenants of Marines had no business betting their lives on the fidelity of Pashtuns as long as the Taliban were active. No one who'd been in country for a six month tour could possibly fathom the layered intricacy of tribe and khel connections, and the playing out of ancient feuds, and the ways that Afghans had devised over centuries of invasion to use the powerful but stupid invaders for their own ends.

Under such conditions, it was easy for the Americans to decide that the best thing was to kill them all and let God sort it out, and while that might not be the way it went down in Mir Puza, because they'd actually been ambushed and were receiving fire until almost the last moments, Nora knew that these feelings had flourished in her heart during the scant minutes of killing in the Maidan.

She didn't share any of that with Jolae, who was still raving, replaying her afternoon in the shit, instead saying only," I'm sorry. I was in over my head. I'm truly, truly as sorry as I can be that you had to go through that."

The air in the booth had become like jello, the words moving whale-like through the dense medium, and it took what seemed like a while for her words to penetrate. Then Jolae stopped talking and her face took on the stricken cast of a Greek mask, her features pulled down as if by fingers, and she went *ah-hunh, ah-hunh, ah-hunh,* as her face turned rose-red and the tears gushed.

Jolae yanked at her thick hair and rocked and flung about. Nora came around to the other side of the booth and tried to hold Jolae, but the woman fought and struck out blindly. A beer bottle smashed. The men in the bar stopped talking. Nora managed to pin the other woman down in the corner of the the booth, throwing her weight on her like one of those mats they use to stifle explosions. After a few nasty minutes of struggle, Jolae relaxed into grief and merely sobbed her heart out, the tears flowing free. The conversation picked up again among the men.

After a indeterminate while, both women became aware of an insistent shrill wailing nearby, and the sound of sirens from the street.

Jolae snuffled and stopped the sobs. She said, "Get off me, that's my cell."

Nora did and Jolae pulled a smartphone from her bag. She listened intently, and swabbed at her face with a ball of paper napkins.

“That was the hospital--I have to go.”

“What’s wrong?”

“A gentleman just shot up the post office,” said Jolae, pushing to get free of Nora and the booth. “It’s payday. It was packed with Mexicans buying money orders to send back home. It’s a mass casualty call.”

“I’ll come with you.”

“I’ll be up to my neck—that’s not a good . . . “

“No, I mean I can help. I’m a qualified EMT.”

Without waiting for Jolae to agree, Nora followed her out of the tavern at a trot; they both leaped into the truck and roared off toward the sirens.

13: Going Postal

It was a comment on America in the 21st century that every town in the nation, no matter how small, had a mass-shooting response plan. West Freedom, KY, even owned an Emergency Coordinator, and she had directed Jolae and her non-official helper to the kill zone itself. Ambulances had been routed in from neighboring towns and counties, but there were people currently dying at the scene and so every medical first responder in the area was being sent there. Jolae, it turned out, had been designated by local and state authorities as an incident supervisor. Nora thought it was a good choice; there must be few people in this part of Kentucky who had seen more massacre than Jolae Ambling.

The post office lived in a squat white building on Court Street, next to the county courthouse and the jail. All the cops in town were there, mostly standing around and looking ready for anything; it would've been a terrific time to rob the bank. Half the ambulances in the county were on site already, lined up in a row like buses at a concert. When Nora and Jolae arrived (the latter flashing her ID at the cops to get through) the place was cordoned off as a crime scene. The EMTs from the ambulances were already at work, but uncoordinated. Jolae jumped from her truck, Nora at her heels, carrying a medical bag similar to the one she'd hauled around for Fairfax County.

Inside, there was wailing, a four-year-old in full cry, and the usual shouts for help and agonized groaning. There were thirty-eight people on the floor of the post office, and so bad were their wounds that the linoleum floor was awash with congealing blood. Nora watched Jolae literally wade through this red sludge, leap up on a table and take charge. She assigned a couple of EMTs to work triage and told Nora, "Get that kid out of here."

The kid was a little tan boy in a stroller. His mother had been waiting in line when the shooting started, she had instinctively knelt to protect her boy, and the shooter had blown her brains all over him. Nora lifted him from the stroller, wiped his face with a wet-wipe from her bag and carried him out. There was a female police officer at the door with the typical bleached look of someone at her first performance of American carnage. Nora handed the child to her and told her to get him to someone authorized to deal with children. She used her command voice; the cop jumped to it.

In the ensuing hour or so, Nora again entered the peculiar psychic shelter of emergency medical work. Your focus narrows; your petty personal issues, like your family's been murdered, say, lose their place in the foreground, which is entirely occupied with the physical task of saving life. Clear the airway; stop the bleeding; treat for shock. Repeat. Repeat. Put on the gloves, strip off the gloves, follow the triage team, ignore the goners, work on that one, not breathing, chest compression, the hand sinks into a pool of bright arterial blood. Start a bag, a probable DOA, but get her off my scene.

Next case, oh good, a mere gut-shot, writhing, screaming with pain in Spanish, but a genuine rescue, pressure bandage, plasma IV, wrap with space blanket, stabilized, call for a gurney, and again, thank God all the casualties are adults, so won't have to find tiny, tiny veins on the small limp arms. Another benefit here: whatever has gone sour in your life, when you do this kind of work you know it's as close to absolute good as can be found in this vale of tears, a kind of vapor emanating from acts of corporal mercy that soothed the sorrowful heart. When it faded, as it had to, many of the morally afflicted substituted drugs.

The total kill was seventeen, with eight more wounded.

To make this achievement easier, the shooter had chosen an actual Chinese AK-47, and so the wounds were familiar to both Nora and Jolae, the awful jagged holes made by military ammunition designed by experts to tumble on contact with human flesh. The last living victim treated on-site was a postal employee—a fifty-three year-old obese white woman with a shattered hip. She had fallen behind her counter when hit and thereby avoided the second killing shot the shooter had dispensed to so many others. She was awake and aware, if shocked, and was bent on describing her experience in detail to Nora, who did not want to hear it, but was happy that the woman was well enough to chatter.

It was that Vern Harrison that done it, according to the victim. She had always known he was a bad one, she had reported it, but nothing happened, until finally the supervisor had realized that Vern regarded sheets of postage stamps as a perk of his employment and had fired him, resulting in the present situation. The supervisor was among the deceased, as was the shooter. He had come out of the P.O. with his gun blazing, fought the law and the law won. He was twenty-two, had no criminal record, and had purchased his assault rifle at a nearby gun show. He was a local boy, an Army veteran, with two tours in Iraq; he had shot his mother and his step-father to death before attending the massacre.

This was learned later. At present, Nora was sitting on the curb with her arms around a police officer twice her size, who was going *"Aww, uh-hah, uh-hah, uh-hah,"* while squirting tears and nose-drip over her blood-stiff t-shirt. Nora stroked his shoulder and whispered, "It's okay, it's okay," and other empty phrases until the man's colleagues gently took him away.

After that, the exhaustion. After that, she was kneeling in the back of Jolae's SUV, changing into a fresh t-shirt and jeans out of a large plastic Goodwill bag Jolae had stashed there; after that, she was in a bar, throwing back shots of Cuervo, washed down with lager. The saloon was out on 430, a concrete block building with barred slits for windows. It was the kind of place—there is one in every community—where cops, firefighters, nurses, and EMTs hang out and seek oblivion from what they do all day.

After that, she was in Helmand again, learning Pashto phrases from Nazanina, a ten-year-old from Mir Puza who had adopted the American Marine woman-man. Nazanina was not as beautiful as the famous Pashtun girl on the *National Geographic* cover, nor would she get the chance, but she had that same wild look, and the same grape-green eyes against dark skin and the thick sooty hair they all had.

The girl was a patient teacher, although she failed to understand why the Lieutenant Nora could not understand her clearly enunciated Pashto. It was said that the Americans did something to their women to make them act like men, but Nazanina had felt the American all over and could attest that she was not a man in her shameful parts. In the latrine, she was just like a real person, and had learned, at least, to use water to clean herself instead of that disgusting paper, and to not use her right hand for it. Among her age-mates, it was understood that the Lieutenant Nora was the personal property of Nazanina and could not be approached by any girl whatever without her permission.

Nora understood that her body was in eastern Kentucky and that Jolae was asking her about stuff and that she was answering and that somebody was setting up shots for her whenever her glass emptied. Her body moved on command, but her mind was less biddable, just now, because she found herself drifting back into the . . . hallucination was probably the right word, but it was also the product of exhaustion. Her mental state had something in common with those odd blackouts everyone has on a freeway drive. You realize you haven't been present for some incalculable time—who the hell was driving your car?

So now she drank, she responded, she generated weak smiles for men who approached her, but at intervals the saloon would fade away and she would be back in the women' quarters of the home of Gorbat Shirani, whose third daughter it was, talking with Nazanina. Nora had not at the time thought of having children; she and Ryan had decided to wait until their careers were somewhat more advanced. They thought that they would both apply for stateside billets and have some extended time together.

But Nora was unexpectedly ravished by the Pashtun girl. She wanted one just like her—bright, funny, curious, charming—and more than that she wanted the connection she saw between Nazanina and Farishta, her mother: the long sessions of hair brushing, and trying on clothing, the whole quasi-erotic life between mothers and daughters. Nothing she ever thought about before but now, in this weird place with different rules about everything, she was seized with desire. She spoke about it with Ryan during one of their phone calls, or maybe it was a Skype, and he had said, "Yeah, I never thought about jumping out of airplanes before I did it, and now I can't hardly think about anything else."

The child was telling Nora about her friends. Nora couldn't follow every word, but picked up the gist. The girls in the town were stupid and old-fashioned except for her and Laila and Khukulay. They were going to go to the school the Americans had built and then attend university in Kabul. Yes it was true! A girl could go to university. What would she study? The family would decide, but she would like to be a pilot of an airplane, not the kind that drops bombs, but the kind that takes people to other lands. She would fly to Mecca! Laila was her new best friend. Before, she couldn't play with Laila because she was a Bazai and the Bazais were allied with the Shiranis; and the Lohanis were in feud with them.

What was the cause of the feud? The girl exchanged a weighted look with her mother, a gentle soul who knew every song, who shrugged and said that the feud was over now, the Shirani had made apology before the *jirga*, so now it could be told to a stranger. The girl fell into the rhythmic chanting of the professional storyteller.

It was during the war. Dost Mohammed Lohani and Baz Gul Shirani had found plunder: a chest that held gold coins. They were far from their camp and the land was thick with enemy patrols. There was bravery, there was trickery in the tale, but at last the comrades broke through the enemy and returned to their village, this very village, Mir Puza, but of course, it was much smaller then, not grand as now, with its own mosque. They got drunk to celebrate their prize and their escape, but in their wine, they fell out over the division of the gold.

Knives were drawn, words were spoken that stained the air. Of course, Dost Mohammed could not kill Baz Gul because they were guest-friends, but they both had lots of cousins and brothers; and so, the killing began. The girl recited a list of who had slain whom. What war was this? Nora asked. Against the Russians? No, they explained, against the *Angrezi.* (That would have been the Second Afghan War, in 1880, Nora had realized with a shock.) But now the feud was over. Bibi Shirani had been entertained in this very house, this very room.

Nora looked around with interest. There was the low-ceilinged, dimly-lit room with the embroidered pillow and the piles of rugs and that spice-perfume-sewage odor that permeated Afghanistan from Herat to China, and in the same space there thumped the American barroom, loud with Carrie Underwood singing *Cry Pretty* and the movement of big American bodies around her and the smells of beer, bourbon, and tequila. She thought that she must be very drunk.

It's hard to get paranoid on alcohol, but Nora was feeling the initial pangs: drunk means out of control; out of control means she might say something or do something that would give her away; she had to get out of here and get sober. Where was Jolae? Dancing? Yes, with a big bearded fellow with okay white guy moves. Nora tried to attract her attention, but Jolae was dancing hard, hard enough to make sweat drops fly from her head and glitter in the colored beer-sign light.

Now they were playing *Texas Twister* by Little Feat. Nora felt herself moving in her chair, which had to be wrong, because Nora didn't dance, although Ryan Graham had been a terrific dancer, and she had delighted in having him fling her around a dance floor, and grind his erection into her butt crack. They had only danced about three times, the last occasion twelve years ago.

On the other hand, the guy sitting at the end of the booth was looking at her again. She'd let him buy her a drink, she vaguely recalled. He was a friend of Jolae's named Trey McKenzie, a tight-knit man of moderate size with an easy smile, who, fortunately for him, shared with the late 1LT Ryan Graham high cut cheekbones, pale eyes, and an air of danger.

Nora tried to recall the last time she had engaged in sexual intercourse. Suffice it to say that sex was not the main draw in the Kehoe-Chase marriage. Nora's libido had dived like a marmot into a hole when Ryan died, and Don Chase, for all his many virtues, was not the man to winkle it out again. From time to time, when her body sent a message, she had taken care of it herself, usually in the bath, usually with a dead man in her thoughts. She would come and then cry, using a form of utterly silent weeping she'd perfected over the years, and then emerge from the tub with a smile for everyone.

He was a cop, was Trey, a statie from the local barracks, she now recalled, and when he gestured to the dance floor she rose and followed him. It was an upbeat Patty Loveless song, and he was a pretty good dancer. She let herself be hauled around, and did not object when his hands clasped her buttocks. A slow one came on: Emmylou Harris, agreeing that if tonight you'll be my tall, dark stranger, I'll be your San Antone rose, and it sounded like a reasonable deal. He nuzzled, he said sexy, stupid things in her ear. She said, "Okay."

He said, "Okay, what?"

She said, "Okay, you can take me somewhere and fuck my brains out. But I need to talk to Jolae first. Wait for me outside."

She left him bemused and elated and found Jolae in the crowded hallway in front of the door that said "Cowgirls" on it.

"I hope you can hold it," said Jolae. "There's one stall in there, and we've had some major puke episodes. I personally am just about to go out into the weeds and squat. Speaking as a medical professional now, I'd advise you to do the same."

"Roger that," said Nora. "But I just wanted to tell you I'm taking off now."

"Leaving with McKenzie, I bet."

"Yeah. He seems nice."

"Uh-uh. I'm guessing an exchange of body fluids is on the menu?"

"So far. Is that unwise?"

"Trey gets around is all. He's semi-famous in the county."

"They fall at his feet."

"We do. So, to speak. I'd insist on a condom."

"Good plan."

"That'll be an XL, by the way. On the condom?"

"Lucky me. Well, I'll see you when I see you."

"I'll walk out with you and find some tall grass," said Jolae and they went out and Jolae walked off into the dark at the edge of the road and Nora picked up her gentleman friend and they drove off in his pickup truck.

He took her to a field growing young alfalfa and fucked her in the bed of his Ford-150 under the stars. The floor of the pickup bed was thick with quilted moving mats, and reasonably comfortable during their remarkably athletic gyrations. As she had expected, her partner, having been blessed with the unit of a porn star, had naturally allowed himself to be schooled regarding sex with a woman by video pornography. So, a great deal of piston-like ramming; the changing of positions like a gymnast going through a prescribed routine without regard to what was happening in the moment; no eye-contact, no remarks, no humor.

It was exactly what Nora wanted, a stupid, meaningless release of animal tension. She wanted to surrender all agency for a time, she had far too much goddamn agency just now, she wanted to be pounded into submission. She encouraged him in his fantasy, she made high-pitched noises, God was much on her tongue, she talked dirty; and he pounded harder. It hurt, sometimes a lot. That was sort of the point: not a bug, but a feature, as her brother Ben might have said.

14: The Furies

The morning found Nora in her bed at The Bonnie Brae Trailer Park & Motel, fully clothed and badly hung-over. As a skilled medical professional and an ex-Marine, she knew what to do and did it, groaning and asking the perpetual question of the hung: why did I drink so much? While she was standing in the shower, the non-drinking elements of the previous evening—Oh, Christ, that guy—Mr. Penis! She couldn't come up with his name, but she remembered he was a cop. She probably had confessed everything and they were assembling the SWAT right now.

Besides that, she hoped that she didn't have to think about having sex for the next ten years. Nora had always had a kind of admiration for whores and other sex workers. They seemed tough and fearless the way Marines were supposed to be and now, soaping her groin, she discovered another reason. Absent the boozy anesthesia the soreness was no joke, although she knew literally dozens on the subject from the forever-to-be-unpublished Girl Marines' Book of Misogynistic Dirty Jokes. It was laughable; she did laugh, and for an uncomfortably long time, there in the little tin shower.

In the cabin that held its office, The Bonnie Brae provided a Continental Breakfast (the continent being North America) and there Nora found black coffee and a blueberry muffin. She was just deciding whether to consume more or to throw up that which she had already consumed when her back pocket vibrated.

"How're you feeling this morning, Lieutenant?"

"I'm fine, Jolae. As soon as I can walk, I'm going to find José Cuervo wherever he's hiding and strangle him with my bare hands. What was I thinking? What did I have—ten shots and three beers?"

"Fourteen, but who's counting? Listen, come over to the house and I'll make you my hangover cure. I have a day off owing to my heroic work in the post office and you can take a day off too. We'll laze around like sluts, we'll watch baseball, people will drift through . . ."

"Will *he* drift through, do you think?"

"Who? Oh, you mean Trey. No, Mr. Penis has a shift today. Are you

heartbroken?"

"No, my heart is not what is broken. You know, I think you set this up. What is it, some initiation, a new girl comes to town and you unleash the Destroyer?"

"It's a natural phenomenon. Fresh pussy in Eastern Kentucky and there he is. I don't know, he may use drones. So, you're coming."

"Send an ambulance."

"You can get off your ass and walk five streets. What are you, a Marine or a little girl?"

That was interesting, Nora thought, after she clicked off the connection. That was me talking and joking, and that was me yesterday at the post office and that was me with Trey and that was me in Vermont, doing my thing with Zulu and Thomas and no one notices that I'm an empty shell. My family doesn't even notice.

My comrades are having their American lives, she thought, and I am so happy for them, that they escaped the plague, the suicides and the murders and the drugs and despair. They're like my dad; they came back home human, despite everything they'd seen and done downrange.

But *her* punishment went on. Her new husband wanted to impose massacre on the people who enabled it, and he had chosen Nora Kehoe to make it happen. And who else was more worthy?

Nora dressed in t-shirt and shorts and walked out into a devastatingly sunny Saturday. The citizens of West Freedom were out in their gardens and in their driveways, trimming, weeding, replacing engine parts, and otherwise acting normal, as if they had not just experienced a massacre. Some people waved to her and she waved back. She walked through the smell of cut lawns, under dogwood and peach blossoms, past yellow forsythia in bloom, and scatters of candy-colored tulips.

She reflected that this town was about the size of Mir Puza, and that at this moment people not unlike her were calling down ordnance on houses full of people like the ones she passed now, but the people she passed seemed unaware of this. They had happily subcontracted national violence out to a tiny fragment of the population, largely teens with few other options, and even an incident like yesterday's, in which one of them had brought the violence back home, was not enough to dent the stainless-steel innocence of the Americans. It was hard to love and hate your country at the same time, but she managed.

Jolae's house was a substantial clapboard with carpenter gothic embellishments that would have cost six million dollars in San Francisco, but was affordable in West Freedom KY on a physician assistant's salary. Nora knocked. The sound of clumping feet, and the door flew open. In the doorway stood a tall, thin boy of about ten, with Jolae's red hair and her freckles spread on someone else's face. He said, "Hi, I'm Cory. You must Lieutenant Kehoe. Please come in."

The boy held out his hand and Nora shook it and was surprised to feel not the dead fish that most kids provided in a shake but a manly grip, if small. She had not known that Jolae had a kid and studied him with interest as he led her through the house. He wore a plaid shirt and tan pants, both swimming on his thin frame, the kind of "good" outfit American parents buy at Walmart and hope will last a growing child for an entire year. He held her hand as they walked, which she thought was unusual and affecting. He told her that Jack Blatt was doing his famous barbecue later, and that he would be happy to fetch her a beer or a glass of wine. They had bourbon, too, but he wasn't allowed to pour it.

The rooms they passed were furnished in an antique style: respectable, small-town-America, mid-twentieth century, but not mid-century modern. People had been living in this house for probably over a century and the inhabitants had not thrown much out. The boy paused outside the substantial kitchen and pointed to the wall. There, framed, was a photograph whose match Nora had recently viewed, the one with the Female Engagement Team squinting into the sun in front of their Humvee.

"That's how I knew who you were," the boy said, pointing. "Auntie Jo talks about you all the time."

"What does she say?"

"Um, that you're a hero. You killed all the hajjis in that town almost all by yourself."

"Uh huh. Are your mom and dad here in town?"

"No, that's why I have to live with Auntie Jo. My dad's in, um, it's a military secret where. And my mom's dead. She was a helicopter pilot in Iraq." Eye-rak.

"I'm sorry."

A shrug. "It was when I was little. I might be a helicopter pilot too, when I get big. Or sometimes I think I'd like to fly AV-8B Harriers. What would you like to drink?"

"I believe your aunt has something special for me."

"Oh, the hangover cure. It's in the refrigerator."

The boy popped the door, retrieved a thick glass flask with smileys printed on it, and poured out a tumbler. He gave it to Nora and she drank it. It was sweetish and tasted of ginger.

"What's in it?" she asked.

"I don't know," said the boy. "Different stuff. It's a family secret."

"So many secrets," said Nora, thinking, I need some aspirin too, or maybe heroin.

The back-screen door sprang open and Jolae entered. “You came,” she said. “And I see you’ve met Cory. And been dosed.” She draped a freckled arm around the boy’s shoulders.

He said, “She wants to know what’s in it. I said it was a secret.”

“It is, but Miss Nora is practically family, so we can spill the beans. It’s Pedialyte, ginger root, brown sugar, eleuthero, and vodka. Drink it slowly until you can’t stand anymore. I myself have been cured and am ready to work on another one. Cory, there’s someone at the door. Go show your manners.”

The boy trotted off. Nora said, “Nice kid. Your sister’s I’m guessing, yeah?”

“Yeah. He looks just like her too, strange to say. Sometimes I have to look away from him or I’ll bawl. I assume he told you about his mother. It’s practically the first thing out of his mouth when he meets a stranger.”

“Yeah. You were close, I guess.”

“Uh huh. Milly was five years older, smart as shit, the pride of the family. Always wanted to fly for the Navy, et cetera et fucking cetera.”

“Shot down in Iraq, he told me,” said Nora.

“No, she was flying Sea Stallions off the *Lincoln* in the Gulf. One night she took off to retrieve casualties and disappeared, went off the radar without a distress call. They searched, obviously, but nada. They suspect engine failure; and you know, those birds have the glide angle of a pipe-wrench. Or the instruments could have been messed up—it was a night flight and . . . oh, crap--I don't care to discuss it any more or ever. Let's talk about *your* sister instead. She's okay I presume?"

Nora said she was and they spoke about Sally's situation in desultory fashion, the way people do when they can't really talk. This conversation was thankfully brief because a small mob of people entered the kitchen laughing and talking and hugging Jolae and being introduced to Nora.

One of these was Jolae's boss, the director of the co-op, who praised Nora's work in the recent emergency and immediately offered her a job as an EMT. She declined, saying she had other plans at present. Shortly thereafter she fell into conversation with a man named Rick, a local PD cop. Rick was a big fellow with brassy candy-floss hair and a face like a cream pie; his wife Marla Jean clearly came from the same batch. It had taken Nora a while to get used to the size of Americans after Afghanistan, and it remained a work in progress. She always felt loomed over, although she was tall herself. Rick and Marla Jean had a kid in the Navy and they talked about the wars for a bit and then conversation switched, as was inevitable, to the recent events.

They had known Vern Harrison all his life, known his folks, his brother was on the same football team as their Dale, everyone was shocked and busted up over how he'd come to do such a thing. Well, some of them were always talking trash about the Mexicans, Marla Jean put in, and Rick said yeah, well everyone goes on about the Mexicans it hardly seems like America around here anymore, when you cross Partridge Street. But nobody expected it to turn violent. Or not like that, although he sometimes had to talk sternly to kids who'd gone hunting for greasers over by Beanertown. They both blamed the war, what it did to the kids who went. The burden of their talk was, we're good people here, don't judge us by this.

Nora was beyond judging anyone else's violence. She asked, "Where did he get the assault rifle?"

Rick answered, "Oh, out at Arno Morgan's gun show. Everybody buys there. He's cheap and he don't ask too many questions. Interesting story: Arno's family owned the drive-in--out on 460 past the Centerville Road? Well, the place closed up years back, because no one goes to drive-ins anymore, what with satellite and all, and the kids don't need no place to go and get inside each other's pants cause they do it right in the basement, or wherever the hell ever they care to, it seems like. Anyway, Arno always had lots of guns and all kinds of junk, so he started up a swap meet on the drive-in parking lot. When was that, Marla Jean? Ten years back?"

Marla thought it was twelve, because she recalled it was just after the flood.

"Right, twelve. Uh huh, he started small and then folks got to hearing he drew a crowd, and other gun sellers started coming, and now I guess it's the biggest gun show in east Kentucky, or near to. You can see the license plates, folks from Illinois, Texas, every damn place. Starts every Friday morning and runs through Sunday evening, with a break for church Sunday morning.

"Anyhow, it looks like Vern went up there a couple of weeks ago and bought himself a Chinese rifle and a couple of banana magazines . . . well, you know the rest. A damn shame, such a nice kid. His family's just all messed up by it." Nora didn't say her thoughts and prayers were with them but made noises appropriate to the situation until it was time to chow down.

The barbecue was terrific. Jack Blatt, a squat, bearded man who referred to himself as a pit-master, had been feeding chunks of hickory into his steel barrel grill since dawn. His pork shoulders had been reduced to tender forkable gobbets, flavored with what he called Lexington dip. Jack had taken a shine to Nora and as she ate he bent her ear about exactly how he managed his creation. Nora let the bbq boredom drift through her ears, and thought about her next move.

As she was thinking thus, her cell rang and it was her sister.

"How's Kentucky?" asked Sally without preamble.

"How do you know I'm in Kentucky?"

"National technical means is all I'm supposed to say. Still visiting comrades I guess?"

Nora said who she was visiting and they had the usual exchange of information, until Nora asked about Barb and the kids and Sally said she hardly knew because she was out in the field working her ass off and barely had a chance to call.

"What field?" asked Nora. "They gave you an anti-terrorism slot?"

"Not exactly, and we're not sure it's even terrorism yet. It's kind of a strange case—we're on it because the Gunsub . . . shit, I shouldn't even be telling you that. Forget I said it. Short version—somebody shot a public official with national implications and took out his bodyguards too, so here we are. But enough about me. How are you getting on?"

Nora let her persona run a mollifying tape while a shaft of freeze ran up from her gut to her chest. *Of course,* her sister was on the case. A dreadful inevitability demanded it, and learning the fact merely reinforced Nora's feeling that she had become a figure in one of history's great extravaganzas, a pawn of the Demiurge, riding on steel tracks to her fate. The United States Naval Academy is not famous for its literature department, but in her junior year there an enthusiastic young professor had introduced her to the *Oresteia.* The tale had penetrated her to the bone, and when she arrived in Afghanistan, she discovered that the world of monstrous deeds and colossal vengeance still lived in that unfortunate, magnificent land.

The young professor had actually made that point: that it was the unenviable task of the American armed forces in the present era to impose modernity (rights, elections, rule-based governances and the rest) on tribal, honor-based societies in which revenge was a primary motivator, and the national sport. The professor did not say that he thought it was impossible, because that would have been defeatist. He did say, and Nora recalled it, that anyone who took that as his mission should bring his lunch, because it would be a long struggle and involve adversaries who didn't mind dying spectacularly to make a point.

Nora was thinking about the House of Atreus, revenge, justice and what the Furies would do to her when they got into gear, and listening to her sister on Barb's discontents, and also planning how she was going to kill Arno Morgan, the gun show operator. She was a good multi-tasker, as infantry officers tend to be, and by the time her sister was done talking, she thought she had the plan of a good operation

15: A Show of Guns

Nora went to the Mitchell County Drive-in Gun Show on Sunday afternoon, carrying her Beretta in a nylon holster on her right hip. She had dressed in jeans and a Maryland Terrapins t-shirt. The high concrete drive-in screen was still there, and on it someone had painted the sacred Second, but left out that uncomfortable first clause about militia. She had skipped church, because the nearest Catholic church was a county distant, and also, even if there had been one right down the street, she would have refrained, not desiring to see the holy water turn black and bubble as she walked by.

They had removed the poles that had once held the movie speakers. Scores of vendors occupied the black asphalt plain, each with a vehicle and a long table. The vendors ranged from locals selling grandpa's old Mossberg, to outlanders with displays of patriotic belt buckles, all the way to guys in mirror sunglasses with vans, who were selling assault rifles by the dozen to dudes who looked like they hailed from south Chicago and northern Mexico rather than eastern Kentucky. Nora knew that gun shows supplied gangsters and *cartelistas*, and that Americans were somehow reluctant to talk about this, preferring to blame those awful people themselves for the murders, because guns don't kill people . . .

There was a table selling t-shirts and bumper stickers with that sentiment printed on it, and others in the same vein. Next to it was a vendor of targets. He had a bunch up on a big board leaning against his van, conventional ones and others bearing the likenesses of Osama bin Laden, Hillary Clinton and a selection of national television journalists. Everyone seemed happy to be out in the sunshine buying and visiting with their neighbors, and pushing around shopping carts full of lethal machinery.

The post office shooting had clearly occasioned no drop-off in attendance. but Nora was not surprised. Gun sales always went up, not down, after a mass shooting. That some particularly awful horror would generate some restrictions on gun sales was the great fear of the gun nuts, and so they rushed out before the blood was dried to stock up, just in case. Of course, the restrictions never came because these people among whom she now walked wouldn't have it. Some deep sense of their own identity and personhood was wrapped up not in character or achievement or affection but in the ownership of firearms.

Nora herself had received her first firearm at age ten, a Marlin "Little Buckaroo" .22 bolt-action single-shot rifle, and her dad had taught her how to shoot it, a process she still recalled fondly. She'd subsequently spent uncounted hours of her childhood with her dad in duck blinds and on tree stands, occasionally with her siblings, but most often alone with him. This was one of the proofs that she was the favored child.

Her family acknowledged that, among the junior Kehoes, she was the best shot and the most engaged in activities requiring gunpowder, but it had never occurred to her, or to her dad, that guns might be fetish objects. Perhaps it was because she had appreciated from an early age the difference, with respect to defending freedom, between a bunch of people with guns and an organized military force, with only the latter being at all up to the task. In Afghanistan, nearly every household owned a Kalashnikov assault rifle, yet surprisingly that nation was not the sort of place any of these nice people would have cared to live. Nora had tired of pointing out this paradox.

She walked up and down the neat aisles, watching America arm itself, until she grew hungry and followed her nose to the food truck zone, which provided a wide selection of fried or frozen substances. She bought a chili dog and a Dr.Pepper, sat at one of the shaded tables provided, and considered her surroundings. The drive-in had been set in a hollow. A wooded hill rose up behind the concrete screen and spread wings out on either side. Nora reckoned that if she had a .50 caliber machine gun emplaced on one of those flanking hills, she could kill half the people at the gun show.

Nora ate and drank and amused herself with the tactical problem. Definitely doable, although not by her. A family walked by, two little boys in camo gear carrying toy (she hoped!) ARs and going *pahpahpah* at each other, and the dad and mom both strapped with pistols, as was their right as Americans, and pushing a stroller with a toddler in it, as yet unarmed as far as could be seen.

She was conscious of a certain tension. Her project might be advanced by a massacre at a gun show or at many gun shows, but she had seen families blown into gobbets by heavy machine. gun fire and knew that she couldn't ever make that happen again, despite its utility. Nora had always been highly competent at everything she tried and the thought that she was *again* shown to be a piss-poor terrorist irked her. She thought this irk was so funny that she laughed out loud around her chili dog.

After she finished eating, she went to view the target. Arno Morgan was not hard to find. He was tall and broad and wore a ten-gallon white Stetson hat and tooled cowboy boots that added a couple of inches to his height. He sported a fat drooping mustache and generous sideburns, and on his face was the look of a man well-content with life.

Nora observed him from a distance as he chatted with vendors and customers. He posed for selfies, armed and unarmed. He had a friendly smile and seemed to wish the world well, except for evil-doers, clearly, because he carried a Western-style tooled leather holster on his right hip that held a large, chromed Colt Army .45 revolver. Nora moved into his field of vision, and when their eyes met, she gave him a wide enthusiastic smile. He had small, nut-brown eyes.

That brought him over. She said she'd heard this was his show, and gushed about how impressed she was by it, and he thanked her and asked her where she was from because she did not talk like a Kentucky girl. She said she was a Maryland girl and was just passing through on the way to a job in Arizona. She was a surveyor, which he thought was amusing; he'd never met a girl surveyor before. He asked her how she liked her Beretta and she said fine and they talked pistols for a while. Nora turned on her brights, which she hadn't done in some time (Trey had been fine with the low beam) and Arno Morgan made the expected response.

He told her an off-color joke, at which she laughed raucously and grabbed his arm. She told the one about the genie and the nine-inch pianist and he hadn't heard that one before and he laughed, and asked her if she'd like to go out for a drink after the show closed up at five. She agreed. He suggested a tavern. She said she'd rather grab a bottle at a package store and go somewhere more comfortable.

His face now showed the nervous but antic look of a married man who had a reasonable shot at some strange pussy. He said that he had an office right here, he'd fixed it up real comfy, had the 50-inch plasma TV and he'd got a whole velour living room set, sofa, chairs, lounger and all--and a wet bar too. She said she'd come by after six and to make sure his bar was really wet. He laughed dirty and asked what her name was, and she said Kathy.

They parted; he insisted on a hug. He smelled of tobacco, Hoppe's gun oil, and a fruity cologne. After, she wandered through the gun show and found that it merged with a swap meet, which is what they call a large group of people gathered to sell each other old tools, car parts, toys, wholesalers overstocks (oatmeal tweed shag carpeting, $1.99 a yard!) and steel racks full of used clothing, or *vintage,* as several hand-lettered signs announced.

Nora bought a pair of skin-tight white jeans, a frilly blouse suitable for a low-end country singer, a denim jacket with outlaw patches, and a pair of vinyl high-heel boots. She also scored a surveyor's transit; it had a cracked lens, but came with a steel box of survey gear—chains, stakes, and other obsolete stuff. She thought the stuff might be useful if she had to make a show out on a street somewhere, and it was only $36. She picked up three traffic cones at a buck each.

She dressed in the van and applied make-up as she had learned to do in the theater course she'd taken in Maryland during what seemed like a prior geologic epoch. The effect was of a dull, somewhat masculine woman attempting sexy. I wouldn't fuck that with *your* dick she said to the rearview mirror before leaving the van. She put her Beretta in a clip-on holster on her right hip., having jacked a round into the chamber and switched off the safety, in contravention of all military regulations.

At ten past six she arrived on her anonymous motorcycle at the gun show parking lot, now deserted except for Arno's black big-cab pick-up truck in its special reserved slot next to the cinderblock office. She knocked on the door. Arno came to the window, looked out, grinned when he saw who it was, and let her in.

Inside, pleasantries with sexy double meanings. Nora played along, and accepted a drink, which was half a tumbler of straight Maker's Mark without ice. Arno had taken a few already, accounting for his rich smell and his hands, which darted out to squeeze her buttocks whenever she came within range. He had music on, Ted Nugent doing a slow one. He still wore his cowboy pistol rig. Nora wondered if he ever took it off, even during sex, and was pleased to recall that she would never find out.

He asked her questions. What did she do, what brought her to Kentucky, didn't she think Kentucky was the most beautiful state in the union, did she have a boyfriend, how come a pretty girl like you wasn't married; and she answered all of them with appropriate degrees of truth.

He seated her on a big brown velour sofa and plopped his bulk next to her. How about a little kiss? No, let's get to know each other a little, she countered, then rose abruptly from the sofa and went over to a wall where photos of Arno with notable white guys covered a considerable patch. Who was this, who was that, she asked.

He told her, with increasing impatience. "Hey, darlin, come sit down here and I'll tell you everything you need to know about ol' Arno."

"Actually, what I want to know about ol' Arno is how he feels about selling the Chinese AK-47 to Vern Harrison so he could kill seventeen people the other day."

"Excuse me?"

"Uh-huh. He was a vet with PTSD, he had a grievance with the P.O. This is a tiny little town, so everyone knew about it. And yet he could waltz in here and walk off with a weapon perfect for a mass killing, no questions asked."

"What the fuck are you talking about, lady? I operate a venue. I don't sell no firearms to nobody. And also, I invited you in her for a friendly drink. I didn't expect a lecture on guns."

"That's okay, Arno. I didn't come here to give you a lecture. Or have a friendly drink."

"Then why the hell did you come?"

"I came to kill you," she said. "I wasn't completely frank when you were interrogating me about my doings. I'm traveling around the country shooting people who sell military weapons to mass shooters. Why don't you stand up now? I'd hate to mess up your nice sofa."

Arno let out a nervous laugh. "Ha. That's pretty good. Come on, sit down here and have another drink."

She stood there with her hands on her hips, with her face saying that this was no joke.

After a long moment, he got the message. "You're serious?"

"Uh-huh. But you still got a chance. Stand up and fill your hand, cowboy!"

He did rise then, a little unsteadily, and after a long, awful period, grabbed for the Peacemaker replica on his hip. He actually cleared the holster before she did, but found that killing someone was harder than it looked in the movies unless you'd done it a lot already. He got one wild shot off before Nora plugged him twice through the pump.

Nora slipped on rubber gloves and did her usual post-murder clean-up/ robbery fake, taking the man's gold Rolex and his wallet and pistol. She pulled open the drawers and cabinet doors and flung stuff around, like a thief delving for loot. In the wide desk drawer she found a framed photograph of a fortyish woman with a stiff blond hairdo and an anxious look, with her three now fatherless children. The boys were clearly little Arnos, but the bored and discontented look on the older girl marked her as one who would not be staying in West Freedom indefinitely.

Clearly, the late Arno had stuck his family in the drawer so as not to detract from what he imagined would be a seduction. Nora set it up again on the desk and looked at it, trying to see if the sight of the soon to be shattered family would raise any feelings in her. None rose; and she reflected that these particular people might be celebrating at the news. Maybe he was a prick who beat them all, although she did not allow herself to hope for that.

She had an interesting thought then and knelt and picked up the dead man's Colt revolver. It was called an Army model, but it was not what she would have considered a military weapon in modern terms. It had occurred to her that this would make it useful in a tutorial she was planning to give.

Leaving the swap meet on her motorcycle, Nora passed two cars on the short gravel road that led to the old drive-in. They would remember a motorcycle leaving at about the right time, later when the cops were canvassing the locality of the crime. She hadn't ridden the bike in Kentucky before and probably no one in the area knew she had a motorcycle, but this sighting meant that she had to get rid of the bike.

Back at the van, she stowed the motorcycle, and brought up Google Earth. A study of Mitchell County revealed a pair of approximately rectangular bodies of water with scarred, brushy surrounds, arguable abandoned quarries. She found a quiet lane in which to wait for the dark, and when it arrived, she drove to the site.

It was surrounded by a chain-link fence secured by a cheap padlock. This yielded in a few minutes to her lock-gun and she drove through and ran the bike off a cliff into what looked like deep water, then tossed her ramp and helmet and her loot from Arno Morgan and everything else she had that suggested motorcycling. She locked the gate behind her and drove back to Bonnie Brae.

She showered and dressed again in her camo pants and her red Marines t-shirt. The clothes she'd worn to the gun show and to her interview with Arno she put in a plastic can liner and disposed of in the dumpster behind the cabins. When she got back to her room, her phone buzzed and it was Jolae.

"What're you up to tonight?"

"I don't know, Jolae. There's ever so much to do in West Freedom. I took in the gun show this afternoon and I'm sort of undecided between the opera and the ballet."

"Funny. You haven't eaten yet? No? Come by, I'll make us something."

"God, she cures the sick, raises the dead, and cooks. And is unmarried. There's a story there."

"Nah, I just got me a shitload of MREs," said Jolae, laughing. "Y'all can have the lemon pepper tuna."

16: Talking with the Dead

That was a lie. Jolae and Cory had gone to some trouble with the dinner. The house had been worked on, for one thing: the casual disarray apparent on Nora's last visit had been whisked away, the floors shone, and furniture polish had been applied, obviously by the kid, who acceded to the kid idea that if a little polish was good, more was better. Every wooden surface glistened damply and the place stank of Old English.

They were having catfish, it seemed. Cory had caught the catfish himself that weekend, and cleaned it and was now helping to cook it, standing on a step-stool and dressed in an apron that brushed his ankles. Nora had brought a couple of six-packs of long-necks and the two women drank beers and stood in the kitchen watching this wonder and pretending to annoy the cook with unreasonable, childish demands, until he made them leave.

They sat in chairs on the veranda and shelled peas into bowls set on their laps and here in the peaceful cricket-chirping, firefly-lit dusk of deep country America, Nora told the story of how their Mir Puza adventure had turned catastrophic.

"We were babies," she concluded. "We were like toddlers packing heavy weapons and air strikes. We had no idea of what we were doing, completely dependent for intel on people who expected to use us as tools to settle local quarrels. And always the pressure—clean this shit up so we can go home, and by the way, we don't want to see any body bags."

"Nothing wrong with that."

"I beg to differ. The point of a military op is not to bring all your guys home safe. The point is to fulfill the mission. If the mission isn't vital enough to put American lives at risk, then don't fucking go!

"I have heard a battalion commander stand up in front of troops and tell them that his highest priority is to bring them all home safe. But that *can't* be his highest priority. Why do they even say shit like that? If that was our highest priority, we should've stayed in Camp Lejeune. What you want them to say is, this mission is so vitally important to the survival of our nation that I will have no fucking hesitation about demanding the lives of each and every one of you to accomplish it. You could have said that in good conscience about Guadalcanal, but not about Vietnam and definitely not about Afghanistan."

"But we filled plenty of body bags anyway."

"Yeah, that's my point. It's one thing to die for Mt. Suribachi. It's something else to die for some miserable town that the Taliban own all night long. You dig a well, you start a school and the next morning the corpse of the schoolteacher is down in the well with his throat cut."

"Let's stop talking about this, okay?" said Jolae. "I wanted to know, you told me, and now I can start forgetting it."

Cory came in and said, "The fish is done. Did you shell the peas?"

The women handed over their bowls. The boy said, "I'll mike them and then we can eat. I already set the table."

When he left, Nora said, "This is robotic control, right. An implant?"

"No, and he's not gay either. He's just trying to make his mom alive again by being her." A small cry escaped her mouth after this and she took an enormous breath through her nostrils. "Fuck. It strikes at odd intervals, doesn't it? The loss. It's like being hit from behind with a cattle prod. I don't have to tell you."

"No," said Nora, although that sudden unexpected shock of pain was familiar. She meant she was used to the pain, welcomed it in fact.

A puzzled look appeared on Jolae's face, but before she could say anything, Cory called, "Let's eat!" from the kitchen and the odd moment passed.

The meal was wonderful. Nora watched herself participate as if watching a television drama, and was at some level amazed that she could do so. Jolae and Cory engaged in a loving, humorous way that included word games and awful puns, and from time to time a question philosopher had been wrangling over ever since Greece. Where does language come from? How can we be happy when sad things are always happening? Why can't we talk with the dead?

Unbidden, there appeared in Nora's mind a vision of her twins, grown to Cory's age, in the kitchen of her house in Herndon, having just this sort of conversations with her. They had been sharp enough at seven, but their minds had not expanded to the goofy wonder that was a bright ten-year-old's, and for a second or two her vision reddened and she wanted to kill, to kill hugely, to commit a horror so vast, so volcanic that everyone would stop dead and say, yeah, let's not be that way anymore, "that way" being the present dispensation that allowed maniacs the means to murder large numbers of children.

She thought of something her grandfather had said once about his experience in 1945 with the occupying forces in Japan. The people who just a few years before had believed themselves to be divinely-inspired invincible warriors of *bushido* seemed to have forgotten that they had ever believed it. They understood that they were misled fools who had ruined their country. Nora thought that something that big had to happen to America, but she couldn't figure out what. All she knew was that, like John Brown, she had to do her part.

"Um, Nora? Is there something wrong?"

Nora sucked Kali back into her box and pasted a fake but convincing smile onto her face.

"Oh, no, just wool-gathering. Sorry, did I miss something?"

"No, we were just talking about communication with the departed and you got this weird expression on your . . ."

"Yeah, said Cory, "you looked like Robert Bruce Banner when he's turning into the Hulk."

"That bad?" said Nora, summoning up a kind of laugh. "I was just thinking about it--speaking with the dead--is all. I mean deep thoughts. And what you saw was only my resting bitch face. I was famous for it in the Marines."

Cory giggled and blushed at the crudity. Jolae asked, "And what was the deep thought, if you'd care to share it?"

"That it's a good thing we can't talk to the dead. The dead are in a different kind of existence and I don't think they remember us the way we remember them. I think if they could talk to us, our feelings would get hurt, because they can't really care about us anymore."

Cory looked stricken. "*I* talk to my Mom," he said.

"Yes, I'm sure you do, and inside you she's still alive. Our parents live inside us forever, for good and bad. There's a part of you that *is* her and always will be. We can all talk to our dead that way, if we want. But the person you knew doesn't exist anymore. She's changed into something we can't understand, not until we die ourselves. Anyway, that's why I don't believe in ghosts or mediums or like that."

"Also, the church's position, if I'm not mistaken," observed Jolae.

"Yes, indeed. Sister Mary Ursula, St. Anthony's in Kailua, Theology 2:The dead are all around us but they keep their counsel."

"But how about vampires?" asked Cory.

"Oh, duh, of course there are vampires," said Nora. "Everybody knows that. And zombies."

General hilarity, each adding a preposterous being to believe in, and then ice cream, with real fudge. In the midst of eating this, the doorbell.

Cory leaped up to get the door and returned with a state trooper. Nora felt the familiar gut punch of terror just for an instant, took a breath, and brought it under control, helped by the trooper being Trey McKenzie. He looked different in his uniform, as everyone does, and his handsome face looked different too, heavy with the burden of his news.

"Would you care for some ice cream, Trooper McKenzie," Cory asked.

"Well . . . um."

"Perhaps Trooper McKenzie would like a drink of whiskey instead, Cory.," said his aunt. "He's just getting off shift and it looks like it was a rough one. Traffic accident?"

"Not this time. Somebody robbed and killed Arno Morgan. I just came from his place."

The two women expressed the usual shock and horror; the boy gaped. Jolae poured a generous splash of Jack, and the trooper tossed it down.

"Yeah, it didn't look like no break-in either. Everybody in town knew Arno sat in that shack on Sunday night counting the take, so we're figuring it's a local boy. Doc Rangel said he couldn't've been dead more'n an hour or so, three at the most. I went around to the nearest neighbors and J.P. Conner said he saw a kid on a motorcycle tearing down Armitage Road from the gun show lot at about the right time. We'll find the motor and we'll find the kid. I don't think we're looking for a criminal mastermind here, by the way."

"Why not?" asked Jolae

"Cause the damn fool forgot to take the loot. He got Arno's fancy watch and his wallet and his dumb six-gun, but didn't bother to go into the back room. There were stacks of bills on the table, maybe twenty grand all told, the whole weekend take."

"Well, it's a crying shame," said Jolae. "Arno Morgan dead! God, maybe I should call Kendra—no, she's a Rogers and they'll be swarming all over her tonight. I'll call over there tomorrow with a covered dish. And those three children! "

She looked at Cory and for a moment Nora though Jolae was going to break down, but she stiffened her jaw, sighed, and said, "Well, if there's anything we can

do . . ."

"You could keep an eye out for that motor. A matte black job, not a Harley. Kid was wearing a mirror faceplate on a black helmet. You give us a call if you see an outfit like that, hear? I know you're a big hero, Jolae, but don't try to take this guy by yourself. He's armed and dangerous."

After Trey left and Cory had gone off to bed, the two women went out on the porch. Jolae pulled a sandwich bag from her pocket and rolled a doobie. She lit up, took a deep toke.

"Just like downrange," said Nora.

"Got that right, Lieutenant. You can take the girl out of the dope but you can't take the dope out of the girl. I guess you'll be moving on now."

"Yeah, I'll be off early tomorrow. It's a long drive."

"Drive to . . .?"

"Pillman, Texas. It's north of Laredo. I'm going to see Chris Gomez."

"Old TP," said Jolae, and laughed. "You think they still call her that in Pillman, Texas?"

Nora said, “They might if she still shits in the boonies at night and forgets the toilet paper and yells at top volume for somebody to fetch her some TP. It started a fire-fight, I heard, the local hajjis figured they could pick off a girl.”

“How wrong they were! Yeah, and the nickname stuck from her old unit when she came to us. ‘Totally pissed’ is what she said it meant, which gave everybody else a ticket to make up new ones. ‘Toxic personality’ was one I remember.”

“Wart started calling her ‘Ting’ for ‘Tingling Pussy’,” Nora said. “Finally, she had to come clean about the toilet paper.”

“So to speak,” said Jolae and this struck her so funny that she had a fit of dope-laughing until both of them recalled that Wart was dead and how she died.

After a silence, Jolae said, “I heard from Gomez, did I tell you?”

She hadn’t. There had been two calls, both late at night. Gomez didn’t know what to do. She was afraid her boyfriend was going to kill her. He’d broken her wrist and smashed up her face and she was terrified of going to the cops. He had a gun he was always waving around.”

“I told her she had to get out of her house and she had to call the cops on him and she said she would, but that’s the last I heard.”

“That sounds bad,” said Nora. “Well, I’ll get out there; maybe there’s something I can do.”

“I bet there is, handy with a gun like you are.”

Nora said nothing to this.

“You know, Arno Morgan was in my mom’s youngest sister’s class in high school. I believe they dated for a bit. And he coached Little League. Cory wasn’t on his team but we saw him all the time at games. I know his wife pretty well. Kendra has some health issues. It’s going to be rough for her now that somebody murdered him.”

Jolae got up from the glider and stretched, yawning. “I have an early wake-up tomorrow, it’s well-baby day in Blair on the other side of the county, so I’ll say good-night.”

Nora stood up too. “Okay, well, thanks for the hospitality,” she said. “I really liked meeting Cory.”

“Yeah, he liked you too. He was fascinated, really, so much so that he peeked in the windows of your van and saw your mirror-face helmet and your matte-black motorcycle. He came and told me about it and wondered whether you’d take him for a ride on it. I said I’d ask, but I had a look earlier and the bike’s gone and the helmet too. I guess I’m not going to ask now, am I?”

Nora nodded her head. “Right. Are you going to rat me out, Doc?”

“Not now. I owe you. You hadn’t done what you did in Helmand, I wouldn’t be here now and God knows what would’ve become of Cory. But this murder is the kind of crime that in Morgan County always seems to be committed by a mentally-defective black man, and if that turns out to be the case here, I *will* have a word with Trey McKenzie. And also, on your way back from Texas, pick another route. I’d rather not see you around these parts again.”

17: Driving Across Texas

Nora left at dawn, taking the small roads to I-80 and then east and south to Bowling Green, where she stopped for breakfast, and then driving hard through the day past Nashville and Memphis and Little Rock. It was a journey of a thousand miles more or less, embarked upon to see a woman she'd spent some months with in an unpleasant and dangerous place, but who was not nearly as close to her as Jolae Ambling, who had just blown her off. Nora was, however, long past pretending that she was in charge of what she was doing. She had to see all her crew and then she could end it in the way she'd planned.

It took her ten hours to get to Shreveport, and there she stopped for the night at the Hilton Garden Inn, because the reviews on her phone said it had good wi-fi. She registered with the name, credit card and ID of Brenda Lisle, the second of Benjy's three-pack of fugazy IDs, and took a shower to wash off the road grime from her actual body. Once she had preferred to soak in a bath, but the thought of a bath summoned up bathing with the twins when they were little girls, one of her favorite parental practices, those slippery little bodies and the giggles and splashing. She didn't take tub baths any more.

Dried, she phoned for a pizza and a Diet Coke. When her meal came, she set up on the bed and ate while she cruised the Internet. As she did every night, she searched for connections between the murders she'd committed. Had anyone associated her targets with the gun rights issue or mass shootings?

And thus she found Elton Morrisey's blog, *SemText*. That was clever, a play on Semtex, the military explosive often at the core of terrorist bombs, and that was what the blog was all about, a sequence of brief speculations about terror attacks and other mass killings along with an encyclopedic sets of links to everything important that had been published on the subject, including the screeds of the mass killers themselves. Morrisey was a reporter for the Baltimore *Sun*. She read some of his postings. He seemed to be a vivid writer with a carefully curated sense of outrage.

Among the posts on the blog was this one:

Is Someone Killing the People Who Put Guns in the Hands of Mass Shooters?

The massacre last week at Keene, NH, that took the lives of three prominent Republican politicians and their police bodyguards has raised fears of a left-wing terror network operating in America. But perhaps the Weathermen have not risen from the grave after all, perhaps there is another explanation. Besides being prominent Republicans, all three victims were deeply involved in 2nd Amendment issues. (You might say that "Republican and "pro-gun rights" is tautological, but bear with me.) The five men who died in this incident were all killed by what police believe to be a 5.56 mm assault rifle.

Lt. Governor Louis X. De Paul was running for governor on a strong gun rights platform. In the last legislative session he led the charge against restrictions on gun-noise suppressors, or "silencers" and armor-piercing ammo.The killer used an assault rifle equipped with a suppressor.

Arthur M. Pauling was not only a major GOP donor but also the largest contributor to a PAC called Liberty Armed, which focused on changing federal regulations so as to make fully-automatic weapons legal for private ownership. He once said, "The Constitution gives us the right to bear arms.The government has no right to bar a weapon just because it fires a lot of bullets in a short time."

Milton P. Evans was on the board of the National Rifle Association.

See the pattern? The punishment fitting the crime? It gets better. A week earlier, William P.Schatz, the CEO of Robbins Firearms, was assassinated in his own home, also by a 5.56 mm assault rifle. His wife, who saw the assailant, described a small man wearing a black mirror face motorcycle helmet. Shortly after the murder, she heard a motorcycle roaring away. Neighbors of Mr. Pauling's Keene estate also told police they heard a motorcycle at around the time of the ambush.

Finally, we have the death of Darren Oglesby, of Harpers Ferry WV. Mr Oglesby didn't have the high profile of the others who were killed, but he had the same politics. He owned a gun shop and was an active NRA member. Even more interesting, Mr Oglesby was the man who sold a 5.56 mm Robbins Reaper assault rifle to Duane Paul Hatch, the so-called Santa killer, who used it to massacre 145 people at a Virginia mall last year.

Coincidence, you say? Then check this out: four days ago, an Iraq vet, Vern Harrison, aged 22, killed 17 people in a Kentucky post office. He had bought his assault rifle at a gun show run by a man named Arno Morgan. The very next day Morgan himself was shot dead in his gun show office. Did witnesses observe a small man wearing a black mirror face motorcycle helmet zooming away on a motorcycle just after the time of the killing? Of course they did.

So maybe it's not some left-wing nut killing Republicans. Maybe it's someone tired of mass killings with assault weapons, someone annoyed that any political process that might restrict these weapons is being blocked by NRA pressure and the cowardice of Republicans, even though a solid majority of Americans wants greater restrictions on assault weapons.

Maybe someone just repealed the Second Amendment all by himself. There's a mass killing every couple of days in the US of A. Our guy is not going to run out of targets anytime soon.

Nora was not particularly dismayed at reading this. Although by no means a data jockey, she had enough awareness of how Internet searches worked to understand how easy it was to connect dots. Just google "murders" AND "gun dealers" AND "second amendment advocates," and her killing spree would be an open book. Her sister would have done such a search already, and she had the more detailed and sophisticated searching facilities of the NCIC at her disposal. Did Sally already know that Nora was—what had she called it?—the Gunsub? It was possible. But if Sally knew, would she tell? Nora wouldn't, had their positions been reversed. Nora thought Sally would want to talk with her sister first. She might even want to bring her in personally, even if it meant breaking Bureau regs, even if it meant blowing up her career.

Of course, some other FBI agent might figure it out, in which case they might be on her trail already. She took up her notebook and studied her Plan, and made a few notes. May 10 was the key date, now less than two weeks away. A day to get to Gomez, two days to hang out with her and fix her issues if she could, if the issues could be fixed by irresponsible violence, four days to drive back to Virginia, and a week to set up the action and finish the plan. It was doable with respect to time, unless there was a BOLO out on her already.

If the FBI was on to her, she would have to lose her cell phone and radically change her physical appearance. Her vehicle was licensed under an alias, and it had been traded for another truck under a different alias and so on back to the beginning. It would be very hard, if not impossible, for the FBI to connect the van she was using with the person of Nora Kehoe.

She looked at her iPhone. She'd kept it because Sally was used to calling her on it and Nora had not wanted to get Sally riled, and because she knew it made her sister feel better if she could track Nora via the only slightly irregular use of Bureau resources. But now, clearly, she had to get rid of it without delay.

She dressed quickly and drove to Elsie's Truck Stop on 173. She bought a roll of duct tape, a pint of Jim Beam, and two burner phones in the store there, then gassed the van and arranged a friendly conversation with a man doing the same to an 18-wheeler in a nearby stall. He was headed to Boise with a load of sporting goods. She bid him good-bye and texted her father that she was fine and was headed to Boise to visit with some Marine buddies.

When the driver was safely in his cab, she dipped down and taped her phone to the undercarriage of the trailer. She had not expected the lift to her spirits that occurred when the semi pulled away, hauling the digital impedimenta of her former life.

She returned to the hotel, drank half a pint of whiskey, fell asleep and awakened just before dawn to the feeling a tiny lip pressed against both ears and small voices saying, "Wake up, Mommy!" and "We're starving to deaf."

With a cry she sat straight up, sweat popping and forming a cold slick over her entire body. She had feared this worse than the flashbacks from Mir Puza, and so far had been spared. Apparently, no longer. She screamed at the ceiling, she cursed God, but did not die. Instead, shaking and mumbling orders to herself under her breath, she packed up and returned to the road.

It took her eight hours to drive across Texas to Pillman, part of that journey being a stop in Dallas to pick up some items that you could only find in a big city. The drive south of San Antonio was dead flat through a landscape of startling monotony: some kind of dark green vegetation amid a semi-desert studded with gray rocks.

There was little traffic on 16 South. Rarely a semi would shake the van with its passing wind, but besides that and the existence of a road the land appeared unpopulated. Nora had once arranged a week of specialized training in Iraq, a scam so she could visit her boyfriend, and the land was like this in places. The last time she had touched his flesh.

The boredom was dangerous. Nora had started to see things out of the corner of her eye that could not be there. Once a small, high voice said, "Mommy, I'm thirsty," and Nora had answered automatically. For long periods she was somewhere else than behind the wheel. The best thing about the journey was that there were probably no IEDs buried at the side of the road.

Pillman proved to be a wide place on the highway with two stop lights at either end of town, a Shell station, a feed and general store, and a Hardees. There was no apparent reason why there should be a town here and not a hundred miles away in either direction. Perhaps it was for the high school, with its outsized football stadium. Why anyone who had escaped this place, like Gomez, would have chosen to return was beyond her, but perhaps the heart commands the feet. Perhaps family and friends had drawn her back to her home town. Or a lover, although from what Jolae had said, that was not working out too well.

The address she had led her to a new double-wide trailer in a sandy yard with a faded swing set and an above-ground pool standing empty, half draped in a blue tarp. A poured concrete driveway on the property led to a parking slab protected by a green fiberglass awning. Through the windows of the mobile home came a child's cry and a woman's scolding voice. Nora walked down a neatly graveled path, stepped around a tiny tricycle, and knocked.

The door opened and a woman stood there with a baby on her hip and a tearful three-year-old clinging to her leg. She was brown and heavy, with the enlarged breasts of a nursing mother. Dressed in cut-offs and a tank top that said "I Am A Miracle" on it, she wore large movie star sunglasses. It took a moment for Nora to realize that she was looking at Chris Gomez.

"He's not here if you're looking for Eddie," said Gomez to Nora; and to the child, "Oh, Cricket, *please*, shut up!"

"Gomez, it's me, Nora Kehoe. I can come back if it's a bad time."

Gomez opened her mouth and stared. The child at her knee stopped grizzling and stared too. Even the baby turned its tan moon face around and directed its dark, half-empty eyes at Nora.

"Holy shit!" seemed to be the official greeting at these reunions and Gomex dutifully said it.

And also, "What're you doing here?"

Nora opened her mouth to explain, but Gomez said, "God, what'm I thinking? Come in out of the sun!" and ushered her into the structure.

The air inside was chilled and smelled of baby powder, oranges and cooked soup.

After a quick negotiation with her little girl, a juice box was produced and the child directed to a beanbag in front of the TV. Nora stood in the living room and admired the interior. The place was neat, ridiculously neat considering that the mom had a baby and a toddler. Marine training? Maybe, but Nora had done lots of Marine training herself and her house had not looked like this when the twins were little. The only defects she could see were cracks and dimples at several points on the vinyl material of the walls, as if something violent had struck the surface.

Gomez returned and, smiling, asked if she could get Nora an iced tea or a beer. She checked her watch, and as she did so a a tiny furrow appeared over her sunglasses.

Nora went for the beer. Gomez poured an iced tea for herself and ushered Nora to a seat on the living room couch, which was covered with some velveteen-like synthetic, colored maroon. It looked virtually unused. Gomez herself sat across a wooden coffee table made from a weathered door thickly encased in clear acrylic. It too was spotless. Gomez adjusted her baby on her lap and said, "God, Loo, it must be what? Ten, twelve years?"

"About that. I see you didn't stay in the Crotch."

"No, my folks needed me here, so I handed in my papers. And then they passed and I met Eddie and stayed. But, Jesus, how come you're in Pillman?"

She checked her watch again. Again, the same little frown.

Nora said, "I was touring the historic beauty spots of America, and Pillman, Texas, was on the list."

"Well, yeah, we have the slaughterhouse. You can go on a tour. The evisceration room is a crowd favorite. Or there's the Hardees. Someone who knew Johnny Cash got a burger there once, or that's the legend."

Nora made herself laugh at this and recalled that Gomez was famous in the Marines for the way she could make up preposterous stories to amuse new arrivals. She had the impression that this talent had not been much used recently; Gomez herself seemed surprised and produced something like her old grin. Then came the expected narrative about her children: Yolanda, or Cricket, was three, bright as a button, could almost read. The baby was Eddie

Junior, a darling, slept the night through most nights, boys are supposed to be hard, but not this one. When the subject was exhausted, Gomez asked, "But really, why are you here?"

"Actually," said Nora, "I came to see you. I'm visiting the old team. I saw Zulu and Jolae and you're the last surviving."

"Wow. All across the country! I guess you heard about Wart."

Nora had. Staci "Wart" Gunther, after eleven years and four days back home in Castle Rock, Colorado, had picked up her two kids at their elementary school, and with her toddler carefully strapped into his car seat, had accelerated her Subaru hatchback to one hundred three miles per hour directly into a bridge abutment on state road 67.

"Were you in contact?" Nora asked.

"A little. We were pretty tight downrange, because we both started in the motor pool. She was the one had the idea of going for the Lionesses. She said fuck this rip-hand shit. We gonna lie on couches and eat roti and talk to the hajji ladies all day long. So after, we kept in touch for a while, Instagram and email, and like that, a phone call once in a while, and then . . . then it sort of petered out. I heard about it on the news. I heard about your, um, thing too."

Nora let the moment drag out. There was nothing to say about her thing, and Gomez was canny enough and enough of a Marine not to make stupid sympathetic noises. The baby started to fret, bringing them out of the shadow of the past and into real life. Gomez lifted her shirt, unsnapped, and gave the baby a broad, brown nipple.

As she watched this Nora worked to bring her breathing under control, crazily afraid that what she had become would do something bad to the milk. She thought that each of the FET women had paid for Mir Puza in the coin of their own suffering. Zulu was the happiest because she'd lost her arm and that seemed more than sufficient to pay the tab. Nora herself—well, that fee was too obvious. Jolae seemed happy enough, but she hadn't fired a shot at Mir Puza. Wart had done the most vivid payback imaginable.

Nora had a pretty good idea of what Chris Gomez's was because she was still wearing the sunglasses, indoors. If asked where the shiner that they must conceal came from, she would have made up a story about falling, how clumsy she was. Nora had also observed a yellow-purple bruise running along Gomez's side when she raised her tank-top to nurse.

"So tell me about Eddie," said Nora. "How did you hook up with him?"

It took some wrangling, but the tale emerged. Eddie had been a little behind her in the local high school. He'd been sympathetic when her parents died. He was a good provider. He loved the kids, always bringing presents. He had some rough years when he was young, on meth for a bit, but he kicked that and found Jesus and he's been clean since. He worked security at the slaughterhouse.

"I didn't know slaughterhouses needed security," said Nora.

"Hell, yeah, they do! There's gangs that go from state to state with reefer trucks. They'll bust into a locker in a slaughterhouse and take the loins—you know, for the steaks."

"And do you love your steak-protecting man?"

"Well, yeah, of course. This is the most expensive double-wide in town. It's got A/C and a built-in microwave, and *three* bathrooms."

"It's really nice," Nora agreed. "You're paying it off, I guess. It must be rough with only one of you working."

"Uh-*uh*. Eddie bought it for *cash*. Eddie don't like having credit debt. He says it's a rip-off and besides, it's against the Bible."

"I see. Chris, you keep looking at your watch. Do you have someplace you have to be?"

"Oh, no, it's just that when Eddie gets home, he likes dinner ready and the kids squared away and the house neat."

"Neat? This place looks like a Parris Island boot camp barracks on Saturday morning."

Gomez shrugged and said, "Well, you know you can take the girl out of the Marines…I like a clean deck too."

"Eddie was in the Corps?"

"No, because of that drug stuff when he was younger." The baby had fallen asleep. Gomez put away her breast and stood up. "Well, um, Lieutenant, it was nice visiting with you, and all, but I got to get dinner started and the kids cleaned up and ready and all."

"I'm not going to meet Eddie?"

"Um, well, he's nervous around strangers. I'm sorry, Loo . . ."

"I'm not a lieutenant any more. You can call me Nora. Or Ice Queen; and I could call you TP."

This produced another grin; it quickly faded. "Yeah, IQ and TP. A long time ago."

"I'll get out of your way, then," said Nora. She engaged Gomez in a brief, uncomfortable embrace. The baby smelled of milk and baby powder, triggering a memory and a pain so acute it darkened her sight. She got out fast and returned to her van.

Down the road a quarter mile she had a thought and almost without willing it, pulled a u-ey and parked on the white dust shoulder of the road, some sixty yards from Gomez's mobile home. She took out her tripod and her broken theodolite, set it up on the road, and after a few minutes in the van emerged with hard hat and clipboard and day-glow vest. She set out some traffic cones and pretended to measure angles and write things down. Every so often she would crouch and make cryptic symbols with chalk on the asphalt.

Forty minutes, and a big pick-up came barreling down the road, a top-of-the-line Ford 350 super-duty Lariat 4x4, red in color. It braked hard, at just the right point and swept into Gomez's double-wide's parking slab. From it dropped a small, broad-shouldered, narrow-waisted man in a gray security guard's uniform, wearing a thick tactical belt that carried a pistol and other cop-like gear. He carefully replaced his uniform cap for the short walk to his front door. On the path he stopped at the tiny tricycle, uttered a curse, and kicked it viciously aside. Nora folded up her equipment and returned it to the van.

A short time later she emerged from the van wearing baggy shorts, a Redskins jersey, and Belleville 500 steel-toe hot-weather RAT boots. In the small of her back, she wore her Beretta in its clip-on holster. She trotted down the road, went to the door she had recently left, tried it, and found it locked. Through the window and the thin wall came the sound of a man yelling and a woman, a child, and a baby screaming. Also, to be heard: regular sharp slapping sounds.

Nora pulled a lock-gun from her pocket and was through the door in ten seconds. She found Gomez crouched on the kitchen floor, with her face pressed into the angle between the refrigerator and a cabinet, her hands crossed protectively over her head. Eddie was standing over her and lashing her back with the wide leather belt from his uniform pants. With every smack of the belt he would hurl an epithet. Stupid bitch. You will learn. To do as I tell you. I told you. Not to leave that damn trike on the path.

Little Cricket was weeping nearby. At intervals she would shriek Mommy! Or Daddy!

Nora said in her command voice, "Stop doing that!"

Eddie spun around. "Who the fuck are you?" he yelled.

"I'm Lieutenant Kehoe. From Afghanistan."

Eddie stared at her, gaping, as if these appellations held no meaning for him. In a moment, though, he returned to his sense of grievance, and began to curse at Nora. He ordered her out of his house. Nora declined to leave: he sprang.

Rushing forward with his left hand extended and his right cocked in a typical wife-beater move, he intended to grab her shirt or arm and hit her in the face. Instead he found himself thrown over her hip and onto the floor, striking his skull painfully on a counter edge on the way down. She was on him in a second, forcing his elbow over one of her knees with her left hand and squashing his throat with her right.

She held her face a few inches from his and said, "I know what you're thinking now. You're think that I'll play along with whatever this bitch wants now, and when she leaves, I'll go back to my wife-beating ways. But you need to change, Eddie. Get a hobby. Get a second job, whatever, but if you try this shit again, I'll find out about it and then I'll come back and kill you. That's not a figure of speech. I mean I will kill you dead. Do you understand me?"

She rendered the famous Ice Queen Glare of Doom to back up this threat, and it seemed to work. The red went from Eddie's face, replaced by something that resembled a sweating cheese. She leaned on his captured arm a little and he yelped and said, "Yeah, yeah, I understand."

She rose and released him. Chris Gomez had vanished into the bedroom with her little girl. Nora backed out of the dwelling, returned to her van, and drove off. She took the first right turn she encountered and circled around until she was behind Gomez and Eddie's place, then worked her way past scrub, piles of junk and other trailers, past the faded swing set and the sad empty pool, and came to the back door of the mobile home. She could hear the baby and little Cricket crying their lungs out.

Eddie had not wasted any time; apparently, he had not understood at all. She came in through the unlocked back door and found that Eddie had duct-taped Gomez's mouth and wrists and was continuing his interrupted beating. Nora stepped silently behind him and kicked him up between his legs with her RAT boot as hard as she could.

As Eddie lay curled on the kitchen floor, groaning and cursing. Nora released Gomez and parked her in the bedroom. She told

Gomez that she and Eddie were going for a little ride. The woman seemed numb and made no objection.

Eddie sat in the driver's seat of his new truck. Nora was behind him, pressing the muzzle of her pistol to the base of his skull.

"Where's the meth lab, Eddie?" she asked.

"What meth lab?"

She hit him in the ear with the pistol.

"You didn't buy a double-wide for cash on a square badge's paycheck. And you probably paid cash for this truck too. So either you're stealing steaks or running meth. Which is it?"

"You're off base, lady, I wouldn't fuck with . . . "

She hit him again. "Where is it?"

He complained. She hit him again. She'd seen this a hundred times in Afghanistan. The demand; the blow. The demand; the blow. Repeat until you got something, usually wrong. It was irresistible for a certain type of person, and she had resisted it pretty well until now.

After a few iterations, he said, crying, that he didn't sell meth anymore, he was in the church now, and he would never steal. It was against the law and the Bible. But he did buy guns with another guy, dozens of guns from gun shows and then drive over the border at Laredo and sell them at huge mark-ups to the many chuteros who infested Nuevo Laredo. It was just business, it was legal.

Oh, thank you, said Nora in gratitude to the saints or demons who were making her do her Plan. She said, “Where do you keep the guns?”

“My man has a trailer.”

“Drive there!”

“What’re you gonna do?”

She hit him again. He drove.

18: Where She Was When

Like every other American of her generation, Sally Kehoe knew where she had been when she learned about 9-11. She was sitting in the bus station at Parris Island, waiting for a bus home to Virginia, two mornings after becoming a Marine. The moment she saw the towers burning on the TV bolted to the ceiling there, she knew that she would never forget the moment, and understood instantly that the world had veered off its old track and onto a new one, and that thereafter we would all live different lives. Then she finally understood what her parents and grandparents had meant about the JFK assassination and Pearl Harbor.

Of course, there were the personal moments like that, too. For Sally, coming out as gay had been one of those, or now this one, the moment when it could no longer credibly be denied that the GUNSUB she hunted was her sister Nora.

It was actually surprising that it had taken her so long, but she had wanted to be a team player and her boss, Brendan Meagher, had lodged in his head the idea that this was a leftist attack, one that had to be stopped before class war broke out and blood ran in the streets. Nearly all of the Boston task force, therefore, had spent months leaning on every source the Bureau had among the violent fringes of the political left.

Sally was the exception, because as sure as Meagher was of his Weathermen redux, he would look like a fool if it turned out that one of the victims had a humongous life insurance policy with a beneficiary who owned a 5.56 weapon, or that all three had, say, cheated a guy with— same deal.

But it was clearly a mere clerical task, backgrounding the five victims, not a patch on real field work confronting Anarchy itself, and so was perfectly suitable for the dyke that fucking Quantico had sent them. Even better, Sally had volunteered to keep the official files of the investigation up to date. No one objected, of course, and so she had the best handle on the investigation, better even than Meagher's because she was more intelligent than him and was not blinded by preconception.

Sally did not mind doing this necessary routine. She loved snooping. It was a positive pleasure to her, finding out stuff her subject would rather no one knew. In the present case, no secret sin or connection bore on the case. One of the pols and one of the cops had mistresses, neither of whom could have done the job, ditto the respective wives.

One of the dead cops had gambling issues and had connections with some hard guys, but no one seemed to want him dead enough to arrange that particular massacre. Sally got a little flutter when she found that Pauling's wife, the discoverer of the massacre, owned a 5.56 assault rifle, a Ruger AR-556, and was an excellent shot, but of course she was at lunch at the time of, with rich white people for her alibi and so she was in the clear.

Meanwhile, she knew the main investigation was going nowhere. The armed left, it seemed, was largely a fantasy of right-wing bloggers and Marxist professors. In any case Sally believed that the shootings had not been accomplished by armed leftists, nor by any ordinary person with a grudge or a yen. Sally had spent hours at the murder scene and studying the forensics of the case. She appreciated how well the shooter had picked his blind. It was the only place along the wall where someone could command the entire gate apron without being observed. And he had killed five men with eight shots in all. It spoke to military training at a high level, SEAL, Delta, Special Forces, Recon Marine.

She kicked herself for not seeing the gun-rights connection sooner, but in retrospect it would have been hard to tease out. It was the litmus testing: when you said "Republican" you already *had* said guns, gays, God and abortion; it was practically tautological. She brought this perception to her boss, who was unimpressed. Some leftist bastard is assassinating Republicans—what does it matter what his particular issues are?

But the gun connection was too obvious to overlook, so Sally ran a simple disaggregating search. Had other people who strongly backed gun rights been attacked? She immediately grasped the connection between the murders in Harpers Ferry and Bridgeport and the Robbins AR used in the Mall of Death.

That the shooter might be her sister remained an observation below the conscious surface of her mind; still, it guided her further research until it became undeniable. Sally had been tracking Nora's movements for a month. Nora had been in Harpers Ferry, *and* Bridgeport, *and* within a few miles of Keene at the time of the killings. She'd been in eastern Kentucky when a man who'd sold a gun to a mass shooter had been shot dead in his gun show office.

Sally did another slightly illegal query and found that Nora's cell phone had traveled through Texas for some days and then headed north to the Boise area. She called Nora without result, repeatedly and with mounting fear and frustration.

Any murders of gun people in the region of Texas through which she had passed? Well, of course there was. A couple of guys who'd apparently been straw-buying weapons for Mexican gangsters had been shot dead and left in a trailer full of guns, which had subsequently been set on fire. The local cops were calling it a gang-related crime. Sally thought that was a fat chance, not with Nora Kehoe in town.

Sally erased the searches and shut down her computer. The book said she had to report these findings and immediately ask for a recusal and a transfer. She couldn't investigate a case involving her own sister, obviously. She began the short walk to Meagher's office.

But she continued walking past that office and to the elevator and down to the motor pool office, where she checked out a sedan and drove off. She had no particular destination in mind, just a desire to get out of the cubicles and into nature. She wanted trees and water around her and air that did not smell of men in enclosed spaces.

Driving slowly through Chelsea on surface streets, avoiding the river-crossing bridges, she found herself in a housing development with nautically-themed streets, and beyond that a small marina and a grassy park overlooking the Charles.

She sat on a bench by the edge of the water and looked across an inlet at a bleak industrial vista, where they were making something that required the movement of white chalky stuff from railroad cars into giant hoppers. She watched this dismal operation for a while, considering her dilemma.

Sally had bought the whole duty, honor, country mix as a small child; indeed, it was nearly impossible to be a normal Kehoe without so doing. (Even the one abnormal Kehoe professed it.) Beneath that patriotic commitment, however, was another: family first, and we don't snitch. This was seared into the Kehoe DNA long before any ancestor crossed from Ireland to America. Sally would have had no hesitation in taking a bullet for her sister, but this one was nowhere near as clear a decision.

Sally had mentors in the Bureau and she thought of calling one of them, but she already knew what the women would say: report and recuse. That was the book answer, but she already knew that. She needed a finer moral discrimination, and for that there was only one source. She took out her cell phone, checked the time, waited seven minutes, and at exactly fifty minutes past the hour, called her wife.

During the day, Barb was available only to her clients, except for the short break between their couch times.

"Hi, listen, I'm in trouble and I need your advice," Sally said when Barb answered.

She laughed. "You, too? Should I cancel the next?"

"No, I don't think it'll take that long," Sally answered, and then told her tale.

A brief silence on the line after she was done; then, "Oh, babe, what hell! What a dilemma! I assume you haven't said anything about this to your bosses."

"No, I just figured it out a little while ago. I've been wandering around in a park feeling like the bottom just dropped out of my life."

"Could she go for an NGI?"

"She killed two police officers, Barb. No U.S. Attorney is going to let her off with an insanity plea. The crimes were planned and executed without flaw. Of course, she *is* crazy."

"Well, she's not normal. I wouldn't expect her to be well-balanced after what she's been through. I noticed something off about her when she was here, but I assumed it was the back-blast of the murders. On top of the Afghanistan thing. Poor woman! And poor you!"

"What should I do, Barb? I mean fuck the Bureau—how in hell am I going to save her? I've always gone by the book, but the book tells me to get my sister killed."

"Not literally, surely. As a matter of fact, what *does* the book say in cases like this? In the course of an investigation, an agent comes to suspect that he has a personal relationship with the unsub. What's the drill?"

"For real? Report and recuse. But it's not something that comes up every day."

"Also, it's just a theory. You don't have proof positive that Nora's doing these murders. It's circumstantial, isn't it?"

"Barb, she's the one. The dates and locations check out perfectly. The GUNSUB is a tactically trained shooter; that's Nora. She has motive, means, and opportunity. Again, Nora. She killed the two men most directly responsible for putting the weapon that killed her family into the hands of the killer. Believe me, when we look at these killings with Nora in mind, we'll find plenty of confirming evidence."

"Maybe, but you haven't got it yet. Look, suppose you go to the SAIC with your theory and present your circumstantial case:

it's not political in the left-right sense, but a vendetta against the people who enable mass shooters, and so forth. There's no need to mention Nora directly, but you can certainly suggest that the FBI look into survivors of mass shootings. Now, what would you expect the reaction to be when a lady agent from Quantico suggests to the big tough FBI chieftain that his theory of the case is bullshit?"

"He'll laugh in my face."

"Of course he will. Then you let your lip quiver and say that you're related to a mass shooting survivor and you really, really think this could be the connection, so maybe you should recuse yourself from this investigation. Then you resign from the investigation and come home."

"How do you make your lip quiver?"

"No, really, Sal. This could work. You'd be clear with the Bureau. You did your job, you found the trail to the killer, but your boss rejected it. You properly recused yourself. And you will have ended the killings without betraying your sister."

"She could be killing someone as we speak."

"True, but that's not on you. That's on what's-his-face. The SAIC."

"I don't know, Barb. He'll talk about it when I'm gone, around the office, in a you know what that crazy bitch said kind of way, but some of the guys there will check it out. It'll take them twenty minutes to find out I'm right. Jesus, a fucking *blogger* already put it together.

"And then they'll run the vics against the lists of recent mass shooting survivors and relatives, and run those against the necessary skill sets and come up with a short list of matches. Of those, how many do you think will have been at the right place at the right time for all five shootings?"

"So what? Your sole responsibility was to report your suspicions to your boss and recuse yourself, which you did. If the goyim figure it all out, let them!"

"So what? For Christ's sake, Barbara! I'm going to lose my *sister*. She'll either be dead or in prison for the rest of her life.

That's not 'so what' to me."

"I meant in relationship to your career. Nora . . . ? Nora's been gone for a while. She never really came back from Afghanistan. You *know* that, dear. We've talked about it, and I know you think you can fix everything, but you can't fix this."

"I can do something."

"Yes, you can try to find her on your own, which won't do any good. If you find her, you won't be able to stop her short of shooting her, and if you find her without informing your superiors of the clues that help you find her, you'll be finished with the Bureau."

"I don't care," said Sally. She said it so vehemently that a passing labradoodle walker gave her a curious glance.

"You'll care when you're the one who has to help Violet with her math homework," said Barb. "And you can do all the cooking, too, since I'll have to start putting in evening hours to make up for the lost income."

"You're being a rat about this, Barb. It's not like you."

"And you're being a man. Unfortunately, it's *very* like you. It's your upbringing, love. Admirable in many ways, it nevertheless taught you that when there's a complex problem, what's called for in every case is violent and precipitate action. Send in the Marines!"

"That's not fair!"

"No it's not, and neither is what happened to your sister, but we're all going to have to live with it, and try to prevent that catastrophe from screwing up more lives than it already has."

"And I resent it when you do therapy on me. I'm not a client."

"No, my client is in the waiting room right now and so I have to get off. Dearest, just recall that our family motto is, be decent but not stupid. I know you'll do the right thing. Bye, now."

Sally sat on her bench and fumed for some minutes. Her need to do something and her understanding that Barb was right fought a short, sharp pingpong game in her head for some minutes. After that, she thought she saw a way to save both her honor and her job. Her sister was probably beyond saving, but she would try that too.

Eddie the Wife-Beater drove his truck to a ten-acre spread with a new kit-built cabin on it, set on a trickle of a creek under a small grove of dusty cottonwoods. It had a shiny log exterior and a green-painted galvanized roof. A small herd of stupid-looking black cattle milled in a small corral. Nora marched Eddie up to the door at gunpoint. She told him to knock, and he did.

A voice from inside inquired as to the knocker and Eddie said it was him. A fat white man in his forties opened the door. He was wearing a greasy t-shirt and jeans cut-offs, in the waist of which was stuck a chromed .40 caliber semi-automatic pistol.

He looked at Eddie and the woman and said, "Hey, my man, what's up?"

Nora stepped away from Eddie, drew her Beretta and shot the man twice, once in the chest and once through the head as he collapsed, the classic double tap.

Eddie took off running, but he didn't get far. Nora assumed the old-fashioned, elbow-on-hip shooting stance she had learned from her dad, and drilled him twice through the center of mass. She waited; only silence. Then she dragged Eddie into the cabin and had a look around.

One of the cabin's two bedrooms had its walls covered with steel racks, and these held guns and ammunition, hundreds of weapons, most in the original manufacturer's packaging. She helped herself to a new Beretta, wiping and dropping the old one near the bodies. She also took a new Robbins Reaper, a brace of 30-round magazines, several boxes of 5.56 full-metal-jacket, and a steel file box full of high denomination U.S. currency and gold coins. A second thought led to her taking another of the nine mm. pistols.

In the kitchen, she pulled the stove away from the wall and yanked the plug that powered the burner igniters. She turned all the burners and the oven on. She found a candle in a drawer and stuck it on the floor in the far bedroom. Outside the cabin in a storage closet, she found a gallon of mineral spirits. She poured it all out on the kitchen floor, then went back to the bedroom and lit the candle. The propane gas would build up in the house until it reached an explosive mixture. Then boom: her first IED.

She drove Eddie's truck back to Chris Gomez's mobile home and carried in the steel money box. When she told Gomez a version of what had happened at the cabin, hysterics ensued, from fear, Nora thought, rather than from a deep sense of mourning. Gomez was afraid she would be arrested in connection with the deaths, and, because of Eddie's little ways, she had less than fifteen dollars on hand. What was she supposed to do now?

Nora said, "First of all, it's going to look like a gang thing, Chris. They were criminals selling guns to the most violent people in the world. Was Eddie the kind of guy who would screw a *cartelista*? I think we know the answer to that one. The cops won't give you any trouble—you were watching two kids right here at the time of, right? In that box is Eddie's money, it's about thirty grand and I've added twenty grand to that, cash. There's a pistol in the box, if you have any trouble.

"The cops will come and tell you about Eddie. Don't act more busted up than you are, because they can tell phony. After the funeral, wait a couple of weeks and move to Dallas or any big city. You can sell the truck, buy a little hatchback. Find an agent to sell this mobile. You'll have plenty of money. Get a place to live, go back to school, get some kind of certificate. You can afford decent child care now. Find something you like to do. Raise your kids. Forget all this ever happened. Have a life."

Gomez blew her nose into a paper towel and dried her eyes. "Why are you doing this? Cause I was in your unit?"

"No, I owe you, because what happened downrange was on me. I was the officer in charge. But you don't have to pay dues anymore. You don't have to take beatings from a piece of shit anymore."

It was apparent from her expression that Gomez had never made the connection between her recent situation and anything that had happened to her in Afghanistan. Now she did. "But . . . you don't owe me anything. It wasn't your fault what happened. You didn't know about the ambush or the women and kids . . ."

"No, but I *should* have known," said Nora. "It was my *job* to know, and I fucked it up bad. But that's on me. You're off the hook, understand?"

She kept at it until she was sure that Gomez did understand, and then helped her pack.

Nora wanted to return to Northern Virginia as soon as possible, with her guns and the other material necessary for the next phase of her Plan, so she found a truck stop where she smiled, and charmed, allowed a grope, and thus was able to purchase a dozen whites—five milligram dextroamphetamine tablets. Leaving Pillman at seven-thirty p.m., she traveled I-30 and 40, picking up 81 in Knoxville and on into Virginia. She drove for thirty-two hours straight, stopping only for food and the toilet. Nora was not much of a druggie, but she liked the amphetamine high and she liked not having to sleep. If she had her choice, she would never have slept again.

Of course she had hallucinations. Pulling out of a gas station near Memphis she saw two little girls dressed in red coats on the side of the road. She pulled over, rolled down her windows and called for them to come in. She waited a while and then got out and saw they were a pair of barrels.

The more intimate manifestations were much worse, little whispers in her ear, Mommy, we're starving, Mommy, and the feather touch of tiny fingers on the edges of her clothing. Still, she drove on. She thought May 10th would see the end of all of that, and she figured she could hang on until. She was a Marine. Marines were not scared of ghosts. She laughed aloud when this thought occurred to her and she found it alarmingly hard to stop laughing.

She arrived in Fairfax before dawn on the second day and sat in her van staring out the window in the parking lot of the

Courtyard by Marriott. Sometimes she ignored the tugs and whispers and the scent of their hair, and sometimes she spoke sternly to them and told them not to bother Mommy, Mommy was busy. When the desk clerk showed at six, she checked in as Brenda Lisle. In the room, she closed the curtains, drank deeply from a bottle of vodka she had purchased somewhere along the way and dove face-first onto the bed.

She awakened fourteen hours later to find that Don was pushing her off the bed as he so often did. She poked him gently, she thought, but her hand went right through him and found the squirmy worms inside.

With a shout she was on the floor, gasping. Maybe this was it, she thought, maybe John Brown had nightmares about the men he had hacked to death in Kansas, maybe St. Joan had a different sort of vision than the ones about the gentle saints.

She checked her burner phone. In was eight-twenty on April 30th. She had just ten days to finish. She thought she'd be able to do it, if Sally kept out of the way.

19: Manifesto

Nora pushed the SEND button and off this went off via Protonmail to emorrisey @semtext.com:

I enjoyed your post about the killings of people who put military weapons in the hands of mass shooters. I am the person doing the killings. Would you like to chat?

Four minutes later the response came:

Yes! Where and when can we meet?

She sent: No meeting. And no calling. If you agree, I'll give you a number for texting me and that's how we'll do it.

She took a break while she waited for his response, pouring a refill of black drip and adding a slab of cake. She was in a Fairfax coffee bar, using its wifi, having just come from getting a haircut from an establishment located in a strip mall concrete box on Route 40. It was a bad haircut and meant to be so. Its chief virtue was that it completely covered her ears, this to confuse facial recognition software; ears are the one feature almost impossible to disguise. She'd had her pale brown hair dyed black too and had applied to her skin a substance that darkened it several shades. Another chemical had supplied a fake port-wine birthmark that started under her left eye and flowed over her cheek to her ear.

A make-up artist in the course she'd taken months ago had said that if you wanted to disguise yourself completely, nothing beat a big, ugly deformity on the face. People would either not look at you at all or would be able to describe only the deformity and nothing else about your appearance. She should have had black contact lenses too, but the thought of using them freaked her out. The birthmark would have to do.

It really worked. Nora felt the eyes slide away from her face as she encountered the world. The young woman who had just served her the coffee would surely be unable to pick Nora out of a lineup or recognize her as the thirtyish matron whose all-American good looks would soon be visible on every TV screen, computer and newspaper in the land.

She went back to her seat and her mail dinged its bell.

Okay. My editor's on board What's next?

I'm attaching a document that I want you to print. When you've printed it, you can ask me questions about it or why I'm doing what I'm doing.

She pressed, the message with its attachment flew off into the web, and she closed the connection. There would not be such an interview, she thought.

She dialed another number and got her late husband's business partner, Andy Bannerman, at the offices of Dominion Building Services. Andy seemed more glad to hear from her than was natural, she having taken little interest in how Don made a living. Some things were inherently dull, especially to one who had lived a life of mortal excitement, but now she put real interest in her voice as she encouraged Andy to bring her up to date on the janitorial business. Getting workers who were okay with the immigration authorities seemed to be the biggest challenge, that and turn-over, which was running seventy per cent a quarter.

"Then I can help you out," she said. "You remember I asked if I found one of my people who needed a job . . . ?"

"Oh, sure, not a problem. Just have her send me her paperwork and I'll take care of it. This is an ex-Marine?"

"Yeah, Maria Foner's her name. A rough case. She had a bad time in her deployment and she, well, she has a blemished face, so it's hard . . ."

"I'll get her set up here right away, don't you worry."

"Actually, Andy, she wants a job with Fairfax Building Services. She lives in Fairfax and doesn't have a car . . ."

"Not a problem. I know the HR girl at Fairfax pretty well. Have her send me her stuff and I'll forward it to Jessica with a cover letter. I hope she's a good worker! Hah hah."

"Really good," said Nora."I personally guarantee it."

By the end of the week, Maria Foner, she of the all-American paperwork and sterling record, had been interviewed at Fairfax Janitorial Services, Inc. in a small, brownish room smelling of microwaved meats. The interviewer was a substantial woman who asked her if she was on drugs or had young children. She wanted to make sure Maria Foner would show up. Her eyes avoided the face before her and spoke to the air some inches above Nora's false defect. Also false was Nora's body, wrapped in the theatrical fat suit she had purchased in Dallas, now clad in tasteless polyester from Goodwill. With the fat and the face, she was as invisible as it was possible for a youngish American woman to be.

She got the job, and started the next evening. She was a hell of a cleaner and she spoke really good English. Her supervisor was pleased and told her she had a secure career at FJS: minimum wage shift work with no benefits for as long as she liked. Nora moved out of the Comfort Inn and found a more role-appropriate room in a former motel on Braddock Road in Alexandria.

It took Nora a few days to learn the identity of the crew chief for the building that she wanted to clean, and to get some intel on her. Deanna Otis was easy to spot at the dispatcher's room at FJS, where the cleaners gathered before being transported with their gear to the various work sites. Deanna was over six feet tall and muscular behind twenty-five years of cleaning offices. One evening, Nora followed her to a bus stop frequented by cleaners returning to DC from cleaning suburban offices, and struck up a conversation. She joined Marva and the other cleaning ladies on their ride down Little River Turnpike to the Metro at Alexandria.

Nora had already found that her supposed facial affliction caused certain people to do her favors. Whether this was because of virtue signaling, or genuine compassion, or the desire to rid themselves more swiftly of her presence, she neither knew nor cared. By the end of several chatty bus rides, Deanna was happy to arrange for the false Maria to transfer to Deanna's own crew, and begin to clean, among other sites, the facility at 11250 Waples Mill Road that housed the National Rifle Association.

The day she began was also the day that the story broke in the Baltimore *Sun.* The headline read, "Someone is Killing Gun Dealers and Gun Rights Advocates," and the subhead, "*A Mysterious Gunman Wages War on Those Who Put Military Weapons in the Hands of Mass Shooters.*" Morrisey had clearly put in a lot of work, traveling to to all the murder sites and sketching the character of each victim.

Nora had no particular feelings as she read descriptions of lives she had ended. Darren Oglesby had coached a Little League baseball team in Harpers Ferry. William P. Schatz had been a vestryman in his Lutheran Church and had a taste for local theater. Her eyes flicked away from the names of the two state policemen she had killed—Otono and Martin—and she did not read the quotations from their wives about what good family men they were. She learned the name of the gun runner she'd shot along with Eddie Spires, the wife beater—Oren Haspell. No one in Pillman, Texas, had much good to say about either of them. She was happy to see that Chris Gomez was not mentioned in the story.

"This reporter was the first to put all these murders together," Morrisey wrote, taking a well-deserved victory lap, "and after posting a story about them on the blog SemText, the murderer himself contacted me and offered his explanation of why he was doing it. He asked us to print it, and we have. This in no way constitutes an endorsement of the gunman by this newspaper, but is presented as news."

They ran Nora's document on the front page:

Why I'm Doing This

> On October 16, 1859, John Brown led a raid on the armory at Harpers Ferry, with the intent of seizing the weapons stored there and starting a slave rebellion in the South. Brown hated slavery. He was an abolitionist, a man who thought slavery should be totally abolished. The other abolitionists believed that slavery could be overthrown by peaceful means, but John Brown did not. At the time, pro-slavery men were raiding into Kansas, trying to push out anti-slavery settlers and make sure Kansas joined the Union as a slave state. Brown joined this fight and gained a reputation as a skilled and courageous fighter. He also committed several murders, hacking five pro-slavery men to death at Potawatomi, Kansas. He saw that the curse of slavery could only be defeated by shedding blood. His own son died in this fight, but Brown fought on, although he knew early on that October day that he would fail in his plan to start up a slave rebellion.
>
> Today, America lies under the curse of military weapons used in mass shootings. As with slavery, political forces (in this case led by the National Rifle Association) prevent a peaceful solution to this deadly problem. I will explain why

it is deadly. I have had a military career, so I know about military weapons. Military weapons use the gas from an exploding bullet to drive the action of the weapon to extract the spent cartridge case and put another round in the chamber, ready to fire. A military weapon will thus fire every time a shooter pulls the trigger, as long as there are rounds in the magazine. Plus it is pretty easy to modify such a weapon to make it into a machine gun.

The reason military weapons are made like that is so that soldiers can fire many bullets in a short time, to produce what we call fire superiority. It makes the enemy keep his head down, so we can do tactical maneuvers and take the position. Military weapons are the favorites of mass shooters because they want to kill lots of people in a short time. No civilian needs a gas-operated military weapon. If you can't defend your home and family and enjoy outdoor recreation with a revolver, a mechanically-loading shotgun, and a bolt-action rifle, you are one sorry loser.

I have always used guns. Hunting ducks and deer with my dad are some of my fondest memories. But my dad would never have used a military weapon to hunt and would have had contempt for anyone who did. We used double-barreled shotguns and bolt action rifles. If you need more firepower than that, you shouldn't be in the woods hunting. You should be in the service, shooting at America's enemies.

I am a survivor of a mass shooting. My spouse and my three young children were murdered. I went a little crazy after that. Some people might think that I still am. There are organizations that lobby for gun control and I considered working with one of those, to try and prevent any other parent from having to go through what I went through. But they are not effective. The National Rifle Association has a political lock on any national debate about military weapons. The NRA is funded by firms that make military weapons for civilian use. Keeping money flowing to these firms is the main goal of the NRA, but they have been able to convince many Americans that owning military weapons has something to do with freedom.

I fought in Afghanistan, where nearly every household owns an assault rifle. I assure you that you don't want to live in a country like that. All those guns have not made it a free country.

I don't care about the Second Amendment. I'm not a Constitutional scholar, but I don't believe Ben Franklin or James Madison thought that anyone should be able to carry a weapon that could kill dozens of people in a few seconds. If the Second Amendment allows that, it should be removed, because that's just wrong. Everyone knows it's wrong, which is why most Americans support controls on assault weapons and big magazines and all the other equipment that enables mass killings. But they don't get sensible controls because of the gun lobby, led by the National Rifle Association and the people who profit from making and selling these weapons.

Therefore I am declaring war on the enablers of mass shootings. I will find and kill the people who sell guns to mass shooters and the people who are responsible for making them. I will kill as many officers of the National Rifle Association as I can find. I urge the thousands of Americans who have suffered the kind of loss that I have to do likewise.

I know that this is wrong and that I have no right to kill people. But this slaughter of innocents can't go on. I am like John Brown here, doing evil so that a greater evil can be destroyed. Like John Brown, I intend to give my life to this cause. I apologize to my family, who raised me to be decent and honorable, and I profoundly regret the deaths of the two policemen killed at Keene. In any war there will be collateral damage. I know it doesn't help to apologize, just like it doesn't help in the places where America and its allies are killing many civilians every day. I did that myself in service of my country. I regret that too.

No one will ever be held responsible for those deaths, but that's no longer true of mass shootings in the United States. I will hold responsible those who enable these killings, and exact justice on their bodies.

GUNSUB

Sally Kehoe was in the cab to Logan heading for the DC shuttle, when her cell rang and it was Brendan Meagher.

"Have you seen it?" he asked without preamble.

"Excuse me?" Seen what?

"The Baltimore *Sun,* but it's all over the media now. The GUNSUB wrote a manifesto. He lost his family in a mass shooting and he's killing the people he thinks are responsible."

There was a pause on the line. She heard Meagher clear his throat.

"You were right on that, Agent Kehoe. I regret dismissing your theory. The bastard even signed his letter, "GUNSUB." He's dicking around with us. Anyway, turn your cab around and get back here. I want you working on the main case."

"I'm sorry, sir, but I have to respectfully decline. I can't work this case, for reasons I've already discussed with you. If you like, I could put it in writing."

Another pause on the line. Then, gruffly, "Yeah, why don't you do that, Agent Kehoe." He broke the connection.

Sally immediately brought up the GUNSUB manifesto and her little screen and read it through several times. She was weeping freely by the time she arrived at the airport, but once out of the privacy of the cab, she yanked herself together, visited the ladies', where she employed techniques not learned at Quantico to expunge the marks of that episode from her face.

Her briefcase held a thick notebook into which she had laboriously copied data from the critical files of the GUNSUB cases. She could have taken copies of the files, but she had no right to them because, as she had told Meagher, she had to recuse from the case. She was going off the reservation, but not far enough off to allow the possession of purloined official files. As she waited at the gate, she extracted from the data a picture of Nora's run. Harpers Ferry was the first, then Bridgeport, Keene, West Freedom, and Pillman, and she matched the dates of these with what she knew of her sister's whereabouts. She knew already that the match was perfect. Now she wanted to explore the details.

Sally opened her laptop and logged into a series of FBI databases, and queried several commercial ones to which the FBI had privileged access. She was checking out something puzzling that had emerged from her researches. The police evidence from the killing sites contained scattered references to vehicles. The famous red, or black motorcycle. A camper that had been spotted at Harper's Ferry. A van with some sort of writing on it that someone had seen in West Freedom. A Toyota Tundra with a different camper top and a motorcycle rack on it, noted in New Hampshire.

She mused on this: one person, many vehicles. That meant either confederates, which she thought unlikely, or that Nora was discarding vehicles and buying others as she traveled. That would make sense. She was working in small towns or wealthy suburbs. Unfamiliar vehicles were noticed, and someone might have written a license number down. If Nora suspected that someone might be tracking her movements using national technical means she would not want her name associated with these vehicles. And when Sally checked a vehicle registration database, she learned that no vehicle had been registered in the name of Nora Kehoe during the period in question.

They called the flight. Sally closed her laptop and shuffled aboard. Once seated, she paid for the airplane WIFI and when they reached altitude, she opened her machine again and continued working. Nora hadn't applied for a federal background check for any weapons purchases, which meant nothing. She might have patronized gun shows. She had obviously patronized at least one, since she'd killed its operator. She might have stolen all the weapons she needed, for that matter.

But Sally didn't think so. Sally thought her sister would have legally purchased or stolen every weapon she had used. That was rather the point of her activities: the same loose system that made it possible for nearly everyone, including the unrevealed insane and potential mass killers, to obtain military weapons, was being used to enable the murders of those responsible for, and benefiting from, that same system.

But no one named Nora Kehoe had registered to purchase the weapons used in the murders (there were at least three assault rifles involved, according to the forensics) and Nora Kehoe's Visa had not been used for anything at all in the past month. Well, she might have brought a lot of cash, but in modern America it was hard to get through a day without using credit. Some places didn't even accept cash anymore.

The implications were clear. Nora was using aliases and making them real with phony driver's licenses and credit cards. She must still be traveling under a series of aliases, making it hard to track her down. But where could Nora have obtained fake ID? High-end bad paper was hard to come by, even for experienced criminals, and Nora, though now a mass killer, was a Girl Scout. So how….?

The light dawned.

There was no cell service on the worn 727 they used for the Boston-DC shuttle so she had to wait and writhe in impatience until the plane landed and she was able to find a quiet corner of the airport to make a call.

A familiar number and a familiar voicemail message: "I hate talking on the phone. Text me instead. If you leave a message at the tone, I might or might not ever respond." Sally said, "Iwo Jima," and closed the connection. She waited and watched people go by. It being Washington, D.C., perhaps many of them had two felons in the family, but this conjecture provided little comfort.

After ten minutes, her brother rang back. "What?" he said.

Sally said, "It's Mom's birthday next week. I wanted to make sure you didn't forget, and also to coordinate presents."

"That's not an Iwo Jima," he answered, with as close to a

snarl as he dared with his big sister.

"What are you getting?"

"Sally, I have a fucking call to China on the other line."

"This won't take a minute."

"Can I call you back?"

"No."

"What I always get her—something from Tiffany's, a pearl thing, maybe. She likes pearls. Now can I go?"

"Yes. Goodbye, kid. Wait!" This last screamed into the little holes.

"What?"

"Ben, this is important. Do you record all your calls automatically?"

"Yeah. So what, California allows...."

"Can you doctor the file to remove everything after me going 'Goodbye Ben?'"

"Yeah, trivial, but why should..."

"Is the record function now turned off?"

"It is now. Sally, what the . . . "

"Nora's been killing people using the fake ID you gave her. Have you checked the Internet this morning? She's the GUNSUB."

He said,"Wait one and let me get rid of China and check it out."

She listened to *Angel of Death* by Slayer for a scant minute and then Ben was back.

"Fuck. That's quite a manifesto. What should we do?"

"Well, you're well and truly busted, baby. We're going to have to figure out a way to keep you out of jail."

"Why am I going to jail? I didn't kill anyone."

"Because providing a false identity in furtherance of a crime is a crime. How many did fakes did you give her?"

"I don't know. Six? Nine? I didn't know she was going to do crimes with them."

"Oh, Christ, Ben! Nine? At ten years per count? And *of course* you knew. Why else does someone need fake ID? Okay, the first thing you have to do is scrub any connections with Nora at your end. How did you get the fakes to her?"

"Fed Ex. I guess I could hack into their system, and get rid of the invoices and waybills. The problem is the other end, with Tormentor."

"Who?"

"Tormentor. He runs a fake ID site on the Dark Web. I got the fakes from him."

"You mean *she* got the fakes from him. But is that even possible?"

"I could have mentioned it to her."

"Right. She asked, you mentioned, and she obtained the fakes from him. Is there any way to phony that all up digitally?"

"I could supply a photograph of Nora sitting on Tormentor's lap handing him cash money for birth certificates that would pass just about any forensic checks. There is no reality any more. The things were bought with Bitcoins, so no traces there. Yeah, it'd take some work, but it could be done. Scrubbing all comm with his site . . . yeah, there's an exploit I could use. Definitely doable."

"Good. This guy's not a pal of yours, I hope."

"I have no friends, as you know. Besides, he's in Ukraine. They can't touch him there."

"Terrific. Send me the names you gave her by encrypted email to my private phone and let me know when you've cleaned this up."

"Yes, Big Sis," said Ben. "Bummer about Nora though. But sort of cool too. She'll be famous forever."

20: Being Famous

Within ten minutes of Nora's manifesto appearing online, #GUNSUB appeared, and ten minutes after that it was the number one trending hashtag on Twitter, with thousands of tweets. Nora scrolled through them reading at random when ever some insight or particularly vivid obscenity caught her eye. By rough count, about a third of the tweeters were cheering her on, about a third wanted the GUNSUB killed in interesting and painful ways, and the rest agreed that something had to be done about the gun problem in America but that this was not it.

Some passionately defended the Second Amendment as a sacred guarantee of liberty, others thought that was nonsense for practical reasons and because the Framers were talking about a national guard, not individual ownership without constraint. As far as Nora could see, no one convinced anyone that they were wrong. No one tweeted, "Never thought of that before. I guess I was wrong on the Second Amendment. LOL!" It was just like the debate on slavery a hundred and sixty years ago, futile, with the whiff of blood in the air.

Her Plan was now in its final stages, with May 10th less than a week away. She had necessarily left certain clues in her manifesto, which the FBI would not be slow to exploit. Nora thought that even if they learned her identity, it would not be easy to find her now. She did not look like her old self anymore, or walk like her. Nora had walked like a Marine; now she imitated the head-down, shoulder-slumping progress common to fat, ugly women. She kept to herself at the ex-motel, and paid her rent in cash.

Each evening she took the bus to Fairfax Janitorial, a white concrete-block-stucco building located in a commercial park off Route 50. There she drew cleaning supplies and boarded a van with the other five cleaners and Marva. She sat with Deanna and talked about what Deanna wanted to talk about, which was reality shows, her rotten kids, her one good daughter, and her generally hard life. She didn't inquire about Maria Foner's life, and Nora did not volunteer any information.

At the NRA building, security let the crew in and Deanna directed them to their duties. Each cleaner worked alone and was responsible for a certain number of offices and hallways. After they had cleaned their assigned areas, they all gathered at the National Firearms Museum and cleaned that, which took the remainder of the shift. Nora thus had at least six hours undisturbed, so that by cleaning like fury she could finish her task early and have enough time to make a thorough recon of the building, and especially of the fifth floor, where the boardroom and the executive offices were located.

On her second night, she found what she was looking for: a locked utility closet on the fifth floor that housed the controls and breakers for the building's electrical power. She opened the lock easily and entered a bathroom-sized space walled by gray panels blinking with colored lights. A set of steel shelves held manuals and a large cardboard carton containing junked electrical components.

From under the thick pads of her fat suit she pulled the front and rear assemblies of the Robins Reaper she'd taken from Arno Morgan in Kentucky and stashed them under the electrical units in the carton. The following night she would bring the magazines for that weapon and the chromed Colt revolver that had once decorated the late Arno's hip.

Then she joined the crew and helped to clean the gallery of the National Firearms Museum that was devoted to movie and TV guns. Nora had heard once that museums could tell the most popular exhibits by counting the finger marks on the glass of the display vitrines. Nora thought it was a toss-up between Clint Eastwood's . 44 magnum from *Dirty Harry* and the .50 caliber Barrett rifle from *The Hurt Locker.*

The museum was a shrine to guns and to the worship of man's ability to fling pieces of metal at tremendous velocity into living flesh. She had a peculiar feeling as she polished the glass that housed the gleaming weapons, that she would have loved this museum, would have taken her kids to it; she *was* a gun person, after all. But now it seemed like a beautiful church in which all the priests were pedophiles, whose altar she had been called to defile. Afterward, Deanna told her she'd done a fantastic job on the glass.

It took the FBI three days to put it together, which surprised Sally. The list of possibles must have been short indeed. She suspected it might have been unconscious reluctance to attribute so vast a crime spree to a woman.

Before noon on the third day Sally received a call from Stewart Nelson, her boss, instructing her to report to his office forthwith. She picked up a file jacket she had prepared against this moment and did so.

When she arrived ,she found Nelson sitting with two other men at the small conference table in his office. One was the director of the National Center for the Analysis of Violent Crime, her boss's boss, and the other was the Deputy Director of the FBI. Nelson gestured her to the one empty chair. He didn't bother to introduce the two other men. Sally could see he was nervous and she felt bad for him.

"I guess you know what this is about," Nelson said.

"I assume it's about the GUNSUB, sir," said Sally.

"You'd be right about that. Um, Agent Kehoe, did you at any time have the suspicion that your sister, Nora Kehoe, might be the GUNSUB?"

"Not Nora specifically, sir, but someone like her. I thought the killings had to be about guns and mass shootings, about revenge against the people who enabled them, and I thought the shooter had to be trained in marksmanship and tactics. I wrote a memo on that theory for SAIC Brendan Meagher last week, while I was attached to the Boston team investigating the Keene murders. He rejected it. I also said that I was uncomfortable about my involvement in that investigation because if it *was* related to mass shootings, then I was compromised because of what happened to Nora, who fit the profile pretty well. I wrote a memo on that too. I have copies of both memos here, sir, if you'd care to read them."

The men exchanged looks. The Deputy Director said, "I believe we've reviewed those memos already. Tell me, Agent Kehoe, do you know where your sister is at this time?"

"I do not, sir. The last time I pinged her cell phone it was in Boise, but it's not responding at all now. I assume she disposed of it."

More exchanged looks. Nelson said, "Agent Kehoe . . . Sally--we appreciate how difficult this must be for you. Clearly, you can't participate in the effort to track down your sister, and since NCAVC is going to be heavily involved in that, it might be best if you took a leave of absence until the GUNSUB situation is resolved."

Sally said, "Yes sir, the book solution, I get that it's a conflict. On the other hand, if Nora's the GUNSUB, she's a clear and present danger to the public, and I'm an invaluable asset. There's no one on earth who knows Nora Kehoe better than I do. And there's not really a conflict of interest. I want her brought in as much as you do, sir. Alive, if possible. My parents lost three grandchildren and I will do anything in my power to make sure they don't lose a daughter too. I want her safe in prison as soon as we can grab her."

The Deputy Director said,"Well, it's irregular, but we haven't had quite this situation before, a decorated veteran turning rogue and making a violent political statement. Anything that will help shut this down . . ."

Then up spoke the Director, NCAVC, a man who'd been a field agent for a dozen years, had two doctorates, one in applied mathematics and one in social psych, and was reputed to be the smartest man in the Bureau.

"Agent Kehoe, do you think your sister will contact you or your family?"

"I'd bet on it, sir. In fact, I think she'll call me specifically. We're very close."

"Do you think she'd want to see you?"

"Yes, but she'd be suspicious of a trap, if I arranged the meet."

"*Would* you entrap her?"

"Absolutely, sir! My goal, as I said, is to bring her in safely, with no further casualties. And, sir . . . my sister is both very damaged and very dangerous. I think the parallel here is the Unabomber. His brother was vital to his capture and I think I would be too in this case."

More meaningful looks, and then the Deputy Director said, "Okay, let's settle this. We're going to move the GUNSUB action back to headquarters and consolidate the other cases—Harpers Ferry, Keene, Kentucky and Texas. Agent Kehoe, you'll be attached to the investigation out of NCAVC in the usual way. No command responsibility *at all*, and you'll report directly to the Special Agent in Charge."

"That would be Agent Meagher, sir?"

"No, Agent Meagher is off the case," said the Deputy Director without further explanation. "I don't think I have to impress on you the extreme delicacy of this arrangement. The reason we have a book at all is so that the whole Bureau knows what to do and what not, so that thirty-five-thousand armed people don't act like cowboys. You're not a cowboy, are you, Agent Kehoe?"

"No sir. Not a cowgirl either, sir."

A tense moment, and then the smartest man in the Bureau laughed, there were smiles all around, and the meeting broke up soon after.

Later, in a stall in the ladies' room, after the howling and the head banging, Sally considered she'd done well. Her stupid brilliant brother was safe for the moment. They could introduce the aliases Ben had provided into evidence without implicating him as an accessory to murder. Besides that, she thought her main task on this investigation was sitting with her thumb up her ass waiting for Nora to call.

On the fourth day after the publication of her manifesto, Nora went to the Lee Highway Walmart to buy bullets and some other stuff she needed when she happened to glance at the rows of TV sets on display there. They were all tuned to Fox News with the sound off and they all showed a photograph of a fresh-faced young woman wearing the camo uniform of a second lieutenant of Marines. Nora allowed the image to pass across her eyes unseen, as one does on such errands, and it was only after she had passed the display on her way to the gun counter that she realized the photo on the screens was an earlier version of herself, and went back.

One of the sets had the closed captions turned on and so she saw her name up there too. An anchor and his guest—a former senator from Wyoming and an NRA board member—expressed horror. Two customers watching wondered why a nice-looking girl like that would turn evil, and one of them said that's what happens when women go into the military and stop going to church. The senator opined that if the Justice Department was doing its job instead of running phony investigations, atrocities like this would never happen. There was a colloquy about the menace of violent leftism before they broke for a commercial about buying gold.

They didn't sell Colt .45 revolver ammo at that Walmart. Nora bought a bottle of ipecac in the drug department and left quickly, resisting the urge to turn around and see whether anyone was looking funny at her. She drove the van deeper into Virginia and found one of the very many gun shops in the region. Although the place mainly serviced people straw-buying guns for New York gang bangers and professional criminals, they were happy to sell the nice fat lady a box of .45s.

Nora had the next day off, which she considered a bit of luck. She spent the idle hours in her motel room, watching the news on the TV and checking Twitter like a teen. Fox had a segment showing the parental Kehoes' house in Falls Church, with the news vans in front and the well-dressed woman talking into the microphone about how there was nothing happening and the Kehoes had no comment. Nora wanted to call her parents, but did not. It was irrational, she knew, but she thought that if her dad got on the line, he would convince her to turn herself in. She felt badly for her parents, in an abstract way devoid of gut emotionality. She was so far from those loving, decent people, and had been for a long time.

Instead, she called her sister, who picked up on the second ring.

"Do you hate me now?"

"Of course I don't hate you, Nora. You're my little sis. I love you. Where are you?"

"You're tracing my location now, aren't you?"

"What do you think?"

"Of course you are. I'm glad you're still with the Bureau. I was afraid you'd get in trouble."

"It probably wouldn't have stopped you."

"No, I guess not. Sally? Remember when we were stationed in Hawaii and we had that house in Kailua?"

"Uh-huh. What about it?"

"Remember the mango tree? Do you remember one afternoon, everyone was out of the house—Dad was on duty and Dougie was out with his surfing friends and Mom had Ben for one of his appointments. We were all alone and we decided to pick mangoes and eat them. I was probably ten and you were twelve, and you showed me how to butcher a mango. And we decided to see how much mango we could eat before we barfed. We were laughing like loons. Remember that?"

"Sort of. Why is it important now?"

"No reason. I was just driving around and thinking about it. I guess you know what I'm driving now. I don't care. I'm ditching it anyway. But about that afternoon—I always thought it was the perfect day, sunny and breezy. We'd been to the beach earlier and then we had the house to ourselves, all alone. When I was real little I used to think we would live together and not need anyone else. It's funny how a day like that will stick in your mind. Every time I smell a mango I think of us sitting there eating. We must have ate ten mangos each. We didn't barf, though."

"No, I seem to recall substantial diarrhea instead. Look, Nora, you have to come in. There's a BOLO out on you and an armed-and dangerous notice on it. Some local cop could blow you up without a thought. Just go to any police station . . ."

"Good-bye, Sally," said Nora. "I love you."

Sally stared at the phone in her hand. She had an overwhelming urge to run down the ladies and do her usual head-banging, but she did not. She felt something vital but insubstantial leave her, like they say ghosts depart from the dying.

Barb had been right. Her lovely brave sister had never come back from Afghanistan, and what had happened here was a Chosin Reservoir, not an Iwo Jima, a defeat, not a victory. But the living would survive and the dead would not be left on the battlefield. Sometimes that was all you could do.

Nora threw the phone into a trash can just as the Uber she had called rolled into the Outback Steakhouse parking lot. The driver was a Palestinian with nothing to say. He drove her back to her Alexandria motel, where she spent the rest of the day. Of course, as she should have realized, Sally would have figured she was using false ID, and she would have got onto Ben, who would have spilled the beans as soon as Sally asked. So, they probably knew about the Maria Foner identity she was using, and if her landlord was one to watch the news, they'd have a SWAT running up the stairs in no time. Or Deanna might have seen through the disguise and made a call.

Or not. The Marines taught you not to second-guess your planning beforehand. Every plan was in error, because no plan survives first contact with the enemy, and so it had proved. But it meant that she couldn't stay here tonight. She tossed what she needed into her backpack and headed for where the homeless dwelt.

21: In the Belly of the Beast

Nora spent the night at Union Station with only a blanket, her clothing and a fat suit between her skin and the marble. It was a fresh spring night, but clear and seasonable, tropic, in fact, compared to the mountains of Afghanistan. She was among a couple of dozen others, almost all men, almost all black or Hispanic. There were comments about her face. Two guys started talking trash about putting a bag over her head, but she moved away and they didn't pursue it.

She ate a meal of hotdogs and coffee from a cancer wagon on Massachusetts Avenue, found a niche in the white stone on the east side of the station and settled down for the night. She was undisturbed except for a fellow who shoved her awake around 0400 to demand a romantic blow-job, offering five dollars. She showed her K-Bar knife and he slunk away, cursing her for an ugly bitch and saying she should fucking pay *him*.

Dawn, and she wandered her nation's capital, humping her pack. She took her meals from the food trucks parked by the fountain in front of the Capitol. Once, when she had finished and was sitting on a low wall, a woman in an elegant suit, about her own age, dropped a dollar into her empty coffee cup without actually looking at her. Policemen did occasionally notice her; she looked them fearlessly in the face and they strolled on by.

She was walking vaguely southeast on the downslope of Capitol Hill, marching actually, with the same tireless stride she had learned in the Corps. Her mind was clear. Although there were many things that could still go wrong with her Plan, she was unconcerned about the future. This was what it was like, her father had told her, when all the prep and plans had been made and the men had been fed and checked for the third time and all that remained was the wait for H-hour. At such moments, Colonel Dad had said, the soldier achieves a sage-like detachment and a strange interior peace. She had told that to Ryan Graham, who had laughed and said, yes, that, or he gets high on bennies or sleeps or jerks off.

This got her thinking about both Ryan and her Dad and the interior peace she was actually feeling came apart for a moment; her knees shook and a pang of sorrow like a hot blade ran up her chest.

And of course when that happened she found herself outside a Catholic church, and of course the church was named St. Catharine of Alexandria, who had appeared to Joan of Arc, and of course, the time she happened to be passing was just the time when they were offering the sacrament of penance, according to the notice board outside the door. She had given up wondering why things happened to her, she felt driven like a beast down a chute, toward a goal not of her choosing. Joan had seen her dauphin crowned, but Nora had only seen dead people as her reward, her apotheosis was a pile of corpses. It didn't seem fair.

She made just this point to the priest, a stupid point she realized as soon as it popped from her mouth, but by that time she could hardly stop herself.

The priest himself was a red-faced man with white hair, about the same age as her father. Nora had insisted on an old-fashioned confessional box, even though she had been raised in a church that rarely used them anymore. The priest offered to see her in a rectory parlor, but she wanted the box. She had seen them in films and thought they were one of the better ideas the church had come up with.

Ensconced in dimness, on her knees, she made the formal request for forgiveness (about which she was uncertain, from a God in which she barely believed) and then spilled her guts, the whole story.

"I wanted to kill them all," she said. "They killed my Marines and I wanted to kill them all. I knew they had the kids and moms in the school. They always do that, they love collateral damage, lots of dead civilians. I knew that and I didn't care, I wanted them dead so bad. I could have gone through the roof, I could've separated the hajjis from the other people, but instead I poured fire into the building until it was a smoking ruin. Then we blew the doors and went in hot, spraying the inside with bullets and grenades."

Nora found she was crying; that was funny, she hadn't cried at the scene. She didn't have any tissues so she wiped her nose and eyes on her sleeve.

"There was a girl there called Nazanina, just the most darling kid, she was like my keeper in the village, bright as a button, just dying for education. Hah! Yeah, right, she actually died for education. She always had on her little yellow dress, with sequins embroidered into it. That's how I knew she was there; you could still see the sequins on the bloody rags we turned her into.

"When we got in, the whole floor of the schoolroom was covered thick with bodies. We killed nearly two hundred people, including practically every woman and child from the Shirani clan. The whole thing was a set-up, engineered by a rival clan, to murder the Shiranis in revenge for something that went down a hundred fifty years ago, using the stupid Americans as killers so they wouldn't have to violate the code of hospitality."

Then Nora continued her story, about what had happened at the Mall of Death, and what she had made of that event, how she had accepted it as a just punishment for her own crimes, and as a spur to her current project. She said she was the GUNSUB, the killer who was on the television, whom every cop in town was seeking. She explained why she was doing what she was doing and named John Brown and St. Joan as inspirations. She had no idea of why she was making a confession here; the last time she had received the sacrament she'd been eight and her sins were less dire.

The priest said nothing while she was speaking. After she stopped there was silence from beyond the grille. Had he fallen asleep? Was he struck dumb by the monstrosity of her crimes?

"So, Father," she added, "what's the deal? Too bad to forgive?"

"No, dear, nothing's too bad to forgive. He forgave the people who were torturing Him to death, and He will forgive you. Forgive *me* for being struck dumb for a moment. All that death, all that horror! But now you've confessed you have to make a good act of contrition."

"I'm sorry, I'm not a practicing Catholic any more. I guess you could tell that." An unbidden laugh escaped her throat, quickly stifled. "What do I have to do?"

"You have to recognize that you sinned, that it was your fault and no one else's, that you regret doing it, and that you commit to never doing it again. It's necessary to reject the sin, do you see?"

"Um-hm. I do. And there would be penance, too, I guess."

"Only after the contrition and the absolution. We do it by the numbers here, just like in the Corps."

"You were in?"

"This is about you, not me. I ask you, can you make a good act of contrition?"

"No. I'm not sorry I killed those ten people, except for the two cops, and I intend to kill more, if I can."

"Then I can't absolve you."

"No, I didn't think you could. I'm not even sure why I came in here. I know I'm going straight to Hell."

"You can't be sure of that. The fact that you came in here suggests you're not entirely depraved. There are people you mention, witnesses, that you might have killed to protect yourself, but you declined to do so. That speaks to a moral center, as does your shame and regret over the killing you were part of in Afghanistan. You're not as bad as you think you are."

"Not even if I intend to kill again?"

"No, the killing is the *result* of sin. Do you understand this? You suffer from pride, wrath and acedia--the surrender of hope. If you had never actually killed anyone, you would still be a grave sinner because of those, and as our Lord reminded us, from the standpoint of God, the thought of violence is the same as the act."

"I don't see the pride. I'm crawling with shame."

"That's the acedia talking. You're as proud as Lucifer. Comparing yourself to St. Joan?"

"What's wrong with that? She caused the death of a lot more people than I ever will. She was fighting to free France from the English and I'm fighting to free my country from guns. It's like an occupying army is killing over thirty thousand Americans a year, year after year, and everything we try to stop it gets blocked. I'm making war on all that, and hoping others will too. What's the difference, morally?"

"Well, there's just-war theory," the priest replied, "which is pretty complicated . . ."

"I know about just-war theory," said Nora. "The bottom line is you only get to kill people if you're a sovereign and your cause is just. "

"That's right," said the priest. "Your cause *may* be just—I'm making no judgment on that, mind—but you're not a sovereign. St. Joan didn't pick up a sword and start killing random Englishmen. She presented herself to her dauphin and begged him to use her to restore his legitimate kingdom and drive out the invaders who were harming his people. But we're not here to chop logic and discuss just wars. You came here to confess sins, not defend your actions, or anyway that's why *I'm* here."

"If I stopped, what would be my penance? A million Hail Mary's?"

"Now you're just being a jerk," the priest snapped. "Your penance would include turning yourself in to the authorities, obviously. God may forgive you, but you have to pay for your crimes. Many people don't get the difference, but I think you do."

"I'm sorry. Not only do I not know why I'm here, I don't know why I'm even alive. I would've killed myself, but I got a . . . a message that I had to do this. It just appeared in my head, like it was from God . . . "

"You can put that out of your mind. God doesn't authorize murder. And if you think you've received a divine message, well, the Devil invariably presents as God."

"I don't think so, Father. If I were a tool of Satan, I would've killed Mrs. Schatz and the other witnesses. But I'm being used by *something*. Maybe something from before God came on the scene. Something Greek?"

"You mean nemesis."

"Right, nemesis. Maybe evil generates a counter-evil that destroys it. Anyway, it picked me."

A deep sigh came from beyond the grille. "I think we can't continue this. You don't have the state of mind required for confession, and I can't absolve you unless you sincerely repent. You might want to seek mental health counseling, but this isn't that. I urge you in the name of Christ to stop what you're doing and turn yourself in. I'm sorry for your agony."

"I'm sorry too," said Nora. "Are you going to call the cops on me?"

"No. And I want to say, I understand how you feel."

"I seriously doubt that."

"I was a nineteen year old rifleman with the second of the Fifth at Hué. I shot a bunch of people, including people who didn't need to get shot. When I got out I stayed drunk for a year. Then I got the call. Which *was* from God, as it turned out."

"You were a Marine?"

"I was. I thought I was too tough for God, just like you. Take my advice. Let go of all this anger and lay the pain on Jesus. He can handle it a lot better than you can."

"Well. I'll think about it," said Nora, to be kind. "Semper Fi, Father. And thanks."

"God bless you my child. May the Lord make his face shine on you and bring you peace."

Nora left the church feeling like she had just emerged from a deep cavern into sunlight. Even without the formal absolution she felt better. She walked slowly west on Constitution to Federal Triangle, and hung around the Metro entrance, watching the tides of people flow back and forth until just after five. After buying a couple of sandwiches and some water bottles from a food truck she took the Metro Orange line to Virginia.

Someone had abandoned a *Washington Post* on the train and she read it with interest. She learned that someone else had shot and killed a gun shop owner. The shooter was the father of a child who'd been a victim of the Emeryville Massacre, where a teenager had taken his legally-purchased AR to a pre-school and killed twelve children under five and two teachers.

It made Nora happy; perhaps she had started a trend. But no: a Congressman from Texas had introduced a bill to make it illegal for authorities to identify where a killer had purchased any firearms used in a crime. He said it was necessary to protect law-abiding gun dealers from murderous fanatics. It had 188 co-sponsors. She was sorry not to have a chance to have a prejudicial interview with that particular Congressman, but she now thought it possible that someone else might.

She left the train at the Vienna stop and took the Number Two Gold Bus to Fairfax Boulevard at Jermantown Road, and walked on thereafter. It was little over half a mile to the NRA building on Waples Mill Road. She sprinted the last five hundred meters, arriving at the entrance panting and covered in sweat.

The security guard recognized her, so she had no difficulty entering the building. There were a couple of men in suits checking things out, and Nora supposed that they were cops or FBI. Of course they would see this building as a target, but it would not occur to them that the killer might be one of America's invisibile servitors.

She hurried past them. Timing was critical here; she wanted to catch Deanna early in the shift, and she did, just after six-thirty, on the fourth floor. She spotted her talking to a cleaner, jumped back in the stairwell, and took a swallow of ipecac. Then she emerged, not having to fake being breathless very much.

Deanna expressed concern when she saw Nora's appearance, and dismissed her apologies for missing the van. Nora said she'd been sick all day, but she needed the day's wage, demonstrating just how sick she was by puking into the cleaner's bucket. Deanna shrank back visibly and ordered her home. Nora thanked her and shuffled back to the stairwell.

Once there, she went not down but up to her hide in the electrical closet. There she stripped to her underwear, ate a sandwich, and tended to her weapons. She had two 30-round magazines for the AR, now fully assembled with the sling attached, and a box of bullets for the Colt pistol. She had a suppressor screwed into the barrel of the AR. She didn't think she would need any more ammunition; the massacre in her plan would be of moderate size.

The Marines had taught her to sleep anywhere; the fat suit padding made a better bed than she'd had many nights in Helmand. And she was tired, colossally tired, more tired than she'd been in boot camp or on the officer's course, or during plebe year in Annapolis. There was a moment as she composed herself for sleep when she feared she would have to endure the little voices and the soft tiny hands plucking at her. But her dead children were otherwise occupied and she slept like a regular person for once. If she dreamed, it left no mark on her memory.

When she awakened it was at last D-Day, May 10th. At ten o'clock today the National Rifle Association would hold a meeting of its Executive Committee in a conference room just down the hall from where she now lay. She intended to make a presentation to that committee, one she was sure that its surviving members would remember for a long time.

She ate her sandwich, drank her water, dressed in fresh camies and her RAT boots, tucked her assault rifle under her arm and stuck the big six-shooter into her belt. Voices and movement sounded in the hall outside the closet door. She waited for these to cease. When they did, she emerged, walked down the hall to the boardroom and entered.

Ten people sat at a long shining pale wooden table and another half-dozen sat on chairs along the wall. They were all white people; four of them were women. The youngest was twenty-four, a secretary, the oldest was seventy-two, and was the immediate past president. The current president of the NRA, a former military gentleman, was seated at the head of the table, at the opposite end of the room from where Nora had entered. He stared at her, as did everyone else.

Nora said, "I guess you know who I am. I came here to kill all of you because you deserve it. You're responsible for laws that get thirty thousand Americans killed every year, year in and year out. This doesn't happen in other developed countries, only in ours, and that's on you people. I'm here because of what you do. I'm representing all the widows and widowers and orphans and brothers and sisters and grandfathers and grandmothers and grandchildren. Somebody has to pay for what happened to them, all the grief that came out of your bullshit. You have to pay for my little girls and my husband."

One of the young women in the side chairs started to weep and several of the men appeared inclined to join her, faces twisted with terror.

"But then I thought, let's make this a teaching moment. You see I have this imitation assault rifle, which you people have made as easy to buy as a can of beans or an egg-beater. Does anyone doubt I could kill every one of you using this weapon? No? It would be poetic justice if I did, don't you think? But I already sort of did poetic justice when I shot Bill Schatz."

She slung her rifle and drew the Colt from her belt.

"And here's a revolver. I think a revolver is ideal for home defense. It's real easy to maintain, it never jams, and let's face it, if you need more than six shots to resolve a home defense situation you're probably toast anyway. Do I sense a disagreement?"

A man three chairs down from the president, a leathery type with a gray buzz-cut, was, perhaps unconsciously, shaking his head in the negative.

"It's not about the guns," he said, "it's about freedom."

"Really? As if a bunch of fat bozos with fake ARs could contest an issue with the military of the United States. Freedom, my ass! No, it's about slavery. You enslaved the whole country. If everyone has a gun, everyone is the slave of the twitched finger, no one has any rights at all, if it's so easy to take a life. It's the ease of it, don't you see? And how easy it is to get one. Before you get to own a gun you should go through ten times the testing you need to drive a car. You should have a full field investigation before you get a little pistol like this one and for an AR it should be like medical school. Otherwise, crazy people like me can walk into a gun show and walk out with a fucking military weapon designed to kill lots of people very fast. You think that's decent? You think any decent country should have laws like that?"

Nora's voice rose to a howl at the end of this, and another woman started to cry. After a pause, she lowered her voice. "Anyway, I'm only going to use this pistol to shoot you. I would have to reload after six shots."

Nora took the box of .45 bullets from her pocket and tossed it on the table. The box popped open and the shiny rounds scattered on the tabletop.

"And so, a lot of you will probably survive," Nora continued. "As you run away and as you're reunited with your loved ones, I want you to think about the fact that the only reason you're alive and not dead is because I chose not to use my assault rifle, and I want you to think of all the dead people who could also have gotten away if crazy killers had to use a puny gun like this. *My husband and children could have gotten away!"*

After she said this, Nora raised her pistol and shot the president of the NRA in the face. The dead man slumped forward. His shattered head hit the table with a thump and gushed blood. A pool of it spread out onto the immaculate blond wood surface. Three of the women were now shrieking as loud as people can shriek. Several around the long table shot to their feet and backed away, as if distance from the dead man would save them.

Nora shouted, "Run away! Run away now!" and for emphasis shot the immediate past president in the chest. This started a general stampede for the far door, although few daring souls made for the open door through which Nora had entered the conference room. One of these was the squat, white-permed woman who had sat on Nora's end of the table, the mom chair. Nora said, "No, you stay!" and gestured her back into her seat with her pistol.

A jam had developed at the far exit. Like many another, the officials of the NRA were trying to escape the consequences of their actions, but the door was very narrow. Nora had no trouble bagging a superannuated movie star, a former U.S Senator, a former White House aide, and the Director of Legislative Activities.

She dropped the pistol on the table and pointed her AR at the seated woman. Nora observed that the woman was trying very hard to be tough. Her jaw was clamped, her gaze was direct and fierce; but skin of her forehead had gone paler than her hair, a remarkable effect, and all the age marks on her forehead looked almost inky. She was trembling all over, like a bird in the hand.

"You're the stand-your-ground lady," said Nora.

The woman's jaw clenched tighter. Nora poked her with her rifle, repeated the question and the woman nodded.

"What is up with that? You thought it a good idea for people to carry guns, if they ran into someone who annoyed them they could shoot them dead? What sick fantasy world do you live in?"

The woman cleared her throat and said, "People have a right to defend themselves?"

"From what? Harsh words? A dirty look? They get to kill anybody who annoys them and your law lets them walk because they, what, feared for their life? Especially if the dead guy is black, yeah, those black folks are really fucking scary. Is that what this shit is all about?"

"You're going to Hell," the woman said.

"Ma'am, I've been to Hell. It's not so bad. You get used to anything, if you have your friends around you. Honestly, you have no idea how much I want to leave this body behind."

Sirens were now sounding. These became louder with the minutes, and then they heard vehicles arriving in front of the building, many vehicles, screeching and roaring as they drove up. Nora went to the window and opened the drapes. The forecourt in front of NRA Headquarters was full of police cars from half a dozen jurisdictions, and a couple of busses from her old outfit, Fairfax Fire. As she watched, a black van rolled in and the SWAT emerged.

The window also afforded a reflection of what was behind her, and so she was able to see the stand-your-ground woman trying to fit bullets into the chambers of the discarded revolver. Nora turned, said, "I fear for my life," and shot the woman three times, letting the rifle ride up with each shot: chest, neck, head. The woman fell face-down on the table. Her blood pool reached out and touched the gelling blood of the late president of the NRA. Nora thought it made a nice effect and hoped there would be photographs later.

The next moment brought another wave of perfect exhaustion. Her knees trembled and she had to take a chair. She had accomplished her Plan, which had been her entire being for months and now that it was finished there was nothing left of her. She felt she'd done her duty, mission accomplished. She'd thrown her body on the grenade, like a good Marine should, to save others.

Maybe she'd be like John Brown, the beginning of something terrible but necessary. She was too tired to care. The important thing was making the stand. If she died for nothing; also cool. Ryan had died for nothing at Fallujah and her family had died for nothing at the Mall of Death. It was a decent club to belong to.

Noises in the hall outside. Nora frowned: no one had taught these guys how to tape down their jingling gear. She went to the rear door, avoiding the corpse pile, and walked into the hallway.

The SWAT was there, black-clad men with assault weapons at the ready, lined up in two columns against the walls, one on either side of the hallway. As she appeared, the red laser beams snapped over to dance small red dots on her chest; a loud voice ordered, "Drop your weapon! Get down on the floor!" Nora supposed that this was the very same SWAT that had arrived to take down the Bad Santa, and was glad about how perfectly squared away it was that they should be the ones who set her free.

She raised her rifle and fired high, not wanting to hurt anyone else.

~~~~~
~~~~~

Made in the USA
Monee, IL
28 May 2020

31367771R00138